MW01712904

CHANGES IN THE MIST

A fictional memoir of New Petrograd

HEATHER J. GRAHAM DIANA VAN GEFFEN

LORETTA SCUTCHINGS

This is a work of fiction. Names, characters, places, and incidents are a product of the authors' imaginations. Locales and public names are sometimes used for atmospheric purposes. Any resemblance to actual people, living or dead, or to businesses, companies, events, institutions, or locales is completely coincidental.

Art by Graham Harris

Assisted publication by Moonshell Books, Inc.

ISBN 9798569724987

Changes in the Mist / Heather J. Graham et al — 1st ed.

Created with Vellum

ACKNOWLEDGMENTS

The authors would like to show appreciation to the following individuals:

Carl Coate, who was very helpful with salmon fishing advice. Milan Gillespie, who advised us on our lighthouse, wildlife, boating and trout fishing. Rob Bryce, UBC, for his knowledge of New Petrograd's location and the surrounding area along the Skeena River and region. Teri Gillespie, who was so enormously helpful in editing. Anna Borosh, who kindly checked for accuracy all Russian names and information. Carol-Lyne Carter, for making all the Russian recipes to ensure quantities and the correctness of the instructions. Deb Moore, for providing support with draft edits. Graham Harris, for creating the fabulous cover. And Moonshell Books, so instrumental in helping with the publishing.

ABOUT THIS BOOK

This book was written by three residents of Carewest Garrison Green, a long-term care facility in Calgary, Alberta, Canada.

We have again enjoyed the experience of working together on the final book in our trilogy that began with *Lighthouse in the Mist* and continued with our second book, *Deep in the Mist*. From a writing perspective, we hope we have matured even further – it has certainly been a challenge to bring in bits and pieces referencing both of our earlier books.

Since the book is set in 1986, a few things will be different. At that time, Haida Gwaii was called the Queen Charlotte Islands, and the First Nations band the Kwakwaka'wakw were known as the Kwakiutl. Cameras contained film, and music came on cassette tapes and 8-tracks.

There is a sadness in the knowing that this is perhaps the end of the road for our writing careers and we will certainly miss the friendly banter and laughter that went with it. But even as the keyboard silences, we look ahead to the next venture that catches our attention, knowing that the bond of our friendship has only become stronger.

We sincerely hope you have enjoyed reading the series. You can leave a review on your favourite retailer's site to tell others about our books. And you can find both digital and print editions of the series online at Amazon.com or in digital at Kobo.com.

Lighthouse in the Mist
Deep in the Mist
Changes in the Mist

IN THIS SERIES

Lighthouse in the Mist
Deep in the Mist
Changes in the Mist

REVIEWS

I thoroughly enjoyed *Changes in the Mist: A Fictional Memoir of New Petrograd*, the third and final book of the trilogy by Heather J. Graham, Diana Van Geffen, and Loretta Scutchings. It is chockablock full of well researched Russian and Canadian Indigenous history, suspense, humour, romance, and some great recipes too! The authors do a fantastic job of bringing their characters to life. So much so, it's easy to picture yourself being right there with them. Great job, ladies!

— TERI GILLESPIE

I really liked this third book in the Lighthouse in the Mist trilogy. It was nice to see how the townspeople work together to solve problems and create new ways to help the town flourish and grow. It was nice to see another generation take the reins and think of creative activities to bring the town into the modern world. I especially enjoyed the information on the Indigenous lore, crafts, skills, and customs. Well done, ladies!

— CAROL-LYNE CARTER

In their third novel, *Changes in the Mist: A Fictional Memoir of New Petrograd*, Heather Graham, Diana Van Geffen, and Loretta Scutchings invite us again for a warm stay amongst well-loved friends. Life is New Petrograd is bursting with celebrations, romance, surprises, friendship, and of course, a dash of mystery! The authors' commitment to research is impressive, informative, and entertaining. Their hard work and gift of storytelling results in a wonderful tale that is intertwined with vivid cultural and historical details. A delicious bonus can be found in the many wonderful recipes that accompany the story. I really loved reading this book and as always with this series, it left me wanting more!

— JACQUELINE SWINDELLS

Changes in the Mist by Heather Graham, Loretta Scutchings and Diana Van Geffen bring us back to New Petrograd, a place we have grown to love. We are reunited with past characters and get to know new ones. This book is filled with romance, edge-of-your-seat mystery, and surprises. A must read!

— CARLY WEBSTER

CHANGES IN THE MIST

INTRODUCTION

It's 1986, and changes are coming to the misty shores of New Petrograd, BC, the Canadian village with the Russian history. The newest residents, June and Marvin Palmer, get surprising and welcome news—their daughter Shelley is coming home as Gaspar Rosso's bride! And with their impromptu wedding reception begins the busiest summer the village has ever seen.

With its fascinating and unique past, New Petrograd has opened its doors as a living history museum, welcoming the public to experience the food, the costumes, and the traditions of its residents. Under Mary Ellen Filipova's capable management, summer staff come on board, and, in the midst of a flurry of building, she learns that New Petrograd may even become an excursion destination for a cruise line.

But along with the influx of tourists and staff comes a perplexing mystery. Every shop in the village reports items missing—items that could mean the difference between success and financial failure. Could it be one of the summer staff? Or Bert, the new gardener who always has a proverb for the occasion? Or could it be a tourist—or worst of all, a new resident? Determined to find the answer before the village's reputation is shattered, Shelley Rosso sets the khaki cap of her 1917 Russian policewoman's uniform firmly on her head and opens an investigation. But with waves of tourists coming all summer for Russia Day, Canada Day, Family Day, and Labour Day, will she find the answer in time?

PART ONE

Changes in the Mist

CHAPTER ONE

Big Changes on the Horizon

The very air in New Petrograd seemed to sizzle as Saturday, the 24th of May, 1986, was fast approaching. After years of seclusion since being settled following the Russian Revolution of 1917, it was primed to open its doors to the world as a living history museum.

After completing an extension to the Borscht Kettle restaurant, the members of the committee continued to meet every Tuesday night. It was assumed by many village residents that it was just to chat and enjoy each other's company. However, it soon become apparent that this wasn't their only reason to get together. Slowly their elaborate plans had filtered through the village: Big changes were on the horizon.

As had been promised to Anna Yusporova, in the late spring of 1985, Gaspar Rosso had built a facade on the addition to the Borscht Kettle. After a long day's work, or on weekends, he had also been restoring other heritage structures. This had been heartily received, as many in the village had felt remorse at the tumbledown state of many of the buildings. On weekends, several village men were eager to support him any time they could. Early Saturday mornings, Gaspar would often collect John Molodtsov's son, Peter, who was also proving to be a great helper.

Shortly after Phil Filipov and Marg Rosnokova's wedding, Kevin Thompson, Gaspar's friend from Calgary, had returned. Sixteen months prior, Kevin, along with their other friend, Greg, had been key figures in expanding the Borscht Kettle. Everyone was pleased to see him again. It was originally thought that he had come for a week's fishing trip. However, when the week ended and he stayed, it caused a lot of speculation. Especially when he and Gaspar were seen conversing with the survey crews as they started arriving and staked out several places. Folks began to be suspicious that something else was in the wind.

Everyone soon became aware that Kevin was spending the majority of his day focusing on the construction of new buildings. While they were expanding the Kettle, Alexander Bolitchyn had indicated to Gaspar that he thought he would enjoy construction work. So, after graduating from high school, Gaspar and Kevin had jointly hired him and John Molodtsov full-time. Kevin also frequently required crews from Prince Rupert, some of which brought heavy equipment with them. These men needed temporary housing.

The two friends, with their respective hired help, had worked tirelessly towards their deadline.

Martin Shatrov had gladly quit his job at a nearby cannery to take up the carpentry trade. *Dedushka* Yusporov, the village's last remaining founding father, seemed to have a youthful step as he instructed Martin in items typical to what in his generation would have been used to in their daily lives. This included crude pieces of furniture, kitchen and garden implements, and even toys. Along with Anna Yusporova's touch, they had concentrated on bringing their home back to its initial state. The dishes and other household items that had been moved from the house of Bob Petrov's *roditeli* were welcome additions.

On opening day, Martin, as Manager of Customer Relations, was prepared to meet the guests. This was such a suitable job for him; he'd been called upon before to perform the duties of master of ceremonies. Anna, likewise, would officially hold the title of Chief Historian because she was sought out anytime someone wanted to learn more about the village's past. Together, they had organized several men, women, and even a few children to volunteer to mingle with the visitors, attired in authentic Russian dress.

Mary Ellen Filipov, Phil's daughter, had moved back to New Petrograd from Vancouver and was using her MBA as she assumed the position of Business Manager. Nick Kutuz had expanded his role as banker and Notary Public to include the accounting for this new venture. The former home of Roman and Katerina Molodtsov, long in ruins, had now been completely restored for the purpose of housing their offices. A window had been built in one of the rooms and would serve as the ticket booth. Jenny Kutuza had also been hired to work there. The Kutuzas were now *roditeli* to a nine-month-old baby girl, Amanda, and Jenny was thrilled that the arrangement would enable them to bring their daughter with them each day.

At the entrance to the new road, the Canadian and Russian flags flew proudly over an honest-to-goodness gas bar. Marvin Palmer had offered to pump gas and do minor services. He and his wife, June, had moved here in 1984 and they both relished any opportunity to become involved with village life.

Within the parameters of the village, they had opted to

maintain the dirt roads that had existed since the early days. In the initial design of the village, these roads had not been much more than trails. Indeed, in some of the less travelled areas, they still were. New land had been cleared across from the entrance and had been graded for a dirt parking lot.

Phil Filipov had, for many years, been a central figure as New Petrograd's lighthouse keeper. In preparation for this endeavor, the lighthouse station had cleverly been turned into overnight accommodations. He and his new wife, Marg, were going to be the custodians. Much to Phil's delight, this meant that they needed to take up residence there.

As if waiting for a chance to move home, Marg's son, Don Rosnokov, grabbed this opportunity and relocated from Whitehorse, taking up residence in his family home. His plan was to operate his fishing and hunting guide business from there. After all, there was ample fishing, with rivers, lakes, and the ocean in the area. And deer and moose frequented the adjacent woods.

Rumour had it that Mary Ellen had been corresponding with Don ever since the wedding of their *roditeli*, though neither Phil nor Marg would confirm this.

Olga Petrova had retired from her position as schoolteacher at the end of the school year in 1985. Marianne Filipov, Phil's other daughter, had moved home and taken over from Olga.

Olga's husband, Bob Petrov, who had operated the Borscht Kettle for many years, had also retired shortly after his wife. Their restaurant was now being managed by their daughter, Anna, and her husband, Uri Golubov. They had planned daily dinner menus to offer tourists authentic Russian cuisine. Of course, the tradition of fish and chips night on Fridays, originally started by Bob's *roditeli*, Nikolai and Margarita Petrov, was still being carried on.

Both Phil's daughters, upon moving home, began boarding with Marvin and June.

A Russian bakery and tearoom had been built near the meadows with a lovely sundeck offering views of the water off Telegraph Pass. Gayle Shatrova was hired to operate this business. June Palmer had been offered, and accepted, the position of hostess. Alexandria Bolitchyn would come to help them whenever school permitted.

Gayle and her husband, Martin, had a daughter, Angela, who was four years old and a son, Christopher, who was just over a year. Their only concern was what to do with their children while they were working. They had decided to talk it over with Anna and Uri as to what their plans were for their eighteen-month old twins, Madeline and Matthew. After some discussion, it was suggested that a daycare service be established at the schoolhouse. Katerina Molodstov would stand in until the school year ended and then Marianne would assume this responsibility.

Near the old church and the founding fathers' plaque, the New Petrograd General Store now had an annex that would only carry souvenirs. Longtime store owners Frank and Betty Yusporov were absorbed in running this new shop. In the future, their son, Alex, would manage the original store.

As one of the final steps in preparation, every store on Sharlotka Street had been spruced up in the last few weeks, courtesy of Tony Rosso. For some thirty-five years, Tony had been the village's sole maintenance man. It had only been a little over a year ago that his son, Gaspar, had moved home to take over his *papa*'s business.

CHAPTER TWO

Shocking News

Good afternoon, Mr. Rosso," John Petrov said to Tony when he came into the kiosk operated by John and his wife Sandy. A major portion of their business was handling mail for Canada Post.

"Good afternoon to you as well," Tony replied. "It's such a lovely spring day out. I've just been strolling about the village observing the various changes that are taking place. I find it so very interesting. Before heading home, I thought I may as well pick up our mail."

"You certainly would find it most interesting." John smiled at him before giving a little chuckle. He added, "This village sure is getting a facelift. I understand every street is to get a new name. I even joked to Sandy last week that I soon won't even know my own way home. I'm apt to think I'm on the wrong street."

"They are," chortled Tony. "I understand the committee thought it would be fun to give them all names with Russian words. I guess that will have to be done this week before the museum opens."

"For sure—we don't have much longer until opening day. Getting back to why you came, I've just finished sorting the mail. Along with your usual papers, I put a very interesting postcard from Mexico in your mail slot. Not that I make a point of snooping at people's mail, mind you, but you have to admit a postcard from Mexico is rather an oddity here."

"How exciting. It will be from Francisco and Alejandra García, whom we met a year ago on our Alaskan cruise. They were so fascinated with everything we told them about New Petrograd and talked often about wanting to visit."

"Well—" John started to say, but Tony talked happily on.

"Daria will be so pleased. Gaspar's friend Kevin is still staying in our guest room, but I'm sure Daria can figure something out." As Tony began to read the message written on the back of the postcard, he stopped as if the message had stung him and looked wistfully at John as if to say, *Help*. "I'd better hurry home and show this to Daria."

"Before you leave, would you mind taking the Palmers' mail with you?" John took it from their slot. "It seems they received a similar postcard," he added as he handed it to Tony.

"I suppose I should," Tony replied, as he hesitantly reached out to take it. Then he made a hasty move towards the door, almost knocking over Olga as he rushed out.

"Goodness, what is up with Tony?" she asked, looking at her son. "He looked very pale. I wonder if he is feeling well. Maybe I should go ask Daria. He also seemed to be in an unusual hurry and didn't even take time to say hello. That's certainly not like him."

"Well, you know how excitable he is at the best of times, but he received some mail today that, well, would certainly fuel this trait of his personality."

"Oh, something like when he received that letter from the

Ministry of Transportation regarding the road being built?"

"No, not quite like that." John snickered as he came around the counter to give his *mama* a kiss on the cheek. "I don't imagine this news will take very long to begin circulating around. You'll have to wait to hear it from others, *Mama*. I'm not going to give you even the slightest hint. It sure is nice to see you. How are you and *Papa* doing?"

"We are both doing fine. Can't you give me even the teeniest hint, dear—" She stopped in mid-sentence as John shook his head.

"So, I guess like everyone else you came to collect your mail." John reached into the mail slot belonging to his *roditeli*.

"Yes, partly, but I also wanted to have a chat with you. I was just thinking of you and Sandy. I know she is starting her last trimester. *Papa* and I would like to offer to take care of the kiosk so you can accompany her when the time comes for the delivery."

"Oh *Mama*, thank you! *Papa* too. That would be awesome! Sandy will be pleased when I tell her. She is quite taken with this idea of me being in the delivery room with her."

"Well, it will be a pleasant change for *Papa* and me, and it's not just a suggestion. I will tell *Papa* tonight that everything is arranged. If we happen to be babysitting Anna's children, we could bring them with us. We keep remarking on these miracles of life as we eagerly await our third grandchild. It hardly seems possible that you and Anna are grown, much less *roditeli*."

"If you do bring the twins, make sure they don't get into any chocolate bars. I don't mind but their *roditeli* might." John smiled as he handed her the mail and walked her to the door.

"Daria," Tony shouted as he came through the door.

"Honey, you don't need to shout. I'm just in the kitchen."

"Well, you best come sit down in the living room," Tony declared, as he began to propel her in that direction.

Daria looked at Tony oddly. "Why are you acting so strangely?"

"We received this postcard from Mexico."

"Oh, from those folks we met on the cruise. What were their names?"

"No Daria. It isn't from them. That is why you need to sit down. It is from Gaspar and *his wife*, Shelley."

"His w-*wife*?" Daria stammered. She snatched the postcard out of Tony's hand as if she had to see it for herself.

Written in Gaspar's sprawling handwriting, the card read:

Having a wonderful time. Swam with the dolphins yesterday. Planning on going deep-sea fishing tomorrow. Expect me and my wife Shelley on the barge next Thursday.

Love,

Gaspar and Shelley Rosso

She stared at the card a few minutes longer before she finally uttered in disbelief, "They eloped." She lifted her face to look at her husband.

"It would seem so."

"Do you think Marvin and June know?" Daria asked, wiping at her eyes.

"No, I don't believe they do. John sent their postcard from Shelley with me. I suppose we should just go across the street now and get it over with."

"Do we have to?" Daria asked, as she got up. "I'd rather do anything else than that."

"Seems to me that we have no other choice, my dear."

June soon answered their knock. "Well, this is a nice surprise. But Tony, Marvin isn't home. He went for a walk to see if anyone needs a hand with anything."

"June, Tony and I haven't come for a visit," Daria said, as she stepped inside. "Tony brought your mail home from the kiosk, and well, I guess there's something we thought you would want to see right away." She handed June the postcard.

June looked curiously at Daria as she led her guests to the kitchen. "Oh," she said, admiring the picture of Puerto Vallarta. Then she turned it over and began reading. After a moment, she said, puzzled, "This is from Shelley. I wasn't aware she was planning to go to Mexico anytime soon."

"I'm sure she didn't, or at least I think she didn't. Read on," Daria said.

We are having a wonderful time. Swam with the dolphins yesterday. I'm planning to relax on the beach tomorrow while my husband goes deep-sea fishing.

"What?" June said, looking at Tony and Daria, puzzled.

"Read on," they repeated.

Next Thursday I will be arriving in New Petrograd with my husband. Can't wait to see you.

Gaspar and Shelley Rosso

June let out a strangled gasp and then slowly sank into a kitchen chair. "No! They eloped, seriously. My only daughter.

How could she do that to me? Not that I'm sorry about who she married. I'm delighted and Marvin will be too, but—"

"Yes, we are also thrilled with his choice," Daria said.

"If my daughter thinks she is getting away with this, then she has another think coming," June declared as she straightened her shoulders. "After all those bridal magazines we used to pour over together—I can't believe it. I can't even imagine what Marvin's reaction will be."

"What my reaction will be to what?" Marvin asked as he came in through the back door. "By the way, nobody could use my unskilled labour." He stopped, and a confused look flashed across his face. "June, why is this tap running? Water is running all over the floor. Aren't you aware of what's going on out here?" He ran towards the sink and turned off the tap.

"Oh, my goodness," June exclaimed as she jumped up, almost colliding with him.

"I was going to do our lunch dishes when the doorbell rang. When I answered it, there were Tony and Daria with our mail, and this postcard."

"Nice picture of the ocean," Marvin remarked, as he took it from her, "Where is it?"

"Puerto Vallarta, where your daughter is currently honeymooning with Gaspar. They will be home next week," June said, her voice quavering.

"Pardon?" Marvin glanced at his wife before quickly turning over the postcard. Then he chuckled. "Good for them. It sure saves me a lot of money." Then he noticed his wife's stricken face. Clearing his throat, he said, "I think I will just get busy cleaning up this water. Tony, can you give me a hand for a minute?"

"Sure can. Then I think maybe we'd best be heading home.

Today is Thursday, so we have another week before they arrive."

As the men got busy, June turned to Daria imploringly. "I guess I have my work cut out for me for the next week. Do you think you could come by tomorrow around ten to help me arrange something for them?"

"Of course, June. Count on me. I feel almost the same way as you. After all, Gaspar is my only child." Daria hugged her friend.

That evening at dinner, Daria casually passed the postcard to Kevin. Upon reading the message, he began to guffaw loudly. "He went through with it, then. Good for him." Sensing an uneasy silence, he peered up from his plate of beef stroganoff and looked into Daria's troubled face.

"You knew," Daria said accusingly.

"Sure. Before he left to go to Vancouver, Gaspar talked about it daily. After all, it really isn't a surprise—he's been dating Shelley for a long time now. It's about time and I'm super happy for him. Shelley is great."

"Well, we can sure agree with you there. We are very happy to have Shelley as a part of our family now," Tony agreed, as he took another bite of his dinner.

"That's not the issue, of course," Daria told them. "Marvin and June are also pleased. The problem is the elopement. June is distraught that her only daughter did this. I admit, I'm not much better when I think I missed my only child's wedding."

"Well now," Tony said, soothingly, "you two agreed that you would get together tomorrow and plan something for them. I trust that you ladies putting your heads together will come up with just the right thing. I'm equally confident you'll be letting Marvin and me know if you need us to help with anything," Tony added, with a smile to Daria and a wink to Kevin.

The meal resumed in silence, but for Daria, the stroganoff had lost its flavour.

When he finished, Kevin set down his fork, and in almost the same motion, stood up. "I think I'll head down to the Kettle and see who is around. I know Gaspar was talking to Don about their moving in with him until he and I can build them a place. I can let Don know that his roommates will arrive next week."

Both Tony and Daria's mouths had dropped open. Daria blurted, "Just how many of his friends did know? I'm surprised he didn't ask one of you to be his best man. In fact, I wonder who was?"

"The only other person I know of him telling is Martin. Of course, for all I know, he could have told others. For a while, he was wondering about Martin being his best man. Finally, they decided it was too risky for them both to be gone. Especially now, with everybody so busy. In the end, he was thinking of asking one of Shelley's brothers. I admit, though, I don't really know."

This last statement was just too much for Daria. She exclaimed emphatically, "June must never hear any of what you just told us."

The next morning, when the mothers got together to plan a reception for their children, there was constant interruption from many folks confirming that the news they'd just heard was true. Regardless of everyone's initial reactions, over and over, it seemed they'd concluded that the news was good. New Petrograd was pleased to receive Shelley as one of its residents.

However, by the end of the afternoon, June and Daria had to admit that they really hadn't accomplished anything other than, as June declared, "Hosting a come-and-go tea party for the neighbor ladies."

"I can come again tomorrow," Daria said, attempting to cheer her up. "Now that everyone's initial surprise is over, I'm sure it will go much better."

"Yes," June replied, "although I did have the thought this afternoon that maybe we shouldn't organize anything. Then next week, when they arrive, we can plan something with them. At least, after telling the story over and over this afternoon, I am getting quite used to the thought of Gaspar being my son-in-law."

"That is true, June. I need to focus on the fact that Tony and I have a smart, beautiful daughter-in-law. I couldn't wish someone better for my son. I'll come again tomorrow at ten and we can discuss plans then. I also have an idea forming in the back of my mind that would be quite fun." Thinking of it, Daria giggled as she prepared to leave.

The barge steered past the craggy point and began gliding towards the pier. A banner strung across the bow declared, CONGRATULATIONS SHELLEY AND GASPAR. Upon seeing it, great cheers went up from everyone on the wharf, which was so crammed it was amazing that it held up under everyone's combined weight. Joe's crew looked on, grinning, knowing that the usual hustle and bustle of bringing the boxes ashore would have to wait.

The happy couple stood on board, their arms entwined, waving. Shelley looked resplendent in a lovely pink dress dotted with splashes of bright flowers, which she had accessorized with a simple white sweater. Standing a little behind her, Gaspar looked very dapper in grey suit trousers and a vest. His wine-coloured shirt was rolled up at the sleeves. Once the barge came to a full stop, Gaspar led his bride ashore amidst well wishes from the crew.

As they took their first few steps, Nick ran up with his camera and shouted, "Stop right there, I need to take your picture. My instructions this morning were to capture this moment on film."

Turning, suddenly they were facing their parents. June and Daria tried to look stern but failed miserably and instead grasped them in a huge embrace.

When they broke apart, June fingered a unique gold necklace Shelley was wearing. "Darling, this is lovely."

"Do you like it, Mom? Gaspar gave me this matching set with these earrings on our wedding day. Aren't they just gorgeous?" She gave her husband a quick peck.

Marvin impatiently broke up their conversation by announcing, "My turn now," and Shelley fairly flew into her father's arms.

"Come on, you too." Marvin motioned to Gaspar, pulling him in also.

Next, Shelley opened her arms to hug Tony, who clasped her emotionally, telling her how delighted they were to have her a part of their family.

Then he thumped Gaspar on the back, declaring, "Good job, son."

The newlyweds then started weaving their way through the randomly arranged receiving line. It began with Kevin, who was grinning from ear to ear and grabbed Gaspar in a huge bear hug. Standing with him was Marianne, whom he quickly introduced to Shelley. Marianne hugged her before presenting her with a large bouquet of flowers.

"Oh, how lovely, Marianne. Thank you so much. I always love the bright faces of daisies, and then to be accented with echinacea and salmon berries—look, they even match my dress. When we get home to Don's, the first thing I'll do is put them in water."

Hand to hand they moved, laughing, hugging, back slapping... from Martin to Gayle, to Anna to Uri, Jenny... all of Gaspar's best buddies.

Towards the middle of this receiving line, Don was standing with Mary Ellen. Suddenly Gaspar realized that they both needed to be introduced to Shelley. Only trouble was, as he introduced her to Mary Ellen, he called her Shelley Palmer. When Shelley giggled, he realized his mistake and bashfully corrected himself. This brought an even bigger spurt of laughter from Mary Ellen, as she hugged her.

Next it was Don's turn to be introduced and everyone chuckled, Shelley the loudest, when Gaspar correctly introduced her this time.

As Don slapped Gaspar on the back, Mary Ellen patiently waited to pin a boutonnière on him.

"Why, thank you," Gaspar said with a grin.

"Look, sweetie, now you match me," Shelley exclaimed as she lightly kissed his cheek.

"But once we get to your place, Don, I will need to put both our arrangements in water to keep them fresh."

Yet still there were the rest of the village folk to greet—a crowd that extended, it seemed, the whole length of the pier. Yet strangely, the line seemed to end at the Borscht Kettle.

CHAPTER THREE

A Wedding Reception

Bob and Olga, along with their grandchildren, Matthew and Madeline, were the last folks standing in this long reception line. As soon as Matthew saw Gaspar, he toddled over to him, arms outstretched. Madeline was just as excited as her brother, but after taking a step, halted when she saw Shelley, and shyly hung onto her *babushka*'s skirt. Gaspar knelt down to pick up Matthew, grabbing him up in a ferocious hug that had Matthew giggling uproariously. Setting him down, Gaspar joined Shelley as she knelt and talked quietly to Madeline. Eventually, she got her courage up and came over, and as she did, she held out the skirt of her dress. It was a delicate yellow floral print made into a sleeveless dress. She wore daisies and pink echinacea flowers in her curly, dark brown hair.

As she came closer, Shelley said, "You look like you're going to a party. And your hair is so pretty, did your *mama* do it?"

She vigorously nodded and then said, "Me go to party but me not tell anyone."

It was only then that Shelley noticed Matthew was wearing grey dress pants with a light blue short-sleeved shirt under a grey vest. Not exactly, she was sure, his usual attire on a Thursday afternoon.

He quickly confirmed this when he said, "*Mama* made me wear Sunday clothes!" His voice filled with disgust.

Shelley's husband, catching the questioning look from her, took note first of the children and then everything else. "What is this all about?" he said to no one in particular.

As Bob and Olga took hold of Shelley and Gaspar's arms, Bob answered, "I reckon this is the grandest reception ever for an errant child. If you or Shelley were mine, I don't think I'd be doing this," he concluded with a grin.

"What do you mean, Mr. Petrov—what reception?" Gaspar inquired, looking very puzzled.

"Really, Bob—" Olga began.

Just then, a shrill voice screeched behind them, causing the four of them to turn quickly in alarm. "Let see, Maddy seeee!"

Shelley stifled a laugh when she saw Matthew on his hands and knees holding out a stone for Madeline to look at, and then turning it over in his hand to admire before putting it into his shoe.

"Children, children," Olga cried as she ran towards them. "Madeline, please honey, don't screech so. And you, young man... you can't walk on a shoe filled with rocks," Olga said, as Matthew held his foot up so she could dump them out of the shoe. "They will hurt and besides, what will your *mama* say to me if you get all dirty?" She then began to wipe his hands clean with a hankie.

Once this little incident was resolved, and Matthew had run as fast as his little legs could go to catch up with his sister, the newlyweds allowed themselves to be propelled the rest of the way to the door.

From farther down the line, Daria and June looked at each

other and smiled; their plan was working out perfectly. Then they locked arms with their respective husbands and walked towards their destination.

Once inside, Shelley sucked in her breath and in a little gasp, causing Gaspar to look at her sharply. "Oh sweetie, this is just like in the bridal magazines I used to drool over with my Mom. Now I know for sure who is responsible for this."

Everywhere there seemed to be huge bouquets. At the end of each table delicate, yet simple, white and pink crepe bells hung. A mixture of daisies and echinacea petals were strewn haphazardly down each table amidst small glass dishes of mints. A huge pink bell and another banner with their names was behind a table obviously intended to be theirs. Just to the right of this, in the corner, a cake stood on a smaller table. More fresh flowers were artfully woven around the various layers.

As they were led towards the head table, Shelley felt a small hand grasp hers. Looking down into Matthew's face, she noticed his eyes glued on the cake. Again, Shelley felt a smile growing inside as she gladly let him propel her towards it. She turned to say something to Gaspar, only to see Madeline just as eagerly pulling him in the same direction.

"Pretty," the little girl said as Gaspar picked her up so she could see better. "No touch."

"No, we don't want to touch," Shelley agreed, as the four of them stood admiring the cake. When they turned, it was then she saw that other children had also crept forward, wide-eyed, to have a closer look.

Gaspar playfully clapped his hands. "Not yet, you rascals. I bet your *mamas* will say dinner first."

Several of them jumped up and down in delight when Gaspar showed them this bit of attention.

Putting his arms around her and drawing her even closer to him, Gaspar told them, "This is my wife, Shelley, and she will be living here now. I know some of you, like Angela, have met her before, but some of you haven't. Can you say hello?"

A chorus of shy hellos went up as the children were now beginning to scamper away.

Angela waited behind and shyly said to Shelley, "You are very pretty today," before turning and running off.

Anna Golubova, who was patiently waiting for everyone around the cake to disperse, directed them to the head table. Then she took her children's arms and led them to a table to the right of the cake. "This is where you will be sitting—at this table with *Dedushka* and *Babushka*. *Mama* and *Papa* have to work."

Once most people were sitting, Martin, in his role of *tamada*, picked up the microphone and announced, "Please sit and relax and soon drinks and some snacks will be served. There will be a bit of a delay while we wait for Joe and his crew to finish unloading, which I understand may take a bit longer than usual because they have some extra boxes with Shelley's belongings. Afterwards, they will be joining us for lunch."

"Yes, I did bring some of my personal items with us," Shelley admitted. Then, speaking directly to her parents, who were sitting nearby, she added, "Lyle and Gordy will be catching the barge later this summer to bring the rest."

"Really," Marvin chuckled. "You finally got them to promise a visit."

"I did. In fact, after all their talks with Gaspar, they seem quite excited. Especially to go fishing with you, Dad."

"I say," June said with a nod, "this is the second piece of good news your dad and I have received this spring. The first, of course, being your marriage to Gaspar."

During this exchange, large platters of herring or sardines were being served on crackers, accompanied by pickles and daintily cut cheese and egg sandwiches.

Martin was again addressing everyone. "I have just been told to start, as Joe and his crew won't be able to stay for long. It is my delight, then, to introduce to you to Mr. and Mrs. Gaspar Rosso. *Za-Molodykh!* Cheers to the young couple who recently got married."

Amongst the cheering, Marvin and Tony started calling, "*Gor'ko, Gor'ko.*" It did not take long for everyone in the room to take up the chant.

Shelley looked around, mystified, especially as her husband scooped her into his arms. However, before he kissed her, he announced to the guests, "You just hold your tongues from counting, you don't need your wine to get any sweeter. You've been drinking it just fine up until now. Not that I mind kissing my wife," he concluded as he folded her into a long kiss.

Just then, the count started... one... two... three... until it reached fifteen, and then the chant was replaced with clapping and catcalls that lasted until the newlyweds sat down.

Martin got up again to speak. "We do not plan to have you redo your vows, but we thought it would be nice if we completed the head table with attendants for each of you. We had many volunteers for this, so we decided we would have a little fun by having each of you choose a name thrown into these old coffee cans. So, Shelley, maybe you would like to go first."

Marvin brought the coffee can over to his daughter, holding it high above her head so she couldn't peek. She drew out a slip of paper and then instinctively handed it to her mother.

After glancing at it, June said, "Oh, how lovely. Anna Yusporova, it's your name she's drawn."

Anna gave her husband a quick peck on the cheek just as someone began to call, "*Gor'ko, Gor'ko*" again. Quickly Alex stood and, winking at Gaspar, bent her backwards, giving his wife a good sound kiss before sitting back down. The room erupted in laughter and Gaspar, with all the attention somewhere else, snuck another kiss from Shelley. Before Anna seated herself at the head table, June presented her with a bouquet.

Then it was Daria and Tony's turn to bring another coffee can to Gaspar who, likewise, chose a slip of paper and handed it to his *mama*.

With a glance at the slip in her hand, Daria declared, "I think the winner is also very appropriate." She turned to Kevin, who seem to be comfortably sitting with Don and the Filipov twins. There was a bit more shuffling in the room as Kevin relocated to the head table. It wasn't until Tony nudged her that Daria recalled that she had a boutonniere for Kevin, which she pinned to his shirt.

Don began to clink his water glass with a teaspoon as many of the other guests looked on, puzzled at what he was doing, because many of them were not familiar with this custom of encouraging the bride and groom to kiss. John Petrov, after staring quizzically at him, soon realized what was happening and, after mouthing the word *"Gor'ko,"* joined in. Before long, others began to do the same.

Gaspar leaned over as if to kiss his bride, but instead whispered something in her ear. Shelley let out a little chortle, smiled and beckoned to Tony, while Gaspar beckoned to June.

Nick was walking up to the front now. "I believe this will be a perfect time to get some group photos."

And for the next half hour, the wedding guests were entertained while he took several pictures of the bridal party, including the bride's and groom's *roditeli*.

"Well, that has been highly entertaining," Martin exclaimed. "Next, we would like to hear if the maid of honour has anything she would like to say."

"I sure do," Anna said as she stood. "I am thrilled to say something—and I think I speak for everyone here. Last week, when we heard that you two had eloped, the comment I heard repeated over and over was 'How positively grand!' We are all excited to think that Shelley is becoming a permanent resident, thanks to my old schoolmate and good friend Gaspar, on your right. Congratulations to both of you."

As echoed words of welcome reverberated around the room, Martin said, "Thank you, Anna. Yes, Shelley, she is correct. I know Gayle and I are sure thrilled to have you become a resident—and our daughter."

"Next, we will ask the best man if he would like to say something."

"I'm not one for making speeches. Shelley, I can attest that Gaspar has been a different man since he started dating you. I do have one important message I want to share, although really it is something Martin told me. Apparently, a Russian saying is that although any baby is treasured, just remember that it takes very little passion to produce a baby boy and a lot more passion to produce a baby girl. Congratulations, Shelley and Gaspar."

The crowd roared uproariously, even though many of them had probably heard it hundreds of times before. Just then, the door opened and Joe and his crew came in. This was a signal to everyone in the kitchen to start serving a light lunch. Gaspar was still laughing when he took Shelley, who had turned crimson, into his arms and kissed her.

Grinning widely, Sandy Petrova began to clink her glass, which started another round of clinking. But this had an opposite effect because abruptly they stopped kissing and this time Shelley beckoned her dad, and Gaspar, his *mama*.

Amongst all this chaos, Martin was barely heard saying, "Before we eat, let's call on Father Nikolas to lead us in a grace."

Father Nikolas, who was also grinning, took the microphone and began by saying, "Shelley and Gaspar, I, too, would like to congratulate you on your decision to enter into the holy state of matrimony. Let us now bow our heads and give thanks."

When grace was finished, everyone settled down to enjoy the bowls of *Okroshka* soup—a hearty meal, accompanied by *Stolichniy* rye bread. To finish the meal, there was a simple dessert of different flavors of ice cream to choose from. Immediately afterward, many of the *roditeli* began gathering their small children together to take them home, as they were already long overdue for their naps.

"Let's give a hearty thank you to Anna and Uri for that lovely luncheon," Martin said, as he again resumed his position behind the microphone. "It has been suggested that we leave some time now for speeches by anyone else who cares to say a few words."

First to speak was Joe the barge captain. "It has been my pleasure to have you with us these last few days. My crew and I would like to extend our congratulations." Then, speaking to his men, he told them that they needed to leave if they wanted to keep to their schedule.

Throughout the afternoon, several folks came forward to

give impromptu speeches. A very touching one was when Marg stood and began, "Gaspar, I feel like you are a third son because of all the time you spent in our home with my two boys. Likewise, I know my sons always felt welcome in the home of your *roditeli*. I am delighted to be here at your wedding reception and to welcome your bride."

Phil then stood, and embracing Marg, added, "We would like to invite you to spend the next three days at the lighthouse."

After the surprise had subsided along with the murmurs of many of the women and a few men, they said, "How very nice, a whole weekend away."

Martin continued, "Next, I call upon the groom's *roditeli*, followed by the bride's."

Tony came forward and beaming at Shelley said, "It sure is our pleasure, my dear, to heartily welcome you into our family. Now I think Gaspar's *mama* has a story she would like to share."

"I'm sure Gaspar isn't going to appreciate me telling this story, but I've been waiting for years to share this on his wedding day," Daria said, laughing. "Gaspar was around seven and Olga was talking to her class about how to use words like *beautiful* and *handsome*. She was teaching this by asking each of her students to repeat, *My mama is beautiful* or *My papa is handsome*. As she made her way around the classroom, her lesson was going well... until she came to Gaspar. He was fine saying, *My mama is beautiful*. But when she asked him to say, *My papa is handsome*, Gaspar said, 'No, he isn't.' So Olga patiently repeated it. *My papa is handsome*. And Gaspar replied, 'No, he isn't, not when he's on the potty'."

Daria could hardly finish as Gaspar glared at her, to a chorus of uproarious laughter and pounding on the tables.

"Olga told me afterward that she could hardly contain her laughter, choosing instead to go on to the rest of her lesson plan."

June and Marvin were still laughing as Marvin picked up the microphone and, despite barely being able to speak, welcomed Gaspar into their family also.

"After that story," June said, "the one I had planned to tell on my daughter seems to pale by comparison. However, the one I have on my mind is, whenever we would go away, she didn't want to come home. You see, Shelley was always a very social girl. One time we were visiting Marvin's brother, her Uncle Melvin and Aunty Wendy. I was telling my sister-in-law that we would be leaving the next morning. Shelley kept questioning me. 'Tomorrow?' she would say, looking at me with those big blue eyes. I would confirm, 'Yes dear, tomorrow.' This went on a few times until she finally said, 'But I still have clean panties.' Then she turned to her Aunty Wendy, put her hands on her hips, and said, 'Aunty Wendy, sometimes I just don't understand my mom.' So you see, Gaspar, she really hasn't always been the easiest to manage. Always questioning every last detail. We sincerely wish you more luck."

"I see," Gaspar said, amidst the laughter going on around him. Then, as he took his wife in his arms again, went on, "I will certainly keep that in mind."

Shelley was enjoying herself immensely—well, with exception of the last few minutes—and could hardly believe it when Martin announced that next, the bride and groom would cut the cake. Everyone gathered around the small table to witness the actual cutting and the merriment that went along with feeding each other. And of course, Nick was there with his camera to take more pictures.

As they sliced the cake into pieces and passed them out,

Shelley felt something was wrong. Suddenly it struck her—there were only a few eager fingers reaching to grab a plate.

"Oh, I forgot that after lunch the younger children went home for naps. We must be sure to send some pieces of cake home for them, don't you agree, sweetheart?"

"I sure do," Gaspar answered, as he kissed her again. "In fact, bring some of those take-away boxes, Kevin, and maybe you and Anna can start packaging some up right now."

"I can help, too," Marianne offered, as she moved beside Kevin.

Finally, it was their turn to thank everyone for making this day so special. As they began, Shelley looked at Daria and June. "I'm sure you're responsible for all this. Thank you, both of you, so much. Gaspar and I never expected this lovely homecoming."

June just laughed before replying, "Trust me, with only a week's warning, it was a communal effort."

"Well, I suppose I should have guessed that. It seems to be the only way anything gets done in New Petrograd. Somehow, though, I feel you two were the masterminds."

It was around five in the evening when all the merriment came to a close and people began gathering their things together. Finally, only a handful of Gaspar's best friends remained—Alex and Anna, Kevin, Don, Marianne, Mary Ellen, and Martin. They were all very pleased to accept Marvin's invitation to stay and have dinner with the families. Soon, platters of roast lamb and pork were served along with a green salad, mashed potatoes, asparagus, cauliflower and cheese, and boiled red cabbage.

"You'd think I had done a day's work, I'm so tired," Shelley sighed during dinner. "Wasn't it a wonderful day?"

"I agree, my love. It was an amazing day. I'm tired, too, yet the only work we did all day was sit at the table and smile. By the way, I didn't add my thanks earlier to everyone along with Shelley's, but thank you."

"All those cameras. I'm sure, right now, I don't ever want to see one again. Talking about photos, Mom," Shelley said, turning towards June, "did you take some pictures of the room when you were decorating? It was so amazing."

"I'm sure Nick would have, honey," Marvin answered. "We asked him to be the official photographer so we will get all the pictures he took. Then you can choose which ones you want to have duplicates of."

"I also noticed several others with cameras," Martin added.

"I know, I saw that, too," Gaspar said. "Sometimes it seemed you didn't know which way to look. By the way, not to change the subject, but Kevin, I've been dying to tell you all afternoon. Can you believe who Shelley and I saw honeymooning in Mexico?"

Kevin shrugged, then after taking a minute to think about it, said, "No idea, really, but if I were a betting man, my guess would be Greg and Barbara. I knew he bumped into her at a coffee shop soon after he went back to Calgary and they ended up having coffee together. I think he told her that night she was crazy to have turned down your proposal." Kevin gave a little laugh before continuing, "In his next letter, he wrote he was occasionally seeing her. Love sure works in mysterious ways."

"That's right. Who would have ever thought it, but they looked great together and very much in love. It was fabulous to see them and, of course, to introduce Barbara to my amazing, gorgeous wife, both inside and out! If you've finished eating, my love, would you care to finish the day by having a dance with me? Then I think it is time that we retired for the night."

This was a signal for all the men present to begin shoving tables and chairs aside to create room for a dance floor. For an answer, Shelley stretched out her hand, and as he pulled her up and into his arms, she looked adoringly at her husband.

As Gaspar led her onto the makeshift dance floor, someone turned on a cassette player and, very suitably, Lionel Ritchie and Diana Ross began singing "Endless Love." When the piece ended and changed to "Juke Box Hero" by Foreigner, the other couples joined them. The space really wasn't big enough to accommodate all these people, but laughing boisterously, they just went on dancing even if it meant skirting around tables and chairs.

Daria was leaning back watching their offspring and friends having this hilarious dance, when she nudged June. "Do you think the Filipov twins might be next to get married? It seems to me that those two young bucks, Kevin and Don, have been hanging around them a lot lately."

"Really, Daria," Tony began, when Daria held up her hand to stop him.

"I was right when I predicted another wedding, wasn't I?"

When the music stopped again, everyone returned to their tables to finish their drinks.

Gaspar picked up his bride and said, "I reckon I had best be getting my wife home," and with the last camera click of the day, he carried her out.

CHAPTER FOUR

A Night at the Lighthouse Station

Gaspar woke early the next morning and sat up against the headboard, his arms folded behind his head, sleepily admiring his wife as she slept. Her long blonde hair was flung loosely across the pillow. I wonder, he thought, if I will ever tire of seeing her like this.

When Shelley stirred in her sleep, she stretched, thrilling at the sound of seagulls mewing just outside the window. Turning another way, she could just make out the sound of the waves gently lapping against the shore. How good it was to come home to such a warm reception! Home. She smiled at the mere thought of the word as she lazily yawned and opened her eyes. She turned to look up at her husband.

Seeing him sitting propped up against the headboard, she murmured, "Good morning, sweetheart," as she stretched up to kiss him.

"Good morning, *moi medvezhono*." He bent to return her kiss before exclaiming, "What do you think we should do today? Of course, we could go grab something to eat and come right back to this room."

"I'm not sure," Shelley answered with a cheeky smile. "I was just thinking how wonderful it feels to call this place home. Perhaps our actual marriage ceremony at the Vancouver Court House was rather clinical, to say the least." Laughter filling her voice, she continued, "You, of course, did cause a bit of a stir, my dear, when just before we went in you couldn't find my wedding band. Then you had to dash after Mandy so you could ask her if she could loan you one of hers. But everything else has been just grand! The outstanding honeymoon in Mexico and the reception we had yesterday have all been beyond words. I feel like I am sliding down a rabbit hole and reality is soon going to hit me."

"Don't remind me," he said. "That was such an awful few minutes when I couldn't find that ring. I'm just glad we found it that night in the hotel room before we left for Mexico. I guess now it will be a story we will laugh about for years. I am so glad you feel that way about the wedding, love, because I think everything couldn't have gone better. Even the trip on the barge was fantastic. Joe's crew went all out to make our journey home memorable."

Shelley nodded before replying, "I couldn't agree with you more. Joe and his crew did everything to make it a special six days. Especially the night Scott and Ray cooked us that exceptional dinner."

"That was fun. However, to get back to my original question," Gaspar said, "I was thinking that after we get dressed, we could walk up to the teahouse and see if Gayle might have something for breakfast. I know she isn't officially open yet, but she just might have something. For the last few weeks, she has been tantalizing everyone with her latest creations. Then perhaps we could wander around and look at a few spots about the village where we might want to build our home."

"Oooh, that sounds so inviting! A place to build our own home! I can't think of anything I'd rather be doing." Shelley gave him another kiss.

Later, when they were both ready, they stepped outside.

As Shelley looked around, she remarked, "Another day I would like to have a closer look at the lighthouse station and all the cabins that Kevin has built. Such a clever idea to turn it into accommodations."

Then Shelley took her husband's arm and they set out on the path leading to the teahouse. Shelley was almost skipping, her footsteps were so light. The warm spring sunshine added its own special touch, inviting anyone to relish the day. As they walked along, content in each other's company, Shelley was the first to break the silence.

"I'm sure this path through the meadows, made out of crushed rock, is new."

"It is," Gaspar replied. "Peter and his *papa* have been very busy putting all these finishing touches on everything. Peter has been amazing, working so tirelessly, and he seems to instantly get the picture of what we want to accomplish. Kevin and I have been thinking that maintaining things like this might be a perfect weekend or summertime job for him."

"I can sure see Peter jumping at an offer like that," Shelley concurred.

Then she paused, lifting her face up to breathe in the spring air. Gaspar took advantage of the situation by enveloping her in a kiss, which lasted a good long while.

When they stopped, Shelley finally exclaimed, "And here all I wanted was to breathe in deeply of these meadows and all the sweet aromas. No wonder my mom finds so much pleasure in them."

"Ah, but wasn't that much better?" Gaspar took her hand

and they resumed walking. "I think the Filipov twins also enjoy these meadows. I'm sure they were responsible for all the flowers yesterday, directed by your mom, of course."

"Who do you think made that amazing cake with all its floral decorations? I am assuming it was done here, especially with my mom's comment that they had only one week."

"I imagine that would be Gayle's creation. Of course, everyone here knows how to bake a *Medovic Torte*, but since Gayle started working in this bakery and teahouse, I think any special orders would be left to her. As you know, your mom is planning on working here, so she very likely did the floral arrangement on it."

"Wow," Shelley responded, "I sure didn't know my mom could do anything like that. She must have developed new talents since she moved here."

By now, they had walked the short distance to the teahouse. Gaspar tried the door, but it was locked. He tried it again. "Maybe I was mistak—"

Gayle opened it. "Why, hello," she said hesitantly.

"Hi Gayle," Gaspar greeted her. "We were hoping you might have something for breakfast."

"Breakfast?" she repeated, raising her eyebrows. "It's almost noon."

"Are you serious?" Shelley asked, looking at her watch. "How can that be?"

"I don't know, Mrs. Rosso, I'm sure," Gayle said, teasingly. "Come in anyway, I'm quite certain I can rustle up something for you."

Upon entering the room, Shelley glanced around and exclaimed, "Oh Gayle, your teahouse is delightful."

Besides the bouquets of brightly coloured flowers, *babushka* dolls of all sizes and colours were displayed on various cupboards. In addition, platters and bowls in Russian designs and blue and white figurines shared the same space. Lacy white curtains hung from the windows and seemed to complete the picture. These were drawn back, offering a perfect view of the meadows and in the distance glimpses of the water.

"It is all thanks to the efforts of Anna Yusporova," Gayle replied, as she brought them big bowls of *Okroshka* soup. "Everything displayed here will be sold in the souvenir shop. My apologies, these are leftovers from your reception yesterday—thankfully the soup is served cold. I did bake fresh bread this morning if you would like some."

"Oh," Shelley said, "I just assumed Anna and Uri prepared the meal yesterday."

Gayle laughed. "Actually, the meal at your reception was a joint effort."

"As for the future plans," Gaspar added, "Gayle will prepare the breakfast menu and light luncheons, and Anna and Uri will prepare everything else. The committee's idea was that this will make everyone's workload more manageable and give our visitors options."

"Well, let me remind you, it is a bakery, so you can come just for bread and other baked goods," Gayle said. "Here, let me get you some slices of the *Borodinsky* bread I made this morning. It may still be warm from the oven."

"This bread," Gaspar told Shelley as he offered her a piece before taking one himself, "is one of my favourites. My *mama* never made enough of it to satisfy *papa* and me. It is a dark brown sourdough bread, traditionally sweetened with molasses and flavored with coriander and caraway seeds."

"Well, I guess that will be one of the next things your mother will have to teach me, then," Shelley said with a grin.

They quickly finished their soup and then Gaspar asked

Gayle, "Do you mind if Shel and I just sit here on your deck for a while?"

"Of course not," Gayle said. "After all, my teahouse is quite secluded. Stay as long as you want. Can I get you something to drink and a dessert perhaps?"

Soon they were settled on the verandah, a couple of cold glasses of raspberry *mors* and a plate of *pirogi* set on the patio table.

"Would you like anything else?" Gayle asked, as she prepared to leave.

"I don't think so, unless my wife does."

As Shelley shook her head, Gaspar said, "Just the bill, please, Gayle."

"Oh, I think for my husband's good friend I can add a few meals in with your hotel package. I will come by later and pick up your dirty dishes. See you tomorrow for breakfast?" she inquired.

"Yes, we will be here for sure. And Gayle, thank you so much."

"Yes, thank you, that is most generous of you," Shelley said, as she stood to give Gayle a hug.

She stood watching Gayle until she had left the pathway. Then Shelley sat down on Gaspar's lap and cuddled up to him. He effortlessly swung her legs around, so she was sitting sideways, and wrapped his arm tightly around her, so she was cradled in his embrace. They sat that way for a very long time enjoying the warmth of the breeze as it fluttered around them, the only other movements being the occasional reaching for a drink or a bite of dessert. It was getting late in the afternoon when Gaspar finally broke the spell.

"If we are going to look for a place to build, we should maybe talk about where. I know you often mentioned you would like to look at the sea through your living room window. Do you still think the same?"

"Absolutely." Shelley turned her head to look out at the water glistening in the late afternoon sun. "Just looking at it, much less the sounds, makes me feel peaceful. I could meditate all day."

"I don't like the sound of that. What about my supper? Or cleaning my house, or for that matter, my laundry?"

"I'm sure I don't know," she replied, grinning. "The maid will take care of it. I'm sure I recall you mentioning you had one."

Then letting out a huge giggle, she jumped off his lap, challenging him to catch her as she raced down the path.

It was a few minutes before Gaspar's long strides caught up with her. "You are so lucky, my dear, that I love you so much," he chuckled, as his arms encircled her, drawing her close. "As I was saying, we can either look at places adjacent to these meadows, or near those of our *roditeli*."

"Oh, near our parents' places, for sure. I don't want our children to have to go far to see their grandmas."

"Right you are," he agreed.

They took a side street to the fields north of their parents' places and spent a lovely couple of hours strolling hand in hand, discussing locations and ideas.

Eventually, Gaspar looked at his watch and remarked, "You know, *moi medvezhono*, it is Friday. Fish and chips night. Should we go for supper at the Borscht Kettle?"

"I'd love some fish and chips. But please, sir, can we have take-out tonight and eat back in our room?"

And so they did.

CHAPTER FIVE

Lighthouse Station

"Today I can say good morning." Gayle greeted Shelley and Gaspar with a huge grin when they came through the door before eight-thirty. "What can I get for you? I am starting to increase my selection of breakfasts. Take a look at the menu board for what I've prepared today."

Menu
Fried eggs and sausage
Blini with honey for dipping
Grenki
Lazy vareniki

"Goodness!" Shelley exclaimed. "All that and Gaspar said you aren't even open yet?"

"Well, I guess, officially that's true. Unofficially, ever since my first batch of bread, folks have been coming to my door. Just look around and see how many tables have dirty dishes," she said with a laugh.

"It is amazing to think that at the end of next week, I will be open from seven in the morning until three in the afternoon. Your mother will start then, and Alexandria will help out when her schooling permits. My day will begin around five, so I can't say I'm looking forward to that."

After reading the list, Gaspar remarked excitedly, "*Grenki*, really Gayle, that is awesome! I think we will have one order of it and one order of *Lazy vareniki* to share. Shelley hasn't had either of them yet, so her taste buds will be in for a real treat."

"For sure, Gaspar. I was informed by Mary Ellen that I should offer various coffees and teas for the tourists. This morning I've brewed a medium and dark roast, plus French vanilla. I also have a variety of teas—Orange Pekoe, Earl Grey, and English Breakfast. Would you care for something to drink and I will bring everything to your table?"

"English Breakfast for me, please," Shelley said. "How about you, Gaspar?"

"I think I'll have a medium roast, please. I got quite used to having a cup when I would visit Shelley in Vancouver. This is great, that you'll be serving it here now, since I won't be travelling to the city very often anymore."

"Gayle, I sure don't mind bussing these tables for you. Just give me a grey bin and I'll get started right away. Gaspar, you won't mind carrying our drinks to a table, will you, sweetie? Just pick one where the lovely sun is coming in."

"It is fine, dear," a familiar voice said. "I can help Gayle bus the tables."

Whirling around, they saw June sitting by the window.

"Mom," Shelley cried, racing over to envelop her in a hug.

Chuckling, June stood, anticipating her daughter's hug, before turning to hug her son-in-law. "I wasn't going to say anything until you offered to bus the tables. Your task right now is to enjoy these last few days of your honeymoon."

"Oh Mom, yesterday was so wonderful."

"Would you care to join us at our table, Mrs. Palmer?"

June squinted at him. "None of this Mrs. Palmer stuff, Gaspar. I am Mom now. I am just finishing my coffee so, no. I will start helping Gayle. I am meeting up with Dad when he gets back from fishing with Bob. So, I'll have plenty of time to clear tables. We'll all probably have dinner at the Kettle tonight, if you care to join us?"

Gaspar looked at his wife, then replied, "Thank you for the invitation, Mom, but I think we might have other plans."

"Today we are planning to tour the buildings of the lighthouse station," Shelley informed her. "Oh, Mom, our room is the most charmiest ever. If that's a word."

Gaspar left then to go to their table, and Shelley spent a few more minutes chatting with her mother. When she saw Gayle heading towards Gaspar with their food, she gave her mom one quick hug and then hurried to join her husband. As Gayle set the plates of food down, she indicated that she had brought two extra plates.

"I will leave you alone now to enjoy your breakfast. Please let me know if you need anything else or a refill of your drinks."

Then she left.

Gaspar began dishing up the food as he explained what the dishes were. "*Grenki* is made of stale bread. *Mama* used to find any bread she had and would bake it in the oven. Then she would fill it with all sorts of things. It looks like Gayle has filled this one with jam. The best way I know to explain *Lazy vareniki* is that they are a cross between Russian dumplings and pies."

"Yum, yum," Shelley said, smacking her lips together after

she took her first bite of *Grenki*. "This seems very similar to French toast."

When they had finished, Gaspar said, "I went to the office this morning while you were showering and spoke to Mr. Filipov. He suggested we come around ten and they will gladly take us on a tour."

"That should give us ample time to have a relaxing breakfast," Shelley replied, sitting back to cradle her tea mug.

"We have thirty-five minutes until we have to be there, so I think I will have a refill of my tea. I should have plenty of time to drink it before we need to go." Shelley pushed back her chair to go get it.

"Did I hear the word refill?" June asked, as she came and stood at the end of their table.

"Mom, I can get it. You don't start work until next Saturday."

Gaspar held out his empty mug to June. She smiled at him as she reached out to take it from him.

"Goodness, getting your refills will be no trouble at all. Remember, I have all day to fill in while I'm waiting for your father to return."

"Good morning," Phil said, "to those who changed our status."

"Changed your status?" Gaspar asked, puzzled. "I don't understand."

"Well, up until now, we've been known as *the newlyweds*," Marg chuckled.

"Ah, I see," Gaspar said with a smile, wrapping his arms around his wife. "I'm pleased Shel and I could oblige you, then.

Although I'm not sure we will hold the title for very long until we have to pass it on."

"If you're referring to my daughters, Gaspar, I imagine you know more than I do."

"The same goes for my son," Marg concluded, smiling at him.

"So, you thought you would like a tour of this new establishment?" Phil asked.

"Yes, I sure would," Shelley was quick to reply. "Gaspar has written me all about the plans, even sent me pictures. I never imagined this finished complex though. How many buildings in total?"

"Seven," replied Phil, "including the lighthouse tower and this building where we are now. It is the original home. Of course, this area will also serve as our office."

"And, I dare say, Phil and I are living right here. Phil may have been fine when he was on his own, but I'll have nothing to do with walking up fifty-six stairs every day," Marg finished, with a gentle squeeze of Phil's hand.

"Fifty-six!" Shelley gasped. "That would be quite a workout even for my legs. I don't blame you, Mrs. Filipova. Mind you, when I came for Thanksgiving in 1984, and you invited us in for a tour, Mr. Filipov, I can't recall there being that many stairs. I must admit I was pretty excited about being invited inside a lighthouse. I'm sure I just raced up the stairs on adrenalin."

"Well," Phil said, "this lighthouse is about sixty feet high. We are planning daytime tours to the watch room and gallery deck. Mary Ellen has suggested they could arrange an evening tour up there to stargaze for the younger hale and hearty clients."

"For those of us who aren't," Marg cheerfully continued,

"we could go out on the wharf and see the same stars. For any of our visitors not from around here, the Northern Lights will be a real showstopper. Of course, they are often not really visible until quite late at night in the summer."

"Why is that?" Shelley asked.

"Because of its being so light until quite late," Gaspar answered her.

"Oh, of course," Shelley acknowledged, "that makes sense. I have so much to learn about living life this far north. Maybe talk to Gayle or Anna about throwing in a light snack and drink. At night, guests could be offered an option of a warm drink."

"You are right, Shelley. Those are all suggestions that Mary Ellen made," Phil replied.

"I have set up pictures of the lighthouse over the years in these photo albums. As well, my daughter has also suggested that we carry a few books on facts and figures of lighthouses through the ages. Betty and Frank will have copies for sale in the souvenir shop. That's about all for this building, so let's carry on to the next site," Phil said as he opened the door, ushering them all out.

It was easy to see the five buildings extending for quite a ways, all in various sizes. Also, it appeared that there was one more building not yet completed.

At the next building, Marg said as she opened the door, "This is the third original one. It was initially used as a storehouse, so we are going to continue to use it that way. This is another one of Mary Ellen's suggestions. She even talked us into getting a set of these commercial washers and dryers."

"An essential suggestion," Shelley agreed.

As they stepped inside, Gaspar commented, "Just look at the mounds of linen, and boxes of toilet paper."

"I imagine that whole row of cupboards will hold a lot of your supplies for cleaning, laundry detergent, and all that. Are those labels for where everything is? It sure looks to me to be well designed and organized."

"Well, again, we can thank Mary Ellen for all her advice," Marg said. "She told us that she is planning on interviewing some people to help clean the rooms, and take care of the mounds of laundry, which will happen every day." Marg laughed.

"Even if I don't learn anything about your lighthouse station, I am learning I like the sound of your daughter, Mr. Filipov," Shelley commented as they exited.

"You can say that again," Phil said with a laugh. "I've learned a whole new side of her. Next is your cabin, which of course we won't need to look into."

"I do hope you find it comfortable and everything is to your liking, though," Marg remarked.

"You will notice it is a quite a bit smaller and, it seems to me, it was Gaspar who was overheard dubbing it *the honeymoon suite* when he was helping Kevin work one day."

"Really, sweetheart," Shelley said coyly. "Did you have your own honeymoon in mind when you said that?"

"Maybe I did, *moi medvezhono*," Gaspar answered her with a grin. "And yes, we do find it most comfortable, Mrs. Filipova. Shelley and I have both mentioned how perfect it is."

"I'm so pleased to hear that," Marg replied with a smile.

"In this next building we have a large room which could be used for a large gathering." Phil stepped into a living room, complete with a piano and fireplace. A kitchenette was on one side, and on the opposite wall another washer and dryer.

"This room was designed with Don's tour groups in mind. Because of course, if you come back wet and cold, you can immediately wash your clothing. There are large dorm rooms on either side with two single beds and four bunk beds in each. Naturally, we can use it for any size group or for two families," Marg finished.

"You mean all told, twenty people can sleep here?" Gaspar asked.

"Yes," Phil replied, "and I understand Don has his first fishing trip booked in two weeks."

"Ingenious, is all I can say," Shelley commented, as she followed them back outside again.

"So, this next cabin can hold two couples or a family of four." Phil waved in its direction. "The building Kevin is currently working on will be the same size. And he plans to build a few more like it. I think any future buildings he puts in will have a similar design."

When they reached the path that led to the teahouse, Shelley exclaimed, "Even this is such a good idea, having a place so close to where your guests can go for breakfast. We were there this morning and the food was delicious. I'm sure the guests will really enjoy it."

Walking back, Marg pointed out to Shelley the flowerboxes in front of each building and said, "Your mom has been giving Mary Ellen ideas of what can be planted here. Then on the other side... here, come through this way to see the view."

When they followed them through the archway, they were looking at a delightful grassed-in area where chairs and even a lawn swing had been set up. The meadows stretched beyond and then, at the far end, a trailhead was visible. The water spread glimmering silver and blue before them as if it were a tableau.

"Your *papa* did this with some help from John Molodtsov," Phil remarked.

"Unbelievable," was all Gaspar could say, while he shook his head. "I didn't know anything about this. That looks like a barbecue pit in the middle?"

"It is. That was Shelley's dad's suggestion."

"Can we try it out tonight?" Shelley tentatively asked her hosts.

"Of course, if you know how to use it. We have some wiener sticks, wieners and buns, marshmallows and some cold drinks in the office."

"Let me guess," Shelley said, amused. "It was Mary Ellen who suggested all that."

Chuckling in return, Phil and Marg replied in unison, "Yes."

"Are you okay with us having a barbecue, sweetie?" Shelley asked, as if in afterthought.

"I couldn't be more in agreement, my love," Gaspar replied.

"Mind if Phil and I join you?" Marg shyly inquired, after briefly looking at Phil.

"Of course not. We'd be delighted."

"Until supper time, we'll stay right here. Or maybe check out where that trailhead goes," Gaspar added, as he took Shelley's hand.

CHAPTER SIX

Oasis Coming to an End

"Sweetheart, this is the last day in our little oasis," Shelley murmured on Sunday morning, as she gave Gaspar a kiss. "I suppose it's only appropriate we attend church."

"I suppose so, but I have been quite enjoying having you exclusively to myself. I have an idea for afterward where we can spend the afternoon together. We just need to get my truck at the home of my *roditeli*. We can maybe have lunch with my folks, but right afterward escape for the rest of the day."

"Where to?" she asked.

Kissing her, he answered, "That's my surprise, love, okay?"

They did show up in church, but intentionally arrived a few minutes late and sat at the back, then left early to avoid conversing with anyone. Hand in hand, they strolled to the Rosso home, arriving about the same time as they did.

"Isn't this a pleasant surprise to find coming home from church?" Daria chortled. "You will stay for lunch, won't you?" Without waiting for an answer, she went on, "Tony, go across the street and invite Marvin and June."

"I agree, this is sure good having you both home," Tony smiled, hugging them both. "I'll be right back."

"Where's Kevin, *Mama*?" Gaspar asked, after he'd waited a few minutes and he hadn't arrived.

"Well, uh, your *papa* may have loaned him his Bronco."

"Whatever for? He's not working today, is he?"

"Oh no. It is getting busier the closer it gets to opening day, but so far, he still manages to take Sundays off. But quite often, of late, he borrows the Bronco for his personal use."

In a few minutes, June came bustling in, followed by a grinning Marvin, and went over and hugged them both.

Then she said, "Daria, I had started to make a taco salad, so brought it along." She handed it to her.

"Um, *Mama*, we were discussing why *Papa* loaned Kevin the Bronco."

June said, her eyes twinkling, "I think I know, just ask—"

"Well, that's simple," Tony answered him. "It's a lovely spring day so he thought he and the twins would go for a drive. They left right after church. After all, I sensed the last few days that he feels you deserted him," Tony said teasingly.

"I do agree with Kevin that it is a nice day for a drive," Gaspar replied. "In fact, that is why Shel and I came home to get my truck—to do the same. So, tell me, *Papa,* is Don with them?"

"Don Rosnokov?" Tony shrugged. "I don't know, nothing was said about him."

"Lunch is ready. Please, everyone, grab a spot at the table," Daria interrupted.

"Afterward, don't worry about the dishes, you kids go and enjoy yourselves," Daria and June said, almost in unison. Then looking at each other, they burst into laughter.

"Can we go to Rushing Falls?" Shelley asked tentatively, when they were backing out of the driveway.

Gaspar gave her a quick kiss. "That is the first place I have in mind. It's always my favourite place, since it's where we had our first date. Mind you, we still need to travel on bush roads to get there, not the new road. Is that okay?"

"Absolutely, sweetheart. First, you say. Is there more?" she inquired.

"There is." His dark eyes twinkled with delight.

She waited a few minutes, and when he didn't say anything else, said, "I can see that you're not going to tell me."

"You're right. But that is because I don't know anymore. I think the most enjoyable way to spend our time is on a whim."

"I like that idea. You do think of everything, don't you?"

"It is my goal to have you always feel that way, my love," he said, wrapping one arm around her.

For an answer, Shelley reached up to give him a peck behind the ear.

"None of that," Gaspar playfully growled, as he took her hand in his. "No messing with the driver."

The day was gorgeous. Gaspar opened the window to let in the warm spring air. At Rushing Falls, they walked hand in hand through the evergreen forest, listening to the songbirds chirping, and the scolding squirrels that called from the trees. Continuing along the path to where they could see the water rushing as it spilled over, they shared their memories of their first time coming here. Then they sat in the grass to quietly enjoy each other's company.

Back in the truck and driving on the new road, they spotted some gentle deer before they bounced across the road.

A little further along, they had to stop while a porcupine slowly crossed in front of them. Then a black bear made a surprise appearance as it lumbered across the road. Beauty seemed to surround them.

"It's not far to Port Essington from here," Gaspar said, after a while. "I'll treat you to dinner there, *moi medvezhono.* They have a Canadian Japanese restaurant that Kevin mentioned to me recently. He told me it serves a delicious meal."

"You planned that all along, didn't you?"

"You think so, do you?" he inquired as he lightly kissed her upturned face. "Let me tell you a bit of history about Port Essington. In its prime, it was a very industrious town, boasting seven canneries built along the estuary of the Skeena and the Ecstall Rivers. Amongst the businesses were three hotels, which was a very good marker for a town's prosperity. But by the early twentieth century, the population was declining and now it is primarily a ghost town. Another day we can drive straight here and enjoy strolling amongst the dilapidated old buildings. There is a gas station with a general store, much like the one we have at New Petrograd."

"Sounds absolutely delightful," Shelley replied as he turned into the restaurant's parking lot.

"Of course, anywhere with you—" Shelley exclaimed, "Look, sweetheart, isn't that your dad's Bronco two spaces over?"

Gaspar looked where Shelley indicated. "You're right, it is. So this is why Kevin's been asking to borrow my *papa's* vehicle on Sunday afternoons. *And* was able to recommend this restaurant," he added, as he got out of the truck.

"You're not disappointed that it's not going to be just the two of us?" she asked, as he helped her out.

"Nope, not a bit. Are you? In fact, this is going to be fun. I'll bet you Don is here as well."

Upon entering the restaurant, Gaspar briefly acknowledged the hostess's greeting and then walked straight to their table, cleared his throat, and asked, "Excuse me, mind if we join you?"

Four heads immediately lifted from their menus and then they all started chuckling.

"You bet," Kevin and Don said, leaping up. "We just need to move this table over and there will be places for you and Shelley to sit."

Gaspar looked at Shelley, grinning as he pulled her chair out.

"We didn't see you at church this morning," Marianne said, "so we thought you were still in seclusion."

And as if she'd just made a hilarious joke, everyone broke into gales of laughter.

"We were there," Shelley replied. "We snuck in the back, late, and left early, not really relishing mingling. Next Sunday will be time enough for that."

"When we left, we went home to my *roditeli*, had lunch with them and Shelley's folks, then collected my truck and headed out on the highway. *Papa* was telling me he often loans you his vehicle, Kevin. I sure didn't expect to see anyone we knew, but when we were parking, Shelley spotted his Bronco."

As Kevin turned a bit crimson, Marianne drew their attention to her by saying, "Wasn't the trip here splendid, Shelley? Reminds me of places we used to drive to from Vancouver."

"It sure was. Gaspar put the windows down so a lovely breeze could come in. Especially some of the scenes following the water. We saw a few animals also—a deer, a porcupine and a black bear."

"Oh, lucky you. I'd love to have seen the bear," Marianne said. "We did see a couple of deer, and one with twin fawns."

"Where did you see the bear?" Don asked.

"I haven't the foggiest." Shelley chuckled. "Do you know, Gaspar?"

"Oh, I'd guess about fifteen miles back. She looked to be in great shape, especially since it's still spring. I suspect she probably had a cub or two, but if she did, they must have been still in the bush. We didn't see them."

"I'd sure like to get a look at them," Don commented, "A Kermode cub has been spotted in the area around where you saw her. It's rather unusual for them to be this far north, but this area is still in the Great Bear Rainforest, so it's not an impossibility. I am wondering if it might be hers—the parent bears can be black."

"I've never heard of a Kermode bear before. What is it?" Mary Ellen inquired, her gaze riveted on Don's.

"It is a rare subspecies of the black bear and is often referred to as a *spirit* or *ghost bear* because of its colouring," Don replied, smiling at her. "A little known fact—it's our provincial animal here in British Columbia."

"Wow," said Shelley at the same time as Mary Ellen, whose face was upturned to Don's. But Shelley wasn't commenting entirely on what Don had just said but on the look passing between the two of them.

Gaspar asked, "Don, how do you know the difference between them and a regular black bear, then?"

"Well, I guess in truth the black ones are just black bears," Don said, turning to his friend. "It is a rare gene that causes sometimes two black bears, or sometimes a combination of both colours, to have a cub with a dirty vanilla or cream-coloured coat. The spirit bear does have black pigment in their noses, eyes, and paw pads so they aren't all white, like an albino. Just enough colouring to give them their name."

"Interesting. From what Don is telling us, it's too bad that you didn't see the cub," Kevin declared.

"I'm not so sure," Gaspar grinned at him. "I might have thought I had seen a ghost," attempting to shiver for effect, just as the waitress began to set bowls of miso soup and the rest of their orders in front of them.

Conversation flowed freely for the remainder of their meal.

As they finished eating, Kevin interrupted everyone by saying, "Well, it is seven and we have a bit of a drive ahead of us. I reckon we should start for home. I think all of us work tomorrow. Even you, Gaspar."

"You're right. Although I haven't the foggiest idea what I need to be doing."

"Well, old chum, I do," Kevin said with a wry laugh.

"And every night this week, we will need a meeting to make sure every detail has been considered," Mary Ellen added.

"That's right, this is the last week before the museum opens. I need to do the same for my business," Don acknowledged.

"Mary Ellen, we had a tour of the lighthouse station yesterday," Shelley told her. "Wow, am I impressed! But what I was going to say was that Mrs. Filipova told us you were interviewing for housekeeping staff and I wondered about applying."

Mary Ellen snickered before saying, "I'll be interviewing you, all right, but it won't be for any position in housekeeping. Can you come by my office tomorrow at eleven and we'll talk then?"

"Well yes, for sure. Gaspar can point out your office to me and I'll be there."

As they turned onto the road, Shelley sighed contentedly as she put her head on her husband's shoulder. "Thank you, sweetheart, for a perfectly lovely day. You know, I almost feel I'm ready to become a full-fledged resident of New Petrograd tomorrow."

"That is music to my ears, my love. But we still have twelve more hours that are solely ours."

CHAPTER SEVEN

The Countdown Begins

In her opening statement on Monday night, Mary Ellen began, "I am so glad everyone could come tonight. In fact, it looks like we have the whole village here. I am panicking inside, knowing there are only six days left until we open."

"Well you sure don't look panicky. You look as cool as a cucumber, my dear," Marg assured her.

"Or like a swan gliding across a lake," Shelley added.

As Mary Ellen looked up and saw Shelley seated in the crowd, a smile crossed her face. "Well, that is something that did go right with my day. I interviewed Shelley this morning and she has graciously accepted the position of Security Manager."

Great cheers went up as Alexander exclaimed, "Shelley did such an amazing job of solving the skeleton mystery."

"I didn't solve that mystery, Alexander," Shelley retorted. "I only worked as a liaison between you residents, the RCMP constable, and that rather stern coroner, Dr. Brown."

"Yes, you did," Alexander argued and from the muffled

responses of others, it sounded like a few more agreed with him.

"Well, at any rate, I'm glad we have an answer for one of the items on my to-do list," Mary Ellen stated. "I also received a shipment containing replicas of some of the wooden implements and toys that Martin made to be sold in the souvenir shop. If I do say so myself, they are absolutely adorable."

She held up a few for everyone to see before asking Alex if he could find time in the week to come by her office and pick up the boxes and take them to the souvenir shop run by his *roditeli*.

"I can," Alex said, at the same time turning around to ask John Molodtsov if Peter might have time to set them on shelves in the store.

"I will certainly ask him, though our biggest problem with him these days is getting him to focus on his schoolwork. He'd much rather be helping with all this, in his words, 'awesome stuff'."

"What about you, Gayle?" Mary Ellen was saying. "Would you like some on display at the teahouse?"

Gayle thought a minute. "No, they are awfully cute, but I think the ceramic pieces and *babushka* dolls are much more fitting for the teahouse."

"The biggest disaster of my day," Mary Ellen went on, "was when the Prince Rupert tourist information office called and said that they received brochures which had many blotches on the back cover. I need to contact the printers and get this sorted out. Thank goodness, I used a local printer so hopefully they can turn things around fairly quickly. This about covers my agenda tonight, but I'm sure others have concerns to bring up."

Anna Yusporova was first, reporting that she had finished

sewing the authentic Russian costumes for the adults, plus a costume each for a boy and a girl. "I am having some difficulty finding time to work on more. If anyone can help me, I would appreciate it if they could let me know at the end of the meeting."

Then Marg asked if anyone had been hired to do the housekeeping and laundry yet.

"No, *Mama*-Marg, not yet. I do not think we have anyone in the village that is appropriate. I put an ad in the paper in Prince Rupert for several positions that have been identified and have received a lot of responses. Thankfully, most of the available jobs are for the summer season, so I will be able to hire students. My plan is to spend Wednesday in Prince Rupert interviewing. I know *Papa* and you feel anxious, but it is really the best I can do."

"Don't worry, Mrs. Filipova," Shelley said. "I'm sure there won't be any security issues right away, so I will be able to help out until Mary Ellen can hire her staff."

"Well, thank you, Shelley, you are such a dear," Marg responded with a smile.

"That's my wife, Mrs. Filipova," Gaspar commented smugly.

"Shelley's right, we won't leave you trying to do everything yourselves," Mary Ellen agreed. "It is much too big a job for you and *Papa* to handle by yourselves. Marianne and I will certainly help as well."

"Yes, and I will certainly support my wife," Gaspar quickly noted, "and it won't surprise me if some of the other guys help out too."

"That's right," Marianne added. "You and *Papa* don't have anything to worry about."

"Another thought—what about first aid?" Tony asked. "I

know that was something else you needed to work on. Do we have anyone lined up to cover that position?"

"Good question, Mr. Rosso. I do have a very good lead, which I also plan to follow up on Wednesday. I recognize having someone responsible for first aid is certainly a top priority in our venture," Mary Ellen replied, her eyes briefly flicking in Bob and Olga's direction.

"I think we'd best let this be all for tonight, as many of us have an equally busy day tomorrow regardless of what we are working towards."

"Today went a little better than yesterday," Mary Ellen reported Tuesday evening. "Thank goodness. I was able to solve the problem with the printers. Our brochures will be distributed shortly at every tourist information office between Prince Rupert and Prince George. I have arranged for some to go to Vancouver as well. Also, some at various locations in the Queen Charlotte Islands. The last place I want them to go is Hartley Bay. I plan to pick some up tomorrow when I am in PR and Don and I will hand-deliver them on Friday."

"Should be an exciting date," Alexander called out.

Mary Ellen felt a blush rising in her cheeks, so quickly averted her gaze and changed the subject. "We received an extra order of toilet paper. I have it in my office so anywhere there are public washrooms, please feel welcome to come and get some. I think that means you, *Papa,* for the lighthouse station, Gayle for the teahouse, and Frank Yusporov for the souvenir shop."

"What about us?" Uri asked. "For the two washrooms at the Borscht Kettle."

"Absolutely, Uri. If I missed anyone else, please speak up."

"We need some for our house," Alexander loudly called out.

Alexandria responded by frowning at him and then landed him with a solid punch in the arm. "Mary Ellen said *public*."

This quickly stifled any more comments from her brother. However, it did start a wave of snickers, which meant they had to wait until they subsided before the meeting could continue.

"Getting back to the brochures for a minute... Mary Ellen, I think you should also include Whitehorse," Don advised. "Many people knew me both personally and professionally and were interested in my plans to relocate here."

"Good idea, Don. Just give me the address for their tourist information office and I will send them a package. I went around to the souvenir shop today," Mary Ellen continued. "It really looks attractive. I must admit I felt tempted to buy quite a few items."

Chuckling, Betty responded, "We will be open from eight to five on Saturday."

"No, you'll only be required to be open from nine to five, because the gates don't open until nine. You could perhaps even get away with opening at nine-thirty because that probably won't be the first place people go," Mary Ellen advised her, with a smile.

"Oh, my goodness, it is this Saturday that we open!"

"Mary Ellen, I really don't think you need to worry about anything. From what your *roditeli* told us when we were touring the lighthouse station and from what I've heard in these meetings the last two nights, you have everything well under control," Shelley declared.

"Three cheers for Mary Ellen," Alexander bellowed.

Amongst the ensuing clamour, Mary Ellen managed to say,

"I have a big day of interviewing tomorrow so I don't think we will plan a meeting for tomorrow night."

"I was very pleased with how everything went yesterday," Mary Ellen reported Thursday evening. "I must have interviewed about twenty people. I hired three people for the lighthouse, plus two floats. This will mean one person in the laundry, and two women cleaning rooms. Of course, when they have finished cleaning, if there is any time left in their shift, they can assist with folding the laundry or re-stocking supplies. I hired one person for general cleaning of the buildings, which I know is not enough. But they were the only ones I interviewed that seemed to be suitable. In the meantime, this will be another job for the float's position." She glanced at her list. "I also hired two people to help maintain the grounds and flower beds. Mrs. Palmer, we will still appreciate any help you can give us in designing them. I know my sister and I also will want to be involved in this. So, eight new people are moving to our village over the next week and will require places to live. Please come and see me if you, or anyone you can suggest, will be interested in hosting them."

After this long speech, Mary Ellen stopped to catch her breath.

"You didn't say anything about first aid," Tony reminded her.

"You are right, Mr. Rosso, I was just getting to that, and what I am about to tell you is very, very exciting. I have hired Nikolai Petrov, who recently retired from Alcan, where he has worked for thirty-two years as a first-aid supervisor. He and his wife, Margarita, will naturally be staying with his brother. That is, until a house can be built for them. No pressure, of course, Kevin," she said, as her eyes searched the faces until she found his.

Mary Ellen's news of Nikolai created a happy uproar, especially amongst the older folks.

"I actually feel I have lost count of how many people are or will be boarding here, maybe fifteen or so," she added.

The excited conversations finally reached such a crescendo that when she realized she was failing to take control of the meeting, she shouted, laughing, "I think that concludes our business for tonight. I don't think we need to have a meeting Friday night. It is much more important that everyone gets a good night's rest and is up early for our grand opening. However, I would like to do a debriefing of everyone's observations after the first three days."

"Oh dear," Mary Ellen said to Nick first thing Friday morning, "I almost forgot something. I couldn't sleep last night for fear I'd forget to mention it to you today. It also makes me anxious as to what else I may have overlooked."

"Don't worry. Don't worry. Tell me what it is and I will see it gets done."

"It's the big banner we were going to hang over the front entrance welcoming everyone."

"Consider it done. I'll get some of the construction men to bring their ladders and see to it. Now, Mary Ellen, I think you had better take the rest of the day off and you and Don get an early start to Hartley Bay. And to wherever else your little heart desires! If you thought up to now you were busy, after today, I suspect your days are going to get a lot busier."

She was just stepping out the door to take his advice when she came rushing back in. "There are two banners, remember. One in English and one in Russian."

"Right you are," as he pointed to the two rolls on his desk. "Now *go*."

Again, Mary Ellen left, only to return a few seconds later.

"What now? Honestly, Mary Ellen, I have everything under control."

"I know, but I just wanted to say thanks, Nick." With a brilliant smile she left the room. This time he could tell she was really going as he listened to her retreating footsteps.

CHAPTER EIGHT

Grand Opening Saturday

On Saturday, opening day, a cluster of the village residents stood just outside the gates watching cars going by on the road. As each car passed without stopping, Mary Ellen could just feel disappointment deflate everyone like balloons losing air.

Then, excitement reverberated through everyone when finally, a red Volkswagen van slowed and turned off the road into the entranceway to the town.

The driver hopped out and asked, "I'm getting low on gas. I saw your sign so can I get a fill-up here?"

"Absolutely," Marvin said, as he stepped forward. "Just pull your van beside the pumps and we'll get that taken care of right away." After Marvin put the pump in the gas tank, he went around to the front to clean the windshield. "Anything else you need? Would you like me to check the oil?"

"I think it's okay, but I suppose it's not going to hurt to check it. My wife sure won't be happy if that's the next thing I start fussing about. I should have stopped for gas in Port Essington, but you know how it is, we just got off the cable ferry. I was sure pleased to see your sign, otherwise we would have had to turn around and go back. "What's going on here, anyways?" the middle-aged man finally asked. "What are all these people standing around here for? And why are that man and woman in costume?"

"This is the village of New Petrograd and this is our first day to open our doors as a living museum. Would you care to visit it? Have a look at our brochure," Marvin offered, as he handed it to the man. "Today is our grand opening so our entrance fee is half price."

The man briefly looked at the brochure and commented, "Looks interesting, but nah. We better keep going. Good luck," he said, as he got into the van and pulled back onto the road.

Around nine forty-five, as they watched two more cars whiz past, Gayle sighed and said, "I reckon I had better bring some of the coffee I prepared this morning and serve us here. It is only going to get bitter and then we'll have to toss it out."

"I'll give you a hand," June offered.

Not long after Gayle and June had disappeared, another car slowed, turned off the road, and pulled into the parking lot.

"Is this the Russian Museum they told us about at Prince Rupert tourism? They told us to take the cable ferry by Port Essington and just follow the new road," the gentleman said as his wife and children got out of the car.

"It is," several eager voices answered at once.

"Oh good, we found it," his wife replied, as the four of them began walking towards the entrance sign.

"You can purchase your tickets here from Jenny," Martin said. "We have a special this weekend, for our grand opening."

"The way it was described to us sounded most interesting. We also understood we could stay at the lighthouse. Our children are very excited about this. Well, I must admit, so am I," the man exclaimed.

"Yes," Phil said, as he stepped forward. "You may set your luggage inside and leave it over by the office building. One of the employees will take it to your room. We also offer a tour of the lighthouse or a couple of choices in stargazing, if that's of interest to you. We can explain more about all the attractions we offer when you visit the lighthouse station."

"That's really neat," the boy said, coming alive. "In science class this year, we've been learning lots about the stars."

Turning to the adults, Phil said, "You can either choose to pay for the tours now or at the lighthouse. Come by when you're ready and we will get you all checked in," Phil informed them, waving to Marg to follow him.

Just then, there was a flash of red as the Volkswagen van pulled off the road and into the parking lot. It had barely stopped when two teenagers hopped out.

"Cool!" the boy said. "After we stopped for gas, Dad was telling us about your museum and we made him come back."

"Yes," his sister added. "Those clothes are the best. Are they for real?"

"Hound, hound, hound, until I finally gave in," their father sighed, feigning annoyance as he and his wife joined them.

"Where is Brian?" his wife asked, looking around. Then she opened the back door and yelled, "Brian, put that comic book down and get out of the van right this minute!"

Once Jenny had checked them through, Martin greeted them and produced a map showing the various exhibits.

"There is no right or wrong way to see everything," he explained. "We have a few people who are dressed in traditional Russian clothing, and yes, they really are for real," he said, smiling at the young girl, who was listening to him very attentively. "They are available to help you in any way. If you need directions or answers to any questions, do not hesitate to stop them. The teahouse serves a light lunch, or snack. And you can be seated either inside, or out on their deck, which offers you a relaxing view. For your convenience, we have included an insert showing their daily menu. Everything to see is shown on this map. The museum closes tonight at five for all our day visitors. If you are staying overnight, we also have another insert telling you what they are serving for dinner at the Borscht Kettle. Are there any questions? If not, please enjoy your day."

Anna Yusporova then greeted everyone next, encouraging them all to come to her history talks beginning at one-thirty, and then every second hour after that until closing time. "You will find me by the founding fathers' plaque near the souvenir booth."

Bob and Olga then stepped forward and offered to get them started by leading them to the first house.

As the families began walking together, Bob congenially asked, "What are your names?"

"Our family is Brian, Luke, and Stephanie. My wife is Mary and I'm Bob Watson," one of the men offered.

"I'm Bob too!" Bob chuckled. "And you folks are?"

"I'm Jennifer, and this is my brother David. Our parents are Peter and Susan."

"Well, welcome everyone!"

After a few minutes, as they walked along a path bordered with honeysuckle, its fragrant scent filling the air, Olga said, "Here we are at our first exhibit. As indicated on this name-plate, it used to be the home of Alexander and Anastasia Yusporov. This is one of the original homes constructed by some of our founding fathers. Inside, you will meet *Dedushka* who, incidentally, is our last remaining founding father. He can tell you much about his former home as well as any items displayed in the rooms. When you leave, the house next door on the right was Pyotr and Elena Filipov's house. You will notice that it is quite dilapidated."

"Pyotr and Elena were also the *roditeli* of Phil Filipov, who you briefly met earlier, when he responded to your question about staying here," Bob added.

"We will leave you now but I'm sure we'll see you again. Enjoy your day."

A half-hour later, a beaming *Dedushk*a waved good-bye to the two families. Brian was saying as he left, "That's pretty cool stuff they have in there. That old man told us we could buy some of those cool toys at the gift shop. Mom, where's the gift shop?"

"Brian, don't speak of him as an old man. I am not sure where the gift shop is. We'll have to look at the map, but not right now."

They looked briefly at the house next door as they continued on the path until they came to a crossroads.

Checking their map, Peter said, "It looks like the teahouse goes to the right. I wouldn't mind going for some lunch now. What do you think, Susan?"

"Sure, that sounds good," as she called after their children who were deep in conversation with their newfound friends.

"That is a good idea! Do you mind if we come with you?" Mary asked.

"Not at all," Susan replied.

"Oh, look at the water. It looks so placid and still with the sun bouncing off it. I suppose it is part of Telegraph Pass."

"It is, my dear," Peter said.

"Oh, and there's the lighthouse." Susan said, smiling at her husband. "And I imagine those buildings in front of it are the accommodations. Doesn't it look splendid?"

They turned to follow the new path. As they paused to admire the picturesque scene in front of them, Mary commented, "I can sure see why people would enjoy living here. It seems so lovely and peaceful."

"Mom, Dad," Stephanie enthusiastically called as she came running up, "there's a sign back there that says tonight there will be stargazing from the lighthouse. Can we stay for that?"

Her father looked at her before exclaiming, "No, and that's my final answer. We were just passing through on this road on the way to visit your grandparents. Remember, I would like to do that sometime today."

"But Dad," Stephanie pleaded, "Jennifer told me they're staying tonight. Can we do that?"

"What did I just say? No." He turned and started up the path towards the teahouse.

When Mary caught up to her husband, she said, "You know, dear, she is learning about the galaxy at school."

"I said no. And Mary, please don't encourage them. I admit though, that I am glad they hounded me to come back. I am quite enjoying this."

Gayle greeted them as they entered the teahouse. "I see you have our insert explaining the options we offer today. Also, for desserts we have Baked Apple, which is quite different from what you are likely familiar with, and *Chak Chak*. What would you like to try?"

"First, please tell us about these soups," Susan asked. "I know *Borscht* soup, but what is *Rassolnik* soup?"

Gayle chuckled. "It is one of our classic soups, made with barley, beef, potatoes, carrots, and... pickles."

"Pickles?" Brian and David asked, wide-eyed.

"Yes," Gayle replied, grinning. "It is a very filling soup and we serve it with a slice of rye bread."

"I'll have that," David exclaimed excitedly. "That's the coolest thing ever."

"Okay, how many orders of *Rassolnik* soup?" June inquired, coming up to the counter to assist Gayle.

Enthusiastic shouts of "me, yes please, me, yeah, yes please" were returned until finally June said, "I think I heard five yesses so I am assuming the rest would like Borscht, which is served with a dab of *smetana*, which is really just a Russian word for sour cream. And rye bread. Over here," June continued, "are our desserts, Baked Apple and *Chak Chak*."

"The other lady said you don't bake your apples like we do. I am curious how you prepare them differently," Susan commented.

"The Russian way is to core the apples, and then soak them in different syrups and sweet concoctions. Then the apples are stuffed with a sweet filling and baked. The other dessert we have is *Chak Chak*. You start with a soft dough and form it into strips. Then the strips are deep fried and a hot honey sauce is poured over them. My husband and I moved here a couple of years ago. When I see this dessert it always reminds me of Rice Krispy squares—not that it is anything like them. Now, how many orders of each? Or would you like me to put an assortment together and you can share?"

"Oh, I think an assortment."

"Certainly," June said, as she smiled at them. "Now Gayle will tell you about our drinks and take your payment."

She then turned to greet the next customers in line, a party of three.

"Hi again," Gayle said. "We have an assortment of teas, coffees, and cold drinks. This weekend we are featuring *Mors*, a cold drink. Traditionally it was made from lingonberries, but it can also be made from blueberries, strawberries, or raspberries. This is how we are offering it today. I might also mention, ladies, that on the rack by the door are sheets with the various recipes of items we offer. You may be interested in picking up a few. When we have your order ready, we will bring it to you."

"Thank you, I will certainly have a look," Susan said, as she put her change away.

Mary called after her, "Can you please pick up copies of both *Rassolnik* soup and *Chak Chak* for me?"

"Yes, I'm interested in those ones, but also the Baked Apple sounded delicious. I'll pick up copies of everything for you as well." To Gayle, she said, "You really have thought of everything to make our visit special."

"These are our manager's suggestions," Gayle laughed. And as she said good-bye, she added, "I hope you and your family enjoy your food."

As they were finishing their meals, Bob studied the map. Suddenly he exclaimed, "It really looks like we have barely touched on everything there is to see. There's the lighthouse with a guided tour to the gallery. Then there is a street with a restaurant, a general store, and both a beauty and barber shop. Over by the souvenir shop, there are a couple more homes, and it looks like a church in ruin. I guess though, we can walk past most of them quickly enough, so they shouldn't take too much more time."

"Is there something indicating where the founding fathers' plaque is?" Mary asked. "Because we must remember the nice lady who told us she would give us a talk about the history. Besides Bob, you know I won't just be walking past the souvenir shop."

Bob nodded, then continued to scan his map. "Oh, and there is a kiosk with a Canada Post Office. It says here that they stamp everything with a special stamp showing that the items are mailed from New Petrograd. It sure is good we're having an early lunch, but it still looks like we only have a few more hours to accomplish everything."

"Susan and I thought it sounded like it would take a good two days to see everything," Peter replied. "Especially if we don't want to feel rushed. That is why we decided we would stay overnight. Of course, it also meant we could consider taking in both the day and nighttime lighthouse tours."

Mary glanced across the table at Bob, who chose that moment to turn and look at their children. "Eat up kids, we still have a lot to do."

"Hi everybody," Alexandria greeted the Watson family when she approached their table. "Can I get you anything else? I just started work because this morning my *mama* made me stay home and finish my homework. I was really annoyed and pouted all morning because I really, really wanted to be a part of the excitement of opening day. Tonight, they're stargazing in the lighthouse and my *mama* won't stop me from doing that." She chatted away while clearing the table. "We're used to seeing the northern lights from here, but to see them way up there, well, I imagine that it will be amazing. How about you all? Are you going? Hey, if they don't need me here, how about I take you around? I've lived here all my life so I could even show you places that are not on the map."

"Can we, Dad?" Stephanie and Jennifer asked their respective fathers, perhaps sounding a little too enthusiastic.

"I don't see why not," Bob said. "Do you have any concerns, Peter?"

"No, except I think it best, Miss, you only show them things on the map, not off. What did you say your name was?"

"My name is Alexandria Bolitchyn. I'll just take this bin in and see if they need me. Oh, I forgot to ask, did you want anything else?"

"Not a thing," the mothers replied together, exchanging a smile, as they stood.

The two couples retraced their steps until they again reached the crossroad. Their five children were once more racing heedlessly down the path and, at the end, turned towards the lighthouse.

"I guess we have to follow them," Peter said wryly. "Although I would have liked to consult with everyone before a decision was made. Susan, at least while we are there, we can ask a few more details about the tours they offer and get checked in."

"I like Peter's idea, Mary. Maybe we should do the same and learn about the day tour. I have to admit, if we are not able to fit everything in today, this activity really interests me."

"Hello again," Phil greeted Peter when they walked in to the office. "Would you like to check in to your room now?"

"Yes, please. Also, I would like to inquire about your tours?"

"The daytime tour to the gallery deck is included in your room rate. Nighttime stargazing, also in the gallery using the telescope, is half price for our opening weekend promotion.

From the wharf, it is of course free, unless you want to purchase a snack or hot drink to take with you."

"I suppose I should inquire how long the day tour takes?"

"That's up to you, really," Phil chuckled. "I give it, so my talk is perhaps a half hour up in the watch room. I need to put my personal feelings aside, because as the former lighthouse keeper, I feel quite at home there. I am going to suggest that you would at least want to enjoy another half hour at the top."

"Well," Susan then inquired, "do you know how long the history talk takes?"

"Again, I'm not really sure, but my guess would be roughly an hour."

"What are you thinking, Susan? Do the lighthouse tour one day, and the history talk the next?"

"Yes," she said with a nod. "That's what was on my mind. But my suggestion would be to do the lighthouse tour when we can start first thing in the morning. Where is the founding fathers' plaque, sir?"

"Hand me your map." Phil reached out his hand. "I'll show you." Then, as he handed them their room key, he glanced at his watch and added, "There should be plenty of time for you to walk there."

Bob and Mary had been standing to one side listening, and as Peter and Susan were about to leave, Bob cleared his throat and said, "Oh well, I guess I may as well book in also," amid cheers from his offspring and ignoring the smug grin from his wife. "Do you mind waiting for us to check in? I like what you're thinking. It makes a lot of sense."

"Not at all." Peter laughed. "We may as well spend the weekend hanging out together."

"I guess if we are staying the night, is there a pay phone I can use?" Bob asked, turning to Phil. "I would like to call my parents and let them know not to expect us today."

Phil pushed the phone forward, advising Bob to make his call quickly. "I suggest you go take in the history talk and check in afterward."

Looking out over the few people gathered in front of her, Anna began, "Glad you all could join me for my talk of the historical events that led to our forefathers' settling this land. First, I want to point out the founding fathers' plaque, which displays the original eighteen brave souls who came."

The listeners gathered around it.

This plaque is in memory of the first settlers of New Petrograd who came to the Dominion of Canada after fleeing the Russian Revolution of 1917.

Pyotr Rosnokov and Nadeshda Rosnokova
Roman Molodtsov and Katerina Molodtsova
Pyotr Filipov and Elena Filipova
Vasily Filipov and Tatyana Filipova
Yaroslav Pagodonov and Tatyana Pagodonova
Alexander Yusporov and Anastasia Yusporova
Pavel Katovik and Yulia Katovika
Nikolai Petrov and Margarita Petrova
Mitslav Golubov and Olesia Golubova

Anna went on, "Beside it are the ruins of the original church. Then next is what once was the home of Pavel and Yulia Katovik. Next door, their neighbours were Mitslav and

Olesia Golubov. Inside their home, we have created a pictorial scene of our founding fathers' journey."

Anna took a deep breath and a sip of water.

"Some of you children, and maybe you adults as well, may remember hearing of the Russian Revolution, which took place in 1917, led by Vladimir Lenin and a group of revolutionaries called the Bolsheviks. This band of peasants and working-class people revolted against the government of Tsar Nicholas II. Our forefathers left Russia during this terrible time. They had to be so discreet, not wanting to draw attention to themselves. Eventually, they made their way to London, where they caught a steamship sailing across what was in their eyes a massive body of water to Halifax. That is where they first set foot on Canadian soil. I have been told that many of our forefathers, with tears in their eyes, bent to kiss the earth. None of us, I'm sure, can even imagine how they felt. There they met with Canadian immigration officials, who told them of homesteading land in the west. So, they boarded a train to travel across miles of endless land to the Pacific coast."

Anna's audience was riveted.

"Again, they met with authorities in Vancouver, who informed them of this land we are now standing on. Before leaving the city, they purchased many items they felt would be useful to them, including fishing boats. They knew the boats would be useful as transportation to their destination, as well as for fishing when they arrived. Often when we were growing up, our *babushkas* would speak about how thankful they were for safety in this new land. I am very proud to be a part of this heritage and thrilled to think that today we have opened our doors to you all."

"How long did this journey take?" a ginger-haired boy, standing in front, asked.

"My husband's *dedushka* has often mentioned to me that it took them the best part of two years."

"Expensive journey for that many people," Peter noted.

"Yes, it would have been. Our suspicions are that it was paid for by Russian jewels sewn in their clothing as they planned their escape—but that is another story."

"Would Canada even have been a country then?" a tall man at the back of the crowd asked.

"Yes, it became a country in 1867, when it was called the Dominion of Canada." Anna smiled at the little crowd. "In closing, I just want to draw your attention to the gift shop beside me. Though sadly, we have no Russian jewels for sale."

"I think we've done enough for one day, so why don't we see the gift shop while we're here?" Mary suggested. "Then Bob, I think you should retrieve our luggage, seeing you have finally agreed to stay the night. I didn't say it before, darling, but thank you for deciding to do this. I appreciate it, and I'm sure our children do as well."

Bob grinned at his wife's praise. "I'll leave the gift shop to you, and Stephanie if she wishes. Then the boys and I will catch up with you both in about twenty-five minutes." He called to his sons, "If I can interrupt your conversation for a moment, I'll need you to come with me to get our luggage."

"We left our luggage just inside the gate because they said an employee would bring it to our rooms," Susan said. "So maybe while you're doing that, Peter and I will have time to stroll along the main street and visit the general store. We'll meet you in the lobby in approximately forty-five minutes to discuss supper."

As Peter and Susan exited the general store, Alexandria raced up to them.

"There you are," she exclaimed, triumphantly. "I've been looking for you guys everywhere since I got off work at three." Then she stopped speaking, and looked around puzzled. "Where are your kids?"

"Well, just stick with us," Susan chuckled. "We agreed we'd meet in the lighthouse lobby around now."

"Wow!" Alexandra said when they arrived. Looking around in amazement at everyone, she said, "I didn't expect you would all still be here."

"There is perhaps something my husband didn't mention to you earlier," Marg said to the two families gathered in the lobby. "But telling isn't really the best way. Showing is much better." She led them outside to the garden area. "If you would care to make use of the barbecue pit, we do store all the fixings for a wiener roast in our office."

Susan looked around her. "That does sound like a good idea. Much less expensive than taking a family of four to the Borscht Kettle. Besides, I imagine we can just stay here for the whole evening until it is dark enough to gaze at the night sky."

"Or what do you think of this idea?" Alexandria spoke up. "I could roast wieners with your kids and let you guys go by yourselves to the Kettle."

"Now there's an idea," Susan said, smiling at Alexandria. "That Chicken Kiev on the menu insert did sound tempting. What do you say, Mary?"

"It sounds like a perfect idea. A lovely ending to what has become a most enjoyable day."

"That was absolutely delightful," Susan said, as she left the restaurant holding Peter's arm. "And I'm not referring to this unexpected date night either. Although that's pretty special, too."

"I know what you mean," Mary agreed. "Everything has been flawless today and for us so unexpected."

"It sure was a great meal," Bob stated. "That Russian Honey Cake they served for dessert was something else. It was so filling I could hardly finish mine."

"Yes," Mary replied. "The waitress gave Susan and me the recipe. Well, where to now?"

"I don't know what everyone else thinks," Bob said, as he put his arm around his wife. "I'm for joining our children for a hot drink and then calling it a night."

"A fine suggestion, Bob," Peter agreed, as he reached for Susan's hand. "Because after all, we'll see the same stars from there."

CHAPTER NINE

Grand Opening Sunday

On Sunday morning, as Susan walked into the common area where the two families were staying, she greeted everyone and then said, "Peter got up early and went back to the garden just to savour the quiet and tranquility. He did come back to tell me that Mrs. Filipova informed him that guests are welcome to attend their ten o'clock service in that delightful little church. We are planning to do that after we have breakfast at the teahouse."

"Good morning to you as well," Mary said, as she turned from the kitchen sink. "That certainly sounds like a nice way to start the day. I was saying to Bob last night, I would like to look at the tombstones in the cemetery anyway. I have an interest in it."

"Alexandria told us last night that they found a skeleton in an old cold storage space a few months ago. It had been buried for almost fifty years and nobody knew about it," David said breathlessly.

Mary and Susan raised their eyebrows, while Brian exclaimed, "Nobody knew but that old man we met in the first house yesterday, remember? He had to tell the whole story to the RCMP."

"That's where my dad works," Jennifer said.

"Yeah, that's what your brother said last night."

"I told you before," Mary admonished Brian. "Don't call him an old man."

"Okay—*Dedushka,* then."

"They didn't put him in jail or anything because it was so long ago," Luke continued. "Alexandria told us the skeleton belonged to a nurse who used to come here. She accidentally fell and hit her head and died. Last year, at the cemetery, they erected a memorial and plaque telling the whole story. I was going to ask if we could go see it, because Brian's right, the story was cool. I'm glad we're going—well, not to church but to see the plaque."

"You guys," Jennifer broke in, "I liked the story she told us about the Russian jewels they found a whole lot better. Now if we're talking cool, that's cool."

"Okay," Susan said. "Tell us. Mary and I are all ears."

"Remember the lady at the teahouse who said she and her husband moved here two years ago? Alexandria told us she always liked to pick wildflowers. One day, she came home with a bunch of flowers and turned the knob on the front door. It fell off and all these Russian jewels came tumbling out."

"How did she know they were Russian?" Susan asked.

"It seems her great-aunt was one of the people who fled Russia. She had written her niece, who was the mother of the lady we met yesterday, about these jewels. They had brought them from Russia for the Tsar and his family. After the Tsar's family were all killed, they didn't know what to do, so it seems they kept them."

Peter, who had just come into the room, said, "Remember

when I mentioned yesterday that it would have been an expensive journey? And her response was, 'Our suspicions are that it was paid for by jewels they would have sewn in their clothing —but that is another story'."

"And as Paul Harvey would say," Bob said with a laugh, "now we know... the rest of the story."

"That wasn't what was so cool about that story," Brian said, looking at the girls in disgust. "There were these two guys who sailed in one morning. This couple hired them to do renovations and they were taking up the flooring in their living room. It turned out they were really looking for the jewels. How cool is that?"

"Very cool, son," Bob said, ruffling Brian's hair. "It sounds like you all had quite the time in the garden last night prior to our joining you. For now, I think you all should finish getting dressed and ready to go."

"I agree," Peter said, "if we want to have breakfast and then get to the church service, we'd all better get a move on."

"How long do you plan on staying today, Peter?" Bob asked, as they trailed behind their wives, who were meandering around the cemetery.

"I imagine midafternoon. I know Susan mentioned earlier she is interested in seeing the pictorial scene of the forefathers' journey. I suppose that's about it. After that, I imagine we'll grab a quick bite to eat before we leave."

"Sounds much like what Mary was saying this morning. It won't surprise me, though, if she wants to visit the souvenir shop again."

"Susan did say something about her and Mary going there

before we leave. It sounds to me we might as well stay together for the rest of our time here. Our children are inseparable now, anyway."

"I agree. Your family coming at the same time has just made this weekend all the better. At lunch yesterday, when I was checking out the map, I knew I was going to cave and book us in for the night, but I had to tease my family a bit first." Bob chuckled.

Peter suddenly blurted, "I'd meant to get up this morning and go do the day tour of the lighthouse. I guess the idea slipped my mind when we decided to attend church. I really want to do that."

"You're right, it was probably the primary reason for my decision to stay. Let's get everyone together to discuss it." Bob called Mary, hoping to get her attention.

"Before we start the tour, let me tell you that the lighthouse is sixty feet high and we will be climbing fifty-six steps to reach the watch room."

"Fifty-six steps!" Susan repeated. "You go with the kids, Peter. I think I'll stay here. I don't know about walking all those stairs. Besides, I'm really not good with heights."

"If you don't mind, Susan, I'd like to go."

"Not at all, Mary, you all go and enjoy yourselves. I don't mind waiting here."

"While you wait, please feel free to look at the photos or other picture books we have in the lobby," Phil invited as he opened the door, motioning everyone to file out in front of him. "Before we begin, let me please remind you to be careful on the stairs. They were built a long time ago, so they are very steep and narrow. This makes them very difficult to maneuver if you're not accustomed to them. After every eighteen steps, there will be a small landing and a window. Feel free to look out at the view. Please stop as often as you need to," Phil advised, remembering at the last minute that Mary Ellen had warned him to make sure no one overexerted themselves.

She'd even talked to him about limiting the numbers of tours he would do in one day. Maybe he'd discuss it with her in the debriefing Monday night.

"If you children want to go ahead of me, go on. Although it's not a good idea to run on the stairs for many reasons. Just wait for us at the top, and don't touch anything."

"You must have children of your own, Phil," Bob said. "That was spoken like a true parent."

"I have twin daughters, Marianne and Mary Ellen," Phil said with a smile of pride. "They went to Vancouver for university, but I am so happy they have both moved back here. Marianne has taken the position left open when the previous teacher retired, and Mary Ellen, well, she's the brains behind this whole living museum operation."

When everyone had reached the watch room, Phil began his presentation by telling them his *dedushka* had been the first lighthouse keeper. "He witnessed a devastating shipwreck just off that craggy point to the right," Phil told them, pointing. "Which left everyone realizing the need to build a lighthouse."

He explained how his *Papa* and other young men had to be taken from their work of building their homes to construct the lighthouse.

"At sixty feet high, assembled of wood, this was a real feat. I have always taken great pride in knowing my *Papa* had a part in its construction. I think I chose my career to follow in my *dedushka's* footsteps because I was always fascinated by the tales he told me when I was growing up. This watch room or service room is where, as a lighthouse keeper, I spent my days preparing items I needed in the lantern room. Looking to the right we can see an additional eighteen even steeper stairs. They go to the cupola, which is a glassed-in housing containing the lantern, lamp, and lenses.

"Can we go up there?" Brian asked, already moving towards the stairs.

"No, son. That area is only authorized for the lighthouse keeper."

As Brian took another step towards them, looking up the stairwell, Bob spoke sharply, "Brian."

"I'm only looking, Dad," Brian replied, looking at his father sheepishly.

"I suggested to Susan to have a peek at the books we have in the lobby," Phil went on. "One of them describes in more detail how the lens and prisms work for making a brighter beam. This is a picture of the foghorn on the roof. It was useful to sound a siren assisting sailors to safely navigate in foggy conditions. In these later years, we didn't use it much because more recently, they set a foghorn at the entrance to the Skeena River, which is still in use today. I would have liked to have brought the one from our roof in for display, but it is far too awkward and heavy."

He moved to another window, and the little group followed.

"If we look to the east, we get a great overview of the village, and to the forest beyond. When you look towards the Pacific, looking far past all the islands, you can see miles and miles of water. The last few days it has been inky, dark and quiet. It isn't always this serene. Sometimes the water lashes the rocks very angrily. Take a few minutes to look around and when everyone is ready, we can step out on the gallery deck to feel the fresh air. If you brought your camera, this is a great place to take pictures."

"Can we walk all the way around?" Stephanie asked excitedly a few minutes later, as she raced ahead of everyone towards the door Phil had just opened.

"Yes," Phil told her.

"Just be careful," Mary called after her. "All of you children."

"We only have one telescope outside for stargazing, but we are thinking of getting more. Of course, if it is too windy outside, we can always stay in the watch room and use the mobile one. When everyone is ready, we will start back down."

At the bottom of the stairs, the children ran to find their mother. "Mom, you should have come. It was really neat!" David said.

"Not *cool*?" she playfully asked him. "I was beginning to think you children had only a one-word vocabulary."

"That's because this place is cool," Brian said, as he skipped outside. "Where to next?"

"Very informative, and the view is spectacular. I'm not going to kid you and say those steps were easy, but I will say the climb was very worthwhile," Peter told her, as he flexed his leg.

"So, after that little interlude, shall we get back on track?" Mary asked. "I think we should visit that other founding father's house. And then we plan to wander down Sharlotka Street to the kiosk where they sell stamps, so we can mail our postcards we purchased in the gift store."

"The founding father's house where they have a display of their journey from Russia is fine. Afterward, I think I'll go to the wharf and view the craft they have docked there," Peter said. "When you're done spending all my money, come and get me."

"Oh, Peter, really," Susan retorted, playfully.

"Hey, I like that idea of going onto the wharf and viewing the craft, Peter," Bob said. "After we see the display, I suggest my family take an hour and have some free time to do what they wish. Then we can meet at the gate before we leave."

"And I like that suggestion, Bob," Peter remarked. "It sounds like a good idea for my family, also."

"Good-bye. Come again," Nick and Martin said as they were locking the entrance at five o'clock.

"We will," came back five enthused voices.

The last thing either of them saw was Brian looking back and continuing to wave until their van disappeared around a bend.

CHAPTER TEN

Grand Opening Monday

On Monday morning, to Jenny, Anna, and Martin's delight, a couple with their young daughter were waiting when Nick opened the gate. After that, there seemed to be a slow but steady flow of people coming through.

Mary Ellen took great pleasure in walking around the village observing folks in various activities. Around Anna there were a few eager faces listening attentively to the village's history. Another couple stood in front of the founding fathers' plaque in the midst of an animated discussion. She had just seen another couple leave Alexander and Anastasia Yusporov's home. Another family had asked her for directions to the lighthouse and souvenir shop. As she made her way back to the teahouse to check on activities there, she let out a contented sigh. Everyone's hard work was paying off.

June had mentioned last night that there had been a few broken dishes at the teahouse. She had also heard of a few other small mishaps over the last few days. That, of course, could be expected. After all, everyone was just getting into the rhythm of things. But by now it seemed that already everyone had found the tempo of the day. Greeting guests, feeding guests, touring guests, answering questions of guests, and accommodating guests.

Over the weekend, there had also been a few minor first-aid incidents which Bob Petrov had handled.

"I am most interested to hear anything you would like to discuss regarding the opening weekend," Mary Ellen said, smiling brightly at everyone when they gathered for the debriefing. "Before we begin, I would like to thank you all for your continued hard work these past three days. Certainly, you can see where all the previous months of your preparation and hard work has paid off."

"I'll start," Jenny eagerly replied. "I have tallied the daily totals. I am most pleased to report that the first day we had fifteen people come through the gate. Of that number, seven people chose to stay overnight. Sunday, there was a two-person increase, plus of course the families who had stayed overnight. Sunday night, Phil and Marg hosted a family of four, and a honeymoon couple. On Monday, we had twenty-one people come through the gate. Plus, of course, our guests from the previous day. Tonight, there is still a family of four staying here."

Everyone cheered as she read out the final number of sixty-six visitors, indicating the success of their grand opening.

When the cheering subsided, Mary Ellen said, "Now *Mama-Marg*, I trust someone helped you with cleaning the rooms and laundry?"

"Yes, thank you. Your *papa* and I were thrilled with the exceptional help we had all weekend. A variety of people came by offering to help, surprisingly—one of them was my own son."

"I am very pleased to hear that. I thought of going often myself, but it seemed something always came up requiring my attention. You will be pleased to hear I can confirm that over the next couple of days all the staff I hired will be arriving. I am now eager to hear from the rest of you. Questions, or just comments," Mary Ellen went on. "I want to hear it all."

Taking the initiative, Daria spoke up. "From Tony's and my perspective, I think everything was lovely. It was so pleasant just strolling around. We were able to give directions and answer many people's questions. Sometimes they just wanted to admire our clothes or pose for pictures with us. Is that what you found as well, Olga?"

"I agree, everyone was so enthusiastic. I can add that over the three days, we received many positive compliments. One couple asked about staying for dinner and stargazing, even though they weren't staying the night. I told them yes. I hope that was the correct response."

"Yes, Mrs. Petrova, you certainly gave the right answer. We are in the hospitality industry now, and want to give our guests the best experience. However, a problem arose when later that night they wanted to leave and couldn't because the gate was locked. *Papa* had to come and get me to unlock it. So, I suggest that in the future, if this occurs, please let me know about it in advance."

"Oh, my dear," Olga exclaimed, horrified. "I apologize. I never thought about it and I caused you and Phil all that trouble."

"Mary Ellen," Nick said, as he stood up, "I'm not sorry this incident happened, because it has really identified a huge problem. I agree with Mary Ellen, Mrs. Petrova, that you answered our guests correctly. The solution I am going to recommend is that we adjust the gate so no one can enter after five, but they can exit. I am also going to remind everyone that we have a second entrance at the far end of the office so anyone living here can come and go at any time."

"Thank you, Nick," Mary Ellen responded. "An excellent recommendation, and we can have our locksmith come to make this adjustment right away."

"I agree with my mother-in-law, and Mrs. Petrova," Shelley said. "From my perspective, I just saw people walking around enjoying themselves."

"Frank isn't at this meeting because every night he takes *Dedushka* home right at five. Every night, he's been complaining about his cheeks being sore," Betty chuckled. "He says it is from too much talking but I think it is from constantly grinning. He's beamed all weekend, even while we're eating supper. I think he's having the time of his life."

"I am pleased to hear that," Mary Ellen replied. "I was worried this would be too much for him, but he insisted that he could do it. Please let him know if there is a day he doesn't want to work, and I will find a replacement for him."

"I will for sure, Mary Ellen, but I also know Frank will keep a very close eye on his *papa*."

"Mary Ellen," Alexandria said, "I offered to stay with some young people while their *roditeli* went to dinner Saturday night. I am wondering if we could post signs offering a companion and babysitting service to children?"

"That's a good idea," Mary Ellen answered. "Are you interested, Alexandria? Because if you are, come to talk to me after school on Thursday."

"I am very much interested," Alexandria enthusiastically

replied. "Do you think I can keep the extra money for my education fund?"

"Hey, no fair," Alexander retorted. "I have to save my wages for my education."

"We'll see. That's maybe something else we can address when you come to see me," Mary Ellen responded, smiling at her.

And ignoring the tittering going on around her, grinning at Alexander Mary Ellen said, "You can come talk to me also, Alexander, before you start work on Thursday. I'm sure Kevin won't mind your being a little late. And maybe we can think of ways we can top up your education fund, too." She nodded to her father. "Now, *Papa* dearest, I can tell you have something you want to say."

"I have two comments, Mary Ellen," Phil ventured. "You suggested I make a schedule of when I offer the lighthouse tours during the day, and I've decided to take you up on that."

"I'm pleased to hear you say that. Come by my office, let's say just before noon on Thursday, and we can work out the details together."

"The other thing is, last night I heard the folks who were stargazing on the wharf talking amongst themselves and wishing there were telescopes available."

"I think they have a good idea. We had initially planned to get more telescopes for the gallery, but perhaps Gaspar could anchor some of them to the wharf? The last thing we want is for expensive equipment to be knocked over and go to the bottom of the cove. I'm curious, did any of your guests venture to the gallery to admire the night sky from there?"

"No," Marg quickly responded. "I think the children whose families were staying with us Saturday night had earlier indicated they wanted to go. But it seemed they were having too much fun in our garden. At least it sounded to us like they were letting off a lot of steam. Alexandria was staying with them while their *roditeli* went out for dinner, and well, I might add. she seemed to be doing most of the talking."

"Those are the kids I told you about earlier," Alexandria stated. "Their *roditeli* came back and joined us in the garden after their dinner. We all enjoyed the night sky from there, especially the dancing and swaying vibrant green and pink movements of the *aurora borealis*."

"In answer to your question, Mary Ellen," Marg continued, "only the couple Olga mentioned earlier enjoyed watching from the wharf. Phil and I went out also, and I must say even the stars in the sky were brilliant that night, as if they too were celebrating our opening."

"Well, it sounds like everyone had an enjoyable evening, then," Mary Ellen finished. "Mr. and Mrs. Yusporov, do you have anything to report from the souvenir shop?"

"I think everything went very well," Betty answered. "Already I can tell the *babushka* dolls are going to be very popular."

"I agree," Gayle said. "Many people spoke to us about the dolls on display at the teahouse. I just informed them that everything I have on display is available at the gift shop."

"Well, that is good news!" Mary Ellen smiled at the ladies. "Maybe you can let me know which colours seem to be the most popular, when I need to reorder." When everyone became quiet, she went on, "Does anyone else have anything to add? This has all been great feedback. Please be sure and come and see me anytime something else comes up."

"Well," Bob Petrov offered, "I'm expecting my brother, Nikolai, tonight."

"That's right," Mary Ellen said. "He called me and said he'd arrive around six. He didn't think he could come so soon, so I am very pleased this is working out so well. I'm also relieved we got through this weekend with no bigger incident than what a Band-Aid strip could fix. I'll leave you to meet him tonight, Mr. Petrov, but please, just let him know I will meet with him sometime over the next couple of days."

"Oh, that's just great," Alexander moaned. "Another Mr. Petrov running around."

"You'll survive," Alexandria grinned at her brother.

"You're right, he is coming much sooner than we expected," Bob said cheerily. "The reason is, he initially thought he would need to stay to sell their house. In the end, their daughter and her husband offered to take care of everything for them. His daughter, Linda, is bringing her mother, Margarita, sometime this weekend as she wasn't prepared to leave yet. Margarita is very eager to get here because Olga told her Anna was asking for help with sewing, which is my sister-in-law's passion."

"Well, with that piece of exciting news, I think we will call it a night," Mary Ellen concluded. "I'm sure everyone is tired, so enjoy the next two days off."

That evening, the family who were staying gathered on the wharf, oohing and ahhing at nature's glory as they sipped happily on their mugs of *sbiten*. The northern lights dazzled them with their splendor, dancing and rippling like curtains as an eerie glow of pale green and pink weaved its way across the sky. Then a crescent moon became visible and one of the girls pointed Mercury out to her family. It was only through binoculars that Venus was spotted, and the family eagerly passed the instrument between them. Around ten o'clock, the parents left to go to bed.

Their daughters decided to stay out and were soon chatting with Alexander and Alexandria. Shortly after midnight, Alexander led everyone up the numerous stairs to the gallery deck. Through the telescopes aimed up at the twinkling stars, the foursome picked out Mars, Saturn, and finally Jupiter. Some of the constellations were so bright they did not need to use any instrument to see them. Just as the first glimmer of the sunrise was showing on the horizon, Alexander pointed out the Northern Cross. This also alerted the girls to the time, and they scurried to ground level and amidst their thanks, disappeared into their room.

Alexander and Alexandria said good-bye to the closing door and went home, content to know they could sleep in as long as they wanted.

CHAPTER ELEVEN

Moving In

"Hi, Marie," Mary Ellen greeted her Tuesday morning when she pulled up around ten-thirty. "You are the first of my summer staff to arrive. I have a map to give you, so just drive in and park where I've indicated with this mark. You will see gentlemen setting up chairs and patio tables in front of this plaque. Please wait for us there. After everyone arrives, some of the village ladies have prepared a welcome luncheon for the new hires, prior to orientation."

This pattern continued for much of the morning, as Mary Ellen greeted the new hires, checking them off her list one by one.

- Marie Gonzalez, laundry
- Patricia Reynolds, float
- Bert Montgomery, gardens and lawn maintenance
- Andrea Staples, cleaning rooms at the lighthouse station
- Roberta Staples, same
- Magdalia Hernandez, general cleaning

Mary Ellen verified that the last two people were coming on Wednesday and then went outside herself. Walking across the lawn towards the founding fathers' plaque, she could see Daria, Jenny, Gayle, and even shy Agnessa Bolitchyn walking with Marg to join her there.

Once introductions were concluded, they began talking and eating, only pausing occasionally as someone said thank you, asked for more juice, or murmured with appreciation over the taste of the *knish*, a small savory pie. To finish the meal, they served *kissel,* a light fruit dessert. Finally, all the plates were gathered, and after the last glass of *mors* was poured, a hush came over the group as everyone looked expectantly at Mary Ellen. As she rose to her feet, she smiled at everyone.

Following a few words of greeting, she began, "Your actual orientation consists of a typed page outlining the responsibilities which are expected from you. Each sheet includes a line that reads, *Miscellaneous duties as required*. What this means is, if you finish your work prior to your shift being completed, please see me. Or if you are working at the lighthouse station, you can speak to either of the Filipovs. I am sure we can always find something to keep you busy. For example, something as simple as stocking shelves, or a special chore. For the most part, I'm sure you will find your sheets are much the same as the information we covered in your interview. I will give you ten to fifteen minutes to read your job descriptions and then answer any questions you may have."

After about ten minutes, when Mary Ellen saw most people looking up, she asked, "Shall we proceed?"

Patricia wanted to clarify her position as a float. "Who do I report to, and am I to have a schedule?"

"Those are very good questions. When you are cleaning the various buildings in the museum, you are reporting to me.

However, for any work you do at the lighthouse station, your immediate supervisors will be the proprietors, Phil and Marg Filipov. In answer to your second question, when we meet tomorrow, I will give you a schedule. As we discussed in your interview, sometimes it will require you working in the morning, like when you are at the lighthouse station. Then when you are cleaning the other buildings it will require you to do touch-up cleaning in the afternoon and a more thorough cleaning when the museum closes. I am hoping that when the museum gets busier, the need for the touch-ups will become greater. My guess is, after a few weeks everything will become more routine. Incidentally, Magdalia, this information about the touch-ups also applies to you."

"What kind of miscellaneous duties might I have, Miss?" Bert then asked.

"When we are planning a special event, I would like to have particular flowers for that occasion. I'd like you to plant these in some of the beds. Not to worry, this will always be scheduled well in advance."

Mary Ellen waited a few moments and when no further comments came, she stated, "If there are no more questions, I will continue. Tomorrow morning, I would like a half-hour meeting with Patricia and Magdalia to go through the buildings you will be responsible for. I suggest we meet at ten in this location. Another new hire, Warren, will be arriving in the morning and will also be joining us.

"Bert, I suggest you be here then, as well. I'll also be able to include your partner Miles, who I am also expecting in the morning. As we walk around the site you will be able to see the garden beds or planters and I will be right there to answer any questions.

"Likewise, Marg Filipova and her husband will show the

staff who will be working at the lighthouse station what their expectations are. That means Marie for the laundry, and Patricia, Andrea, and Roberta for cleaning the rooms. Warren, who is also a float, will need to take in this talk. They have planned this for eleven-thirty at the lighthouse station. I'm sure you all noticed where it was when you drove in this morning.

"My reason for planning these meetings tomorrow is so I can feel sure each of you are prepared when you show up for work Wednesday morning. We are still closed for the rest of today and tomorrow, so hopefully that will give everyone time to settle in. Feel free to wander around and familiarize yourself with the whole village. You'll also have time off over the next few weeks so you can have the opportunity to see all the museum exhibits.

"I think that covers everything I had planned for today. So, allow me to wrap things up by introducing you to the ladies whose homes you will be staying in." She beckoned to the four women who had been patiently waiting since lunch.

"Marie and Magdalia, it has been arranged for both of you to stay with Tony and Daria Rosso. Patricia, you will be staying with Martin and Gayle Shatrov. Bert, you will be staying with Nick and Jenny Kutuz. Andrea and Roberta, you will both be staying with Agnessa and Mitslav Bolitchyn.

"I'm sure sometime today you will receive help bringing your personal items to the home, but afterward, please leave your vehicle in the space that we have designated for employees at the far end of the parking lot."

The next few minutes were very busy as Mary Ellen introduced everyone to their respective hostesses. Then she sighed contentedly, as everyone departed, still talking. Soon all that was left to indicate the event had even happened were the empty tables and chairs and a few stray napkins, which she cheerfully gathered up.

Early Wednesday morning, it was raining as Mary Ellen made her way to the entrance in anticipation of meeting her last two hires. She was busy looking up at the sky in annoyance and almost tripped over a pair of legs sticking out in the pathway.

"Goodness," she cried, trying to regain her balance, as Bert crawled out from underneath a bush. "Whatever are you doing, Bert?"

"Good morning, Miss. I am just starting to dig up some soil around these plants."

"But you don't start until tomorrow."

"Mother always says there's no time like the present. So I thought I might as well get busy today. Besides, I think this rain will work to my advantage."

"Well, I guess if you're happy... don't feel like you have to. You know, I have an idea, I'm expecting Miles Stewart, who will be assisting you. Why don't you come with me and meet him?"

"I suppose I could," Bert said, as he stood and brushed the dirt off his hands.

Miles was already waiting, anxiously looking at his watch. His face broke into a smile of relief as he watched Mary Ellen approach.

"Good morning, Miles, I'm sorry I am a bit late. Truth is, I almost tripped over your co-worker's feet. Allow me to introduce Bert Montgomery to you. And Bert, this is Miles Stewart. Bert has already started working, even though everyone won't officially start until tomorrow."

"Sounds like a man after my own heart," Miles said as he shook Bert's hand, and which started the men off on a conversation about Bert's first impressions. Mary Ellen was quite enjoying listening to them when another vehicle pulled off the road.

"Ah, my last employee has finally arrived. Greetings Warren, come over and meet Bert Montgomery and Miles Stewart. Gentlemen, this is Warren Spencer. I see each of you appear to have one suitcase each, so if you would like to bring your luggage with you, follow me. We can just leave your suitcases at this office building and someone will bring them to you later. I am very disappointed about the rain. I had intended for us to meet outdoors, but now I'd better take you to the teahouse. But maybe this is going to work out. Everything is closed today, but my suspicion is that Gayle will be there baking."

By the time they arrived, the rain was slowing to a drizzle and a few patches of blue sky were visible.

"Well, Miss," Bert said, "Mother always says, 'It is a good sign if there is enough blue in the sky to make a sailor trousers'. So, it looks like we are going to be in for a fine day."

"Thank you for that charming piece of wisdom," Mary Ellen said, smiling at him. "We're at the teahouse now, so let's see if my assumption is correct. Yes, she is here." Mary Ellen beckoned to Gayle.

When Gayle opened the door, Mary Ellen quickly said, "My last two employees have just arrived and because it is drizzling, I told them I thought we might come here. By the way, meet Miles Stewart, who will be working with Bert, and Warren Spencer, who will be another float."

"Why, yes of course, come in and I will make a fresh pot of coffee. I just took the dessert, *pirogi,* out of the oven, so they will be nice and warm. I will bring a plate for everyone to share."

Once they had selected a table, Mary Ellen said, "I will need to leave you on your own for a time while I get Patricia and Magdalia. I told them yesterday to meet me somewhere else, but I will bring them back here. Warren and Miles, these sheets are your job descriptions. When I return, I can answer any questions you might have. Oh, I almost forgot, here are some maps of the village. You might also find these interesting to familiarize yourself with."

When Mary Ellen came back with the girls, after introducing everyone she said, "We just have two hours until eleven-thirty, so our timing looks good."

"Mary Ellen, I read my job description," Miles commented, "It seemed pretty much what we discussed when you interviewed me."

"You're right, Miles. Any other comments or questions from either of you?"

"No, I'm good. Miles just expressed what I was thinking," Warren agreed.

"All right then, let's move on to the second stage of your orientation. Warren, you will be meeting with the Filipovs at eleven-thirty to learn your duties at the lighthouse station. There will be some others joining you there.

"First, though, you and these women need to walk around and see some of the buildings so I can explain in greater detail what I expect to be done. And after our snack, before we leave the teahouse, we may as well start here.

"Then on the way to the rest of the buildings, we can stop at the barbershop, so I can introduce Miles and Warren to Paul and Christella, at whose home you will both be staying. Warren, as I mentioned earlier, I will need you until approximately one o'clock. Miles, after the introductions, I suggest you continue to accompany us and take note of the various gardens.

"I had mentioned to Bert yesterday that he can come with us. But something tells me, Bert, you will be just fine on your own and will let me know if any issues come up. You decide."

"You have that right, Miss."

When everyone finished eating, and after discussing the requirements of the teahouse, she led them outside. She was pleased to see it had turned into a very nice morning. They stopped at the barbershop to introduce Miles and Warren. After the introductions, Miles did choose to continue with her. Bert did as she suspected and returned to his bushes without a backward glance.

Everyone else continued to the first-aid building, where she explained in detail her expectations, and from there to each place they were responsible for. Before they wrapped up, Mary Ellen gave both Patricia and Warren a schedule. Then at eleven-twenty, she led them to the lighthouse station.

"Hi, *Papa*," Mary Ellen said in greeting, when the group arrived at the lighthouse station. I have brought your new employees so you can provide them with details about the work that needs to be done here. I gave everyone a map, but I'm sure you will help anyone who gets lost to find their way home."

"Marg and I were saying this morning that it will be after twelve noon when we finish our orientation, so maybe we will just have hot dogs in our garden afterward. Don came one night to show me what I need to do to have a wiener roast."

"That sounds lovely, *Papa*. I think I will join you as well, and find my other new hires and see if they might also be interested in joining us. I will leave you now to make your introductions."

The last thing she heard her *papa* say as she left on her mission was that he would begin by introducing his wife. She had at least forty-five minutes because after introductions, they would cover first the laundry room duties, supplies, and then the guest suites. At the corner, she came across Don.

When she explained what she was doing, Don responded, "Ah yes, I was giving *Papa*-Phil instructions the other night. You know, you might even want to recruit me." Chuckling, he added, "I'm not a new hire, so maybe I don't meet your criteria exactly." He fell out of step with her.

She playfully grabbed his arm as if she was dragging him along.

"I see." He grinned at her. "You seem most anxious I come. Are you suggesting I will be useful?"

Bert and Miles were exactly where she suspected to find them—looking at some of the flowerbeds. When she explained her reason for looking for them, they both agreed to join her.

Walking along, Bert offered to help. "Mother always says, 'Many hands make light work.'"

They were cutting across the lawn to come out on what used to be called Marine Street, now renamed Sharlotka Street, heading towards the Rosso house to invite Magdalia. A block away they encountered her strolling along and visiting with Marianne and Kevin. When the invitation to join the group for a wiener roast at noon was extended to Magdalia, her sister mischievously asked her if she and Kevin were invited as well.

"Sure," Mary Ellen agreed. "The more the merrier. Besides,

it will be great for my new employees to start meeting some of New Petrograd's residents."

Mary Ellen looked at her watch and then jumped up with a start. "This afternoon has been quite delightful, getting to know you all better. What a great idea this was. But I've just noticed the time—it is almost three-thirty and I still have work to do. I have a previous appointment I need to keep, so I'd better get going."

She almost ran to Bob's house, arriving shortly before four. But because she was so out of breath, she waited to compose herself before knocking.

Nikolai must have been looking out the window for her, because as she approached the door, he came out. "I was thinking I was going to have to come looking for you myself," he said with a chuckle as he closed the door behind him.

"I do apologize. I could have come much sooner, but all my other new hires, who have also arrived this weekend, were having a lovely wiener roast at my Papa's and I lost all track of time."

"At Phil and Marg's. I think after we've had a look at my facility, we should just head over and say hello. I haven't seen my sister since I came home. Then I can meet your other new employees as well."

"For sure. I don't know how much longer they'll be there, because it is getting close to suppertime. I'm not hungry, as *Mama*-Marg has been spoiling us all afternoon."

"Well, that sure sounds like her."

"Getting down to business, I ordered everything you asked

for, and have hopefully organized them in a way that will be efficient for you."

The small building that was to serve as their first-aid facility really didn't seem very big. It always reminded Mary Ellen of a trailer, but it had been built according to the measurements he had given her. Nikolai took a good look around the first room, a smile crossing his face as he took note of the desk and two chairs. A brief look inside the desk drawers showed some office supplies. In the next area was a sink with several basins neatly stacked on a shelf under the sink. An autoclave was also present. Last was a bed with its disposable paper roll and a pillow at the head.

"I have pillowcases, towels, and facecloths in the storage cupboard in the other room. Everything can be washed at the lighthouse station. The staff are already aware whose responsibility it is to collect and return the linens for you. I didn't want to put a pillowcase on too far in advance as it will just get dusty. I can take a minute to put it on now, if you like?" she offered.

"Oh, don't worry about that. It will just take me a minute to do it in the morning. And many days, I can take the laundry to the lighthouse station at the end of the day. It will give me an excuse to stretch my legs and to drop in and see the folks there."

"Suit yourself, but arrangements have been made, so don't feel like you have to."

They went into the next room where a full-length wardrobe stood. Inside were clean white linen towels, facecloths, and boxes of items, which Mary Ellen quickly explained were extra supplies.

Silently, he continued around the room, opening the drawers in a cabinet and taking note of the various first-aid supplies, nodding as he went. "Well, it looks like you've done a remarkable job of getting this place set up. Tomorrow when I come to work, there are just a few minor adjustments I need to make."

Mary Ellen hadn't realized she had been holding her breath, until she let it out. Shyly looking at him, she said, "I didn't write out a job description for your position. In fact, I'm hoping you can put something together for me, so I have it on file."

"Absolutely, that shouldn't be a problem at all." He looked in the last few drawers and then turned to leave, ushering her out in front of him.

As they were making their way to the lighthouse, Nikolai said, "Tell me about yourself, Mary Ellen. You girls weren't even born when we moved away."

"You must be Buddy Rasmussen," Bob said on Wednesday night just before five, when he approached the bus driver as he exited the bus. "Our office received a phone call informing us to expect you tonight." Rasmussen looked like a middle-aged man, not unlike himself.

"You got that right," Buddy said with a hiccup. "From the Grey North Bus Lines, serving Prince Rupert to Skagway in Alaska. It sounds like you have quite the setup here. My boss has assigned me to make this my regular route. Takes quite a while to drive from Prince Rupert, but that's okay. What did he say? I'd be sleeping at a lighthouse? That sounds like quite the adventure."

"That's correct. We did add some accommodations for our guests at our lighthouse station."

The passengers by now were all huddled expectantly around the luggage compartment, looking rather grimly at the driver.

"Enough talking," Buddy muttered to himself as he walked the length of the bus. Then he unlocked the door and began pulling out suitcases and backpacks.

"Greetings, everyone," Bob said while Buddy was busy. "Welcome to New Petrograd. After you have collected your luggage, just go through the entrance. Then you can drop off your baggage beside the Bronco parked just inside the gate and an employee will drive it to your lodgings. I will wait here and when everyone is ready, I will escort you to your lodgings, and give you an information package that will give you a map of our town, along with an insert for the Borscht Kettle showing their dinner menu this evening."

CHAPTER TWELVE

Fishermen Arrive

"Oh good, you're still home, Gaspar," Don greeted him, coming into the kitchen on a Friday morning a couple of weeks after the grand opening.

"Yes, Shelley and I were about to have some *blini* with honey and *smetana.* It's one of the Russians foods *Mama* taught her to make." Gaspar gazed at his wife adoringly. "Help yourself, they are really good. What's on your mind?"

"Don't mind if I do, but I'll just eat it while I'm standing," he said as he reached over to get one. "I know I'm running late, but I just want to remind you that you and Kevin agreed to assist me when I go fishing tomorrow. If you still want a refresher this afternoon, we can schedule one in. I've had a few cancellations, so there is also room for Shelley."

"That's it! I knew I was forgetting something about this weekend, and I couldn't remember what it was. Fortunately, I have nothing else going on that I can't change. So, I can fit in an hour around two-thirty. I'll just meet you at the wharf." He turned to Shelley. "So, what do you say, *moi medvezhono,* would you like to go? You haven't had a day off in two weeks."

"Well, other than Monday and Tuesday when the museum is closed. No different than you, sweetheart, or for that matter, anyone else," she responded, reaching for his hand and entwining their fingers. "A fishing trip does sound delightful, though. I may not be as much of a fisherman as my dad, but I do enjoy a day on the water. I will ask Mary Ellen if I can take the time off."

"Well actually, Mary Ellen is planning on getting away with me," Don huskily responded.

"Oh really," Gaspar said to his chum. "I suppose Kevin is bringing Marianne with him."

"Now that you mention it, I have heard something about that." Don grinned. "After all, I think allowing you to bring your significant other along on the trip is a small price I am willing to pay to keep my assistants happy. Getting back to Mary Ellen, she has been thrilled since the grand opening. Apparently, attendance is increasing nicely, and I think that can be attributed to all her efforts. So, I thought it was time she took a well-deserved break. We haven't had any time to ourselves since we went to Hartley Bay, and that was just business."

"Umm, of course it was," Gaspar agreed. "And of course I believe you," he added with a grin, tongue in cheek, as he took a sip of his coffee.

"I guess my day off is a given if the boss is going, so sure, I'll be happy to come along," Shelley said.

"I think my clients arrive around ten," Don said, "which gives them some time in the afternoon to look around. I'm not quite sure when the solo person will arrive. I've got to run, so I'll catch you two later," Don said, as he ducked out the back door.

Looking at the clock, Shelley commented, "I guess I best

be getting dressed for work. This 1917 Russian women's police uniform, with the khaki jacket and skirt, plus these big black boots, is already warm. On top of that, Anna wants me to wear this khaki hat. One good thing, I won't have to worry about being sunburnt in the summer. The sun will never be able to find me!"

"But seriously, my love, you do look so charming in it," Gaspar chuckled, as he bent to kiss her nose. "If the sun never finds these dimples, it's all right with me. You're right, though, you'd better get ready. I'll just do up these few breakfast dishes and go too." He gave her yet another kiss. "I will kiss you good-bye now, in case I've left when you finish dressing. I'll see you tonight at the Borscht Kettle for fish and chips."

Don stood by the entrance watching for the van and felt quite relieved when, just around ten, he saw a blue van slowing and pulling off the road. When it came to a stop, the man in the front passenger side got out and greeted him. "Are you Don Rosnokov?"

"I am," Don said, extending his hand. "Who might you be?"

"I'm Harvey. Harvey Mann."

"Nice to meet you, Harvey. How about you unload everything here and then your driver can move your vehicle to the parking lot," Don said as he pointed to it.

Everyone began piling out then, and as they were unloading their fishing gear and backpacks, Harvey introduced Don to the rest of them—Pete Arthurs, Andy Grimshaw, and his brother Charles.

While Charles left with the van, Don commented to

everyone else, "I see you've all brought your own rods and tackle. We can put them in this first building when we get inside the gates. I'll just let Nick know that I've left them there."

When they saw Charles coming back, Don asked, "Anybody need a hand, just say so. Otherwise, follow me."

As they picked up their backpacks, Andy said, "Just these bags of munchies, maybe," indicating with his foot a large box on the ground.

"No problem," Don said, as he heaved the box onto his hip. "Good planning," he told them with a chuckle. "You can get beer or *tarasun,* a Russian beer, or vodka at the Borscht Kettle, but they don't sell Cheezies or potato chips there. The kiosk carries them, but my guess is that when you'll probably be wanting to nibble, it will be closed."

"Hi, Jenny," Don called as they approached her wicket. "These four men have come for my fishing trip tomorrow. I'm not sure when our final guest will be arriving."

"That's okay, Don. I know not to charge him, but just to let him go straight in. Nick will escort him to the lighthouse station. That way he can get checked into his room until someone can find you."

"Appreciate it. Thank you, Jenny. Nick," Don called out, as he made his way into the office with the four men. 'We're just putting our gear here now, until I can retrieve it."

"Just leave them where you think it will work best," Nick called from the other room. "Have a great time tomorrow."

After the men had left their gear, Don led them back under a shady tree to chat. "As you know, I'm Don Rosnokov and this is the village of New Petrograd, where I was born and raised. So, welcome, all of you. I lived for a brief stint in Whitehorse, but when the Ministry of Highways put in this road, I was thinking about moving my business back here. Then I got wind of the talk about making the village a living museum and turning the lighthouse station into accommodations. And the rest is history."

"See, I told you, Harvey," Charles said. "I hoped you were the same person, because I've heard great things about your guiding abilities."

"I am," Don replied. "Thank you for your kind words. Before we go anywhere else, I'll take you to Martin and he can give you a map and some useful information about the museum, in case there is anything that might interest you. After that, I'll take you straight to the lighthouse station and get you checked into your rooms. Then I'll leave you on your own for a few hours."

"Don? *Don!*" Jenny called, leaning out from the ticket booth. "Your last guest just arrived."

"Awesome," Don said, turning to greet him. "You must be Rod Brantford. I was just about to start taking everyone to check into their rooms, so your timing couldn't be better. I'll just take a second to put your fishing gear in the office with everyone else's. Maybe in the meantime all of you can introduce yourselves."

As Don led them through the village, he had to smile at their comments as he was pointing out various things.

"Get a load of this ruin of a building. It's pretty neat. You know how much I like photography. I can tell already there'll be no shortage of photos to take here."

"Hey, look at that dress—it's probably authentic. Would my wife ever like to see that."

"I'm a landscaper," Rod chimed in. "Some of these garden arrangements look pretty interesting."

"It's looking pretty good. Maybe this afternoon we can take

in one of the history talks, and I don't know, if we still have time maybe tour the house Don just pointed out to us. You too, Rod—feel welcome to join us."

"Hey, this map says stargazing from the lighthouse tower. That's got my interest piqued."

"Well, maybe that's fine for you, Charles, but I'm going to hit the hay early tonight."

"I'll take you right to the room that Don has booked for you," Marg offered hospitably as she led the way. "We have a few others who have booked in this weekend."

"This is grand," Charles said, on his first glance. "Great job, Harvey, recommending this place. Now, let's get back outdoors and not waste another minute."

"Are you sure you don't want to do anything more to settle in?" Don inquired.

"Nope, it's noon, and I'm not one to waste time," Charles answered him. "Where did you say the history talks are? That sounds like a great place to start—oh, here it is on the map. Ready, everybody?"

"Hang on, hang on, Chuck," Harvey admonished him, "I just might want to use the washroom before we go anywhere."

"Yeah, me too," Pete said. "Hold your horses, Charlie."

Don laughed. "The history talks don't start until one-thirty, so you have time beforehand to grab a quick lunch or tour the house you were talking about earlier. One last thing I will mention before I leave you. It's a longstanding tradition in New Petrograd to have fish and chips at the Borscht Kettle on Friday night. Why don't I swing by tonight and escort you to dinner? I'll probably have some of my friends along, if you don't mind." Back outside, he said, "See you later. I'll be back to get you for supper."

It wasn't until he left that he realized he'd never gotten an answer to his question.

When Gaspar and Don were getting into the boat that afternoon, Don said, "The first thing I want to remind you is that we'll all have CB radios so we can stay in constant contact."

"Oh sure, and let everyone know that I don't know what I'm doing," Gaspar replied.

"I can always let them know you're just an amateur, which you are."

"Oh no, that's going a little far," Gaspar said. "I liked it better this morning, when you called me your assistant. Anyways, let's get on with your test."

"Okay, you tell me what you're going to do, and I'll correct you if you make a mistake or overlook anything."

"Well, I've checked to see that everyone is safely in the boat, so next I'm going to hand out life jackets to everyone." He pointed to the locker. "Next, I'll check for fishing licenses. If someone doesn't have one, they can't start fishing until we go to the general store at Port Essington."

"You're doing just fine so far," Don replied. "Just so you know, I do get them to send me the number and expiration date of their licenses when they register for the trip. So, really, what we're mostly checking for is to see that they have it with them."

"Right. Next, I'm going to make sure I have everything I need in the boat. Things like extra gas, bait, nets, and downriggers. Then there's the nonessential items that will make the day more pleasant, like lunch, water, sunscreen, bug repellent, and safety supplies."

"Safety supplies are essential and even though with some of the other items you are technically correct, they certainly contribute to making your trip successful. Most people bring their own sunscreen, but it sure gives us points if they don't and we have some. I always equip my boats with complimentary caps with my logo as well, and hand them out. Don't forget that while we're still here at the pier, you can easily ask me a question. Actually, you know, I'll just make a point of coming around to your and Kevin's boats to check that everything is going well."

"Come to think of it, why isn't Kevin here now?"

Don laughed heartily. "Don't you worry, I went through this with him last night. Okay, so far, so good. What's next?"

"I look around my boat to make sure everything is stowed away properly, turn the boat on, and we'll soon be feeling that delightful sensation of the wind on our faces. Do you want me to do that now?"

"Ha, ha. Good try, my friend, but no, everything we need to accomplish we can do right here."

"Rats," Gaspar said, grinning. "Okay, lures and bait. What you recommended the other night is a combination flasher and hootchie for salmon. Sometimes, anchovies work better than hootchies, so we should have some of those along, too. I also need a bucket of water or ice to put the fish in when they're caught."

Don shook his head. "I don't recommend you put your caught fish in water—it makes them turn soft too soon. But since we will be out all day, a cooler of ice would probably be appropriate."

"The men have booked me for eight hours, so I'm thinking

we will stay on the ocean in the morning for salmon. Then go up the Skeena in the afternoon and see if we can get some rainbow trout. For trout, we'll use flashy spoons. The bait I keep for them is fish eggs, and tomorrow morning if I have time, I'll dig up worms." At Don's nod, Gaspar took a breath and went on. "When I bait the line, I'll attach it to a downrigger cable and drop it to a fishing depth. Then we drive to where the fish-finder indicates the fish are. When there is evidence a fish has been hooked, like the rod bending, I'll take it off the downrigger and hand the rod to the guest. I won't be able to coach them too much, but I will sure provide ample encouragement. Then I must pay very careful attention to what is happening so I'm ready to net the fish and bring it in."

"You're doing great. What about when we come back?"

"Oh, that's when the real fun starts." Gaspar guffawed. "We scale and clean the fish. So, did I pass?"

"I'd give you a gold star if I had one," Don exclaimed, chuckling, as they were leaving the boat. "Just a couple of comments I can make. Since we will be fishing for Chinook salmon, and we are limited to two per person, we will only set out two lines per boat. Also, we won't need to set our fish-finders until we get near the area we're intending to fish."

When they arrived at the Borscht Kettle that evening, it was already quite full. "Do you think you can find a table for eleven, Uri, for my five guests, five friends and myself?"

"I can," Uri answered hesitantly, "but you might be waiting a long while before I can accommodate everyone."

Looking behind him, Don spotted Kevin arriving with the twins.

"I've an idea though. Why don't I put together eleven take-out orders for you?" Uri offered.

After a minute's thought, Don replied, "That will work. We can go to the garden where the barbecue pit is. I believe we just might qualify to use it, seeing about half us are staying there. If you see Gaspar and Shelley, just redirect them to the barbecue pit."

Then, while they waited for their meals, Don introduced the two groups to each other. He was just explaining that all of them were planning on going fishing tomorrow when he saw Gaspar and Shelley walking towards the Kettle. Just as he concluded introducing them as well, Uri brought out a box with their eleven meals wrapped and ready to go.

"Off to the lighthouse," Don announced as he opened the door, gesturing everyone out ahead of him.

"Sounds good," Harvey said. "You lead, we'll follow. I, for one, am starved."

As they walked along, Mary Ellen enlightened the men about this part of New Petrograd's history. The original owners of the Borscht Kettle, Nikolai and Margarita Petrov, had begun this tradition of Friday night fish and chips, with ice cream for dessert. They then passed it on to their son, Bob, and his wife, Olga, who had just recently retired. It then changed hands for the third time, but to Anna, Bob and Olga's daughter, and their son-in-law, Uri.

"Because my *papa* was the lighthouse keeper, he was unable to join us, so when my sister and I were growing up, we would come with our *mama*. Often, we shared a table with Don's family."

"When I came for Thanksgiving a couple of years ago," Shelley remarked, "Mrs. Rosnokova, Mr. Petrov's sister, said her *mama* used to make homemade ice cream. She told us when her brother, Bob, took over, he was too lazy to make his own so just ordered it in from the general store."

Don startled laughing, "I'm sure all these names are confusing you. The Mrs. Rosnokova that Shelley just spoke about is my *mama*. Last year, she married Mary Ellen and Marianne's *papa*. And she's the lady who booked you into your room earlier. I don't know why I didn't think to introduce you to her then."

"Well, that explains why you're such good friends, actually more than friends. In fact, you're related now. How about the rest of you? Shelley, you spoke like you're not from here," Andy said, when they made their way around the corner, only to stop and stare at the pleasant scenery before them. "Well, I just found where I'm eating tomorrow night, too! Say, we were thinking of climbing the lighthouse tonight, or at least going down to the wharf later when it gets dark, to stargaze."

"If you want my advice," Don offered, "being as we all have an early start tomorrow, may I suggest you plan on doing that tomorrow night? My plan is to eat my supper and then head home to bed."

Even with Don's good intentions, it was eight o'clock before everyone began to disperse, and already dusk was beginning to shadow their little gathering, bringing the stars with it.

CHAPTER THIRTEEN

Gone Fishin'

It was five-thirty in the morning when Don, accompanied by Kevin and Gaspar, started organizing their vehicles by collecting the men's fishing tackle. When they came back to Don's house, they began loading the rest of the equipment into their vehicles.

"I've asked everybody to meet us on the dock in a half-hour. I'm hoping to be on the water by six-thirty or shortly thereafter," Don was explaining.

Overhearing them as they began work, Shelley exclaimed, "Seems like you've planned things down to the wire. I was just coming out to ask what time I should be ready. Now I know I'd better hurry."

"The twins should be here shortly. I suggested they come around five-fifty," Don replied. "They're bringing us a Thermos of coffee and some fruit and cheese scones Gayle made yesterday, so we can eat while loading the boat. Gayle left some of the scones at the lighthouse station. My *mama* was going to make a fresh pot of coffee and see my clients had room service this morning."

"Sounds like a plan," Shelley remarked, before hurrying back inside to finish getting ready.

When the twins arrived, Don pulled a piece of paper out of his back pocket and handed it to Mary Ellen. He asked her if she could help him check off the items as he called them out. "This may take us a few minutes—we have at least three of each item."

"Of course," Mary Ellen agreed, as she flashed him a brilliant smile. "Fire away."

As the long list of supplies was being called out, Kevin and Gaspar checked it against what they had loaded into their vehicles. As she got to the end of the list, Mary Ellen turned to him quizzically and asked, "Everything checks out, but licenses... Licenses for what?"

"Fishing licenses," Kevin replied. "If you girls want to fish for trout, we can get them at the general store in Port Essington."

"We never worried about them before because we were just on our own land. Well, at least, we thought of it as our own," Don carefully amended. "Now, travelling further afield, we'll have to conform to provincial laws."

"Oh," both Filipov girls said, surprised.

Then Marianne burst into a fit of laughter. "Now look where that fancy new road got us."

As everyone else joined in laughing with her, Don exclaimed, "If we've got everything loaded into the vehicles, I think we're ready to be 'gone fishin'."

They drove the short distance along the wharf to where the boats were bobbing in the water. Don and his assistants made short work of transferring everything from their trucks into them. They had just finished when the five men arrived.

When everyone was standing beside the boats, Don

handed out the complimentary caps, smiling as he handed one to each of his buddies. Then he gave his customers a little more information on his game plan.

"We just missed the spring run of steelhead because they pretty much finish up by the middle of May. At the beginning of June, the Chinook salmon started running. The other name they go by is the Mighty Kings. These are big fish arriving with the high tides out of the ocean. They start to migrate up the Skeena River on their way to their native streams, where they spawn. My plan is to go to the mouth of the river, which should be perfect. Just prepare yourselves for a big fight, because they are the hardest fighting, toughest salmon in the world."

"When you say *big*, can you give me some idea of their weight, in pounds?" Mary Ellen asked.

"They'll usually weigh in between fifteen and twenty-five pounds, but every year it seems some are caught closer to thirty pounds. Even some exceeding thirty," he told her.

"Are you sure the thirty pounders aren't a fish tale?" Mary Ellen asked.

"I don't know—could be." Don laughed.

"I think at the end of Telegraph Pass, we'll head towards Edye Pass. If we set the fish-finders down there, they will indicate where the best spots are. We may find we need to motor as far out as Brown Pass. In the afternoon, I suggest we go up the Skeena River and see if the Rainbow Trout are biting." When the men nodded, he went on, "Your registrations all indicate you've fished before. Kevin and Gaspar are both trainee guides, so are probably best with the most experienced fishermen, leaving me with the least. I did take them fishing a week ago to give them instructions, and did a refresher with them recently. They both passed with flying colours."

They all stood with amused grins as the men had a comical discussion amongst themselves, relating fishing stories to decide who had the most experience. Finally, they concluded that Rod would go with Gaspar, Harvey and Charles with Kevin, leaving Andy and Pete in Don's boat.

"I'll go in the lead boat, but we have CB radios to keep in contact with each other. Now, before we start, can everyone please check to make sure you have your fishing licenses with you?" Don was rewarded when all the men obligingly pulled them out of their wallets. "How do you feel Kevin, Gaspar? Are we ready to go?" Don asked. "Any last-minute questions?"

Receiving a thumbs-up from both of them, he and his passengers got into his boat, he fired up the engine, and pulled away.

"Mary Ellen, did I hear you say you're coming with us today because you are checking out the other tourist attraction in New Petrograd?" Pete inquired.

"Yes, that's right. I'm managing the living museum, but I would like to become better acquainted with Don's business. It's not really what you would call a tourist attraction, but it does attract visitors to the museum. I think that by knowing something about both businesses, perhaps both of us will find it is to our mutual benefit. Don is an old school friend, so I was quite pleased to accept when he invited me on this outing today."

"Ah, yes, I see," Pete said, throwing a wink at Andy. "Very nice of him indeed."

"That's some attraction you have going there," Andy said. "All we had time for yesterday was to listen to the history talk and take in the pictorial scene. We strolled around the area for a few minutes, past the plaque she pointed out. It seemed by then that it was time to hightail it down the main street to meet up with you all for supper. I'm hoping tonight when we get back, after supper of course, to take in some stargazing. Then tomorrow, I'm planning to sleep in. I do hope I get up in time to take in the lighthouse tour though. If there's any time after that, maybe I'll go see the other founding father's house by the entrance."

"I understand you're the brains behind this whole thing," Pete said to her. "You've definitely done a good job. Andy and I were saying yesterday that we need to bring our wives here. Be good to get away for our wedding anniversaries coming up."

"Well, thank you, Pete. I guess you got this 'brains' bit from my *papa*—he's the one who has been telling everyone that. I may have used my business skills, but it was people like Gaspar and Kevin who did most of the manual labour. Plus, the efforts of everyone else in the village. They are the ones who deserve the credit." She added, "By the way, the museum closes for the season after Labour Day weekend, but we do call it a living museum because we will still be here."

"That will work," Pete cut in. "Our anniversaries are the first of August and mid-August respectively."

"So, I understood from something said last night that Gaspar and Shelley are newlyweds," Andy said. "Nice couple. How long have they been married?"

"They are a lovely couple. Of course, I grew up with Gaspar, but I've been enjoying getting to know Shel. I'm guessing they've been married for about five weeks. Do you know, Don?"

"Five weeks sounds about right. Not entirely sure, because they eloped and then went to Mexico for their honeymoon. I must admit, I do have a better idea than most, seeing as Gaspar pre-arranged that they would live with me when they got back. Shelley is a fabulous cook, so I'm not complaining."

"Well, I've only been married six years, but I can tell you it's the best thing that has ever happened to me." Andy grinned.

"We're just entering Edye Pass, so time for me to get this fish-finder activated," Don commented. Picking up his CB, he instructed Gaspar and Kevin to activate their fish-finders as soon as they caught up.

"Sure love that salt spray coming off the water. I also really enjoyed the drive here yesterday. Beautiful country, isn't it?" Rod commented, as soon as they got underway.

"Nice new road too. When was that put in?"

"The road this far was pretty much finished maybe six months ago," Gaspar replied. "It will go all the way through to Hartley Bay, but I'm not sure if it is finished at that end yet."

"Of course it is, sweetie," Shelley told him. "Otherwise, Mary Ellen and Don couldn't have delivered the brochures."

"You're probably right, my love, but there is another way they could have gone. By boat," Gaspar said, realizing he had just cut Rod off.

"Oh, I suppose," Shelley admitted, reaching for his hand.

"Sorry Rod, what were you going to say?"

"Oh, I was just going to say that it must have given you a lot more freedom."

"It sure has. We couldn't travel by land anywhere other than short distances on bush roads. So, really, it's opened up a whole new area for us. I suspect that Don knows a lot more than most of us because he and his brother always spent their weekends with their *Papa* on hunting and fishing trips. I'm sure they ventured far outside the realms where most of us went, but I doubt if even he knows all this new territory very well yet."

"I imagine it must be kind of crazy with everyone having to learn how to drive in the last six months."

"Oh no," Shelley intervened, laughing. "My husband lived in Calgary for five years prior to him moving back home, so that's where he learned to drive. Kevin is also from Calgary, and Don lived in Whitehorse."

When they heard the CB squawk, Gaspar yelled into it and a few minutes later said, "When we reach Edye Pass, it'll be time to turn the fish-finder on."

"Kevin, you said last night that you're from Calgary," Harvey remarked, once they had left the immediate area of New Petrograd.

"Well, actually I grew up in a farming community about an hour north of the city, called Olds. I moved to Calgary after I graduated from high school to start working in construction. I managed to make my way to a supervisory position fairly quickly."

"If I can ask, whatever prompted you to move here?" Harvey inquired, puzzled.

Kevin chuckled. "Gaspar was my roommate for a few years in Calgary. There was another guy also, Greg. Gaspar decided to move back here to take over his father's renovation business. He and some of his friends here decided to expand the Borscht Kettle. They tore down an old house and storage shed and were planning to construct a new building and connect them."

"Oh yes," Charles interjected. "I noticed that newer building when we were touring around yesterday."

"They needed some extra skilled labour, so Gaspar asked if Greg and I would come and help. We were here maybe four months and I don't know ... while I miss living near the Rockies, I kind of got attached to the place. So when he wrote late last year about their plans to develop this museum, I wrote and asked him if they could use some extra help. He said they sure could, for construction of new buildings, so I quit my job in Calgary and moved here. Whether permanent or not, I really can't say yet. But for now, I'm quite happy. There's a lot of things to like. For example, great people." He glanced towards Marianne. "The fishing is great. Beautiful scenery in every direction, and I'm loving living near the ocean. Since the museum opened, it sounds like they are organizing some exciting celebrations. Like next Saturday, for Russia Day."

"Russia Day celebrations have been going on for years," Marianne said. "They began soon after our founding fathers arrived. I'm not sure what they did in the early years, but when I was growing up, there were all kinds of competitions. Then towards evening there are authentic foods and dancing. It was always held just after our school year ended so our *roditeli* would let us stay up for the dance. Mary Ellen and I liked it because *Papa* would always take that day off."

"Oh yes," Kevin said, "you told us last night that your dad rarely came to fish and chips nights with you. So I guess it makes sense it was probably the same for other events as well."

Marianne continued, "I imagine they'll start with giving a welcoming speech."

Kevin looked at her sharply. "Are you being sarcastic?"

"No, of course not. Just telling the truth. When it was just us locals, we never needed speeches."

"Well, even if it is just like you explained, it does sound pretty interesting," Harvey remarked.

"That's just what was crossing my mind. That's next Saturday, you say?" Charles asked. "Is there any way I could phone my wife? Maybe she could drive here with our daughter. I wouldn't mind staying here all week. I think I could easily amuse myself taking pictures."

"Yes, there is," Marianne replied. "When we come back to New Petrograd tonight, just ask Mrs. Filipova if you can use the phone at the lighthouse station."

When Kevin heard the CB crackling, he picked it up, "Ten-four, roger that." After he hung up the handset, he remarked, "I guess you heard that as soon as we reach Edye Pass, Don says to turn our fish-finder on."

By seven a.m., when the men were baiting their lines and attaching them to the downriggers, the sun was starting to show its golden tint in the eastern sky. Some time passed before there were any visual signs of activity on any of the boats. But for the most part, everyone was busy enough concentrating on what was happening on their own boat.

After a couple of hours, Don again came over the CB radio inquiring as to how many fish each guest had caught. Hearing the information he wanted, he came about and headed towards the Skeena River.

As they berthed by the boat ramp, Don informed them, "I admit the cheese scones and fruit we indulged in earlier are starting to wear off. From here, it will be a short walk to the local diner beside the gas station. We should be able to get a more substantial breakfast there. And of course, if the girls want them, fishing licenses are available right next door at the general store. We can talk further, while we're eating breakfast, about my suggestion to travel east up the Skeena River. There are two or three river estuaries we may want to explore where we can try for rainbows."

"I don't need to talk about it any further," Charlie said. "My mind's made up ... that's a capital idea."

Looking around at the five nodding heads, Don remarked, "Okay, if that's the vote. Breakfast first, though." He led the way up the incline.

As soon as everyone finished a hearty breakfast and shared their fish stories from the morning, Don inquired whether there were any licenses they needed to purchase. Marianne thought she would like to buy one, so Kevin accompanied her into the general store.

Then they all set off back to the river. Just before they divided up into their boats again, Don asked Kevin and Gaspar for assistance with loading coolers containing the lunches.

By now, the sun had risen high in the sky and beginning to spread some warmth over the day.

After boarding Don's boat, Mary Ellen leaned back, catching the sun's rays on her upturned face.

Upon observing this, Don quickly cautioned her, "I'm not sure that's a good idea, unless you've got layers of sunscreen on. Even then, I wouldn't advise it, unless you want to end up with a nasty burn, especially with the sun reflecting off the water. It's a pretty calm day, but let's face it, there's always some wind when you're out here."

"Spoilsport," Mary Ellen replied, giving him a cheeky smile.

For an answer, Don threw her the sunscreen along with a

grin. Kevin, watching the antics on Don's boat, quickly started putting sunscreen on Marianne and then himself before handing it over to Harvey.

They ate their lunches as they motored upstream. Gayle had prepared opened-faced sandwiches of rye bread, with Havarti cheese, *kielbasa,* and a cucumber slice on top. She had also packed hard-boiled eggs, apples, and *pastila* for dessert.

Stopping just before one-thirty to cast their lines, they began drifting downstream in hopes that they would be successful in adding more to their day's catch. This strategy seemed to pay off, as fish were soon being reeled in on all the boats. Shortly before three-thirty, they stopped and put away their gear before beginning the return trip.

When they disembarked after mooring at New Petrograd's wharf, Don humbly accepted everyone's thanks before saying, "Tomorrow, you can do whatever you like while I keep myself busy either smoking or freezing your catch. I should have everything ready for you to pick up by five o'clock. Tonight, don't forget the stargazing."

"After such an early morning and the busy day we had," Charles exclaimed, "the only stars I'll see after supper will be in my dreams. Don't let me stop the rest of you from going, though."

Then they all walked across the pier, leaving behind the three men who already had begun putting up a portable table to work on as they started to gut and clean the fish ... the first step in preparing them for the freezer.

Mary Ellen approached Don and asked, "Can we do anything to help you?"

Don smiled at her and replied, "Not at all. Your job was accompanying us today."

As they walked away, the men overheard Shelley say, "I'm glad he said that, because I didn't want any part of that messy, smelly business."

"Me too," Marianne agreed, as she turned to head towards Marvin's and June's place.

As soon as Betty spotted Shelley, she frantically raced over, wringing her hands and calling her name.

"Whatever is wrong, Mrs. Yusporova? What has happened?" Mary Ellen asked, as the five men stopped walking to listen.

"Shelley, I need to speak to you," she wailed. "I went to our storeroom to put out more *babushka* dolls—they are selling so well—and the whole box is gone. Disappeared into thin air." Her anxiety increased as she wailed.

"Mrs. Yusporova, please calm down," Mary Ellen implored, as she moved closer.

"I looked everywhere and couldn't find it," she admitted, sounding even more distressed.

"What about Mr. Yusporov? Did he move it?" Shelley asked.

"I asked Frank and he said that he didn't. We both looked then, and he couldn't find it either. Oh, Mary Ellen, please don't be mad at us," cried Betty, her wail almost ending in a crescendo.

"Be mad at you?" Mary Ellen exclaimed. "That is the farthest thing from my mind. I think the best thing for you and your husband to do is to go home. I will have some supper sent over from the Borscht Kettle for your dinner tonight. And if you don't feel like opening your shop tomorrow, I can. In fact, why don't you let me work there for you?"

"Oh, would you?" Betty asked, showing the first sign of relief.

"Absolutely," Mary Ellen said, reaching out to give her a hug.

"I will come and see you tomorrow to write a full report and start an investigation," Shelley told here. "Please, as Mary Ellen said, try to calm down tonight and get a good night's sleep. I'm sure that in a day or two, we'll figure this out."

As she and Mary Ellen walked towards Don's, Shelley gave a huge sigh. "I'll have to ask her more details tomorrow. In fact, I should probably sit down tonight and write out some questions for her. Oh dear, I should have known that with all these tourists coming, something like this was sure to happen."

"What about all the folks we've hired?" Mary Ellen said anxiously. "I obviously screened them, but..."

"If it is a one-off occurrence, we can pretty well count on its being a tourist. But you're right, Mary Ellen, if it becomes a common occurrence, I will have to question the staff. This is not the homecoming that I would have anticipated at the end of such a perfect day. Good night, Mary Ellen," she said, as she made her way inside.

CHAPTER FOURTEEN

All in a Day's Work

Right after church, Don set up his portable table in his backyard. He was whistling a happy tune as he carried the packages outside from his freezer.

"Quite a job being an outfitter," Gaspar greeted Don, as he came home from church. "I had no idea you have to do all this. I just thought you chose this as a career because it meant you would get to fish all the time."

"I wish," Don replied. "My job includes a lot of paperwork, organizing things, instructing, making sure things go well and if they don't, handling the situation appropriately, and that's just half of it. Afterward, there's cleaning the fish, which we did last night gutting and scaling, preparing them as my clients have requested, and packaging." Hands in the small of his back, he stretched. "When we go hunting, the list of things I need to look after gets even longer. I'm not sure if I will manage to guide the men for hunting this year. I like to do it on horseback, but I sold my stock back in Whitehorse. If I get more, I'll have to hire support, as I can't manage it all by myself. I had an excellent stockman, so ideally, I'd like to hire him back. I love it all, though. Sitting at a desk like Brad, doing accounting, would drive me crazy."

"Whew, you're talking a whole bunch of stuff I never thought of," Gaspar said. "If you need extra staff, too, along with Kevin and Mary Ellen, it sounds to me that Kevin needs to get another crew in here putting up a dorm for seasonal workers. Good thing all we need to do is clear out more bush, and presto, we'll have more land to build on. I'm going to mention my idea to Mary Ellen. Is she coming by today?"

"She is coming after five," Don replied. "I'll be done packaging and delivering the fish and shortly after that, the men will be on their way. Your idea of a dorm for seasonal workers is good. I thought you were going to say a barn and paddock."

"That too," Gaspar acknowledged. "Anything I can help you with?"

"Sure. As I bring all the frozen packages out here, you can start putting on my company label," Don replied. "Be sure to not disturb the sticky notes I put on last night, so I can copy the type of fish, date it was caught, and most importantly, the name of the fisherman. You can probably also help with the last step, which is putting the packages into the correct guest's cooler and packing ice around them for their trip home." Don turned to make another trip to the freezer. "While I'm getting everything ready, maybe you could bring us both a glass of *kvas*. I think it is going to get pretty hot this afternoon, and we may as well be comfortable while we work."

When Don returned, Gaspar said, "All those tricks you taught Kevin and me yesterday about filleting the fish, trimming the blood off, putting it in a salt brine and then vacuum sealing, I must say, are very interesting. The best tip I overheard you give Kevin was about putting the fillets into a Ziploc bag and wrapping them in newspaper before freezing. I can't wait to ask my father-in-law if he knows about that," Gaspar added, smiling. "You sure have impressed me this weekend with all your expertise."

"Thanks for the compliment, but I'm going to be honest. I learned a lot from trial and error. My first attempts didn't go quite so well."

Right after church Sunday morning, Shelley kissed Gaspar good-bye and headed over to the Yusporov home.

"If this isn't good timing, let me know, Mrs. Yusporova. I can come another time. I thought I'd come now, before my shift starts, but I can come after five, too. I made up a list of questions to ask you last night."

"Oh, Shelley dear, I was going to find you right after dinner. I feel quite sick about it all. You see, last night Frank and I were telling Alex and Anna about the incident with the missing box. Alex just started laughing uncontrollably. Frank and I were getting so annoyed, and then he admitted that he had taken the box. Seems people have been asking him if he sold the dolls in the store. We were so disgusted with him and let him know it. He really deserves to be disciplined, but he's much too old for us to do that. Even Anna was not happy with his taking the box and not informing anyone. I'm so sorry for making a big scene. Now you tell me that you stayed up last night working out questions, so I'm sure going to let him know that, too."

"Not to worry at all." Shelley laughed. "I'm just relieved everything turned out well. I'll not disturb you anymore. You go back and enjoy your meal. I'll hurry home to change into my police uniform and start work."

"Oh, thank you for being so understanding. You do look so sweet when you're all dressed up. Even Frank says so, dear."

For an answer, Shelley gave a little wave, and still smiling with amusement, she turned and walked away as Betty closed the door. Whether from the incident or the compliment, she wasn't sure.

"Good afternoon, Mary Ellen," Rod greeted her, as he came into the gift shop Sunday afternoon. "I'm surprised to see you working here today. We noticed last night that you and Shelley were talking to that very agitated lady for it seemed a very long time. Isn't she the lady who was working in here on Friday?"

"Yes, she does normally work here," Mary Ellen replied, with a hint of attentiveness in her voice. "What might I help you with? Anything in particular you're looking for?"

"Yes, I finally made up my mind. I think I will get my daughters the dolls that come apart to make four dolls. They're cute and quite attractively painted."

"For sure," Mary Ellen replied, as she came around the counter. "We have them in blue, red, mauve, green—and yes, there is still a yellow one here."

"Great. I wish my wife was here—she'd know what colours to get. I think I will take a blue and a green one. You might as well throw in the red one, too. Hopefully I've picked colours the girls will like and my wife will be happy with the other one. But really, for Audrey, I was thinking of a piece of pottery, maybe a plate or bowl."

"We have both." Mary Ellen led him to the other side of the store.

"This is why I hate shopping. I never know what I'm

doing. I almost decided to go home without buying anything, but I know my family would be disappointed. Oh, I don't know, maybe I'll flip a coin." He pulled some loose change out of his pocket.

"You could always buy her both," Mary Ellen said, helpfully.

"Thanks, but no. Here's a quarter, so you call it for me."

"Okay, heads it's a bowl," she said with a smile. Then she opened her hand to show him that yes, it was heads.

"I have one more gift to buy—for my son. At least this one is easy. I want one of those wooden ships for him. You may as well throw in a book about lighthouses for me. The five of us did a tour of the lighthouse this morning. Most interesting. Since then, I've just been wandering on my own, mostly looking at the flower arrangements. Now, I think I'm done. What's the total?"

Mary Ellen added it up and gave him the bill. Rod paid and she handed him his package. After a few minutes, she noticed that he wasn't leaving.

"Anything else I can help you with, Rod?" Another family came into the gift shop.

"No, not really. I was just wondering what was up last night. Never mind, it's none of my business. Thanks for the lovely weekend, and bye for now."

Mary Ellen went over to help the other customers and when she turned, she saw both Harvey and Charles in the store looking at the miniature wooden toys.

"Why, hello," she said. "I'll be right with you, after I ring these people up."

"Not a problem," Harvey replied. "We're mostly just browsing, but it doesn't seem quite right not to bring my wife something. Thankfully, I am an empty nester."

"What about your grandchildren? I'm thinking about some of these wooden toys," his brother remarked.

When Mary Ellen came over, Charles said, "You got any trucks, or trains? My one grandson is crazy about trains. The other one is crazy about cars."

Chuckling, Mary Ellen replied, "No we don't. These are all replicas of things our forefathers' generation knew. Like my *papa* when he was growing up—he knew about ships and lighthouses."

"Well, now that you've explained it that way, it makes sense. Okay, I'll take a ship and a lighthouse."

"Harvey, is there anything I can show you?" Mary Ellen asked as she turned her attention to him.

"I'll just pick up a couple of these lighthouse books, for me and my missus. Say, we just bumped into the lady dressed as a policewoman and the minute she spoke, we realized it was Shelley. Got us wondering, is that why that other lady came running up calling out to her last night?"

"Knock it off, Harvey. What do you think, you're some big detective yourself?" Charles laughed. "Pay Mary Ellen and let's get going."

As Mary Ellen was checking them through, she said, "Yes, Shelley is one of our authentically dressed personalities. Her dress is a 1917 women's police uniform. It does seem fitting for her because she did work for the Vancouver Police Department."

"I wouldn't have thought they had policewomen in Russia back in 1917," Harvey mused. "How interesting—and a pretty smart way of having security, I'd say."

"She probably has a lot of experience with all kinds of situations. Makes sense if one of your employees was upset about something, they'd seek Shelley out. We noticed before we went in for supper, it seemed like between the two of you, you managed to get things settled," Harvey finished. "We're off now, just have to pick up our fish and we'll be gone. Nice to have met you."

"It was," Mary Ellen replied, "and to have shared some fishing stories with you. Have a safe trip home."

It seemed a steady flow of customers came in all afternoon. Mary Ellen was about to close when Pete came running in.

"I've got to get some gifts. Oh hi, Mary Ellen, it's you. What can you recommend for teenage girls? I have four of them, all noisy and—"

"These *babushka* dolls seem to charm everyone from the very young to the very old," she said. "See? They come apart four times, always with a smaller doll inside. Plus, they are so attractively painted, and come in different colours, besides being quite collectible."

"Okay, they'll do. Give me four different colours. I suppose I should take a bigger size for my wife."

As they made their way to the till, Mary Ellen said, "I've seen the rest of you today, but not Andy. I'm about to close, but if you think he plans on visiting the gift shop I'll stay open a bit later."

"No, he's not, but thanks for asking. He wanted me to pick up one of these dolls for him and a book on lighthouses. The one that talks about lighthouses all up the Pacific coast. So, I guess I better add that to my order. Boy, would he be miffed at me if I'd forgotten. May as well toss the other lighthouse book in for me as well."

"Sure you've got everything now?" Mary Ellen giggled as she began to tally his bill.

"Well, what I don't have, I guess I don't," Pete answered her cheerily. Bye now, it's been a great weekend."

"Pete," Harvey hollered from outside. "What's taking you? We're ready, so let's get going."

"Bye," Mary Ellen said, as she came to the door to wave. Then turning back inside, she smiled with satisfaction as she tallied her sales for the day.

CHAPTER FIFTEEN

Russia Day

In the morning, a small group of residents wearing authentic Russian dress were standing outside mingling with the visitors as they arrived. Bob was pleased to see a bus pull off the road and recognized Buddy Rasmussen at the wheel.

"Morning, Bob," he called as he got down. "I have eighteen passengers that have been travelling since one o'clock in the morning. When we first left the city, I think they may have slept a couple of hours, but it has been pretty noisy for most of the way here. They're quite excited but not as much as I am that we've finally arrived. One more rendition of 'Ninety-Nine Bottles of Beer on the Wall' and—"

"That explains why we didn't see you earlier this week," Bob said, cheerily. "Everyone wondered if you weren't well."

A petite lady came to stand beside Buddy, and as she smiled at Bob and Olga, she said, "Good morning, I'm Pearl Rasmussen. Buddy came home telling me what a lovely time he had here. I work in the administrative office of a community college, and I was telling some of my coworkers who also became interested. They went home and told their spouses, and next thing we knew, we were thinking of coming here. Then, one of the students approached me and said she had overheard our plans and had mentioned it to some of her friends who also got interested. So finally, she came and inquired if they could come along. Of course, we told them that we would be thrilled to have them join us. But by this time, our party had grown big enough we needed to charter Buddy's bus. We couldn't leave until we got off work yesterday, so we decided it was best if everyone got a few hours of rest before we left." She took a breath. "Look at all these delightful clothes," she said, admiring them as she walked towards the entrance.

Inside the museum, there had been a flurry of activity as everyone rallied to get things set up before opening time. Shelley had been listening for the sounds of Johnny Eagle Feather's seaplane all morning as she was helping to set up booths. She was almost finished when her ears detected a faint humming sound coming from overhead and she ran to the end of the street where the pier was visible. Confirming that the plane was about to land, she let out a whoop of excitement and ran towards the wharf.

"*Moi medvezhono*," Gaspar called after her, "let me get my truck and drive you. Don't try and go running way up to the end of the pier."

When Gaspar and Shelley arrived, Johnny Eagle Feather was helping his passengers alight from the plane—two men and a woman. They were standing on the pier, obviously uncertain what to do next.

"Shelley?" Johnny asked, hesitantly, by then getting his passengers' luggage. "How...? What are you doing here?"

"Yes, it is me," Shelley replied, chuckling. "I live here now. I married a New Petrogradian." She pulled Gaspar forward. "We were married the first part of May. Oh, it is good to see you again. Plus, I see you have brought some guests with you. I am anxious to meet them. Then I'll only have to introduce my husband once."

"Good idea," Johnny responded. "I have with me today Alice and Randy Griffin, plus Alice's brother, David Drew."

"Welcome to all of you. My name is Shelley, and this is my husband, Gaspar Rosso." She turned to him. "I suggest, sweetie, that you help Johnny and take everyone's luggage to the lighthouse station. Afterward, Gaspar can direct you, Johnny, to where the activities are starting at nine-thirty."

Then, turning to the other folk, Shelley invited them to come with her and she would take them to the entrance to get their tickets. "It is so delightful you have come from Sandspit," she exclaimed as they made their way through the village.

"Yes, we had to get up very early, but we had seen a brochure the other day about your museum and made inquiries about how to get here. I thought it would be a nice change for the week," Alice said. "I am a wildlife photographer and was commissioned to do a job by a lodge in Sandspit, so my husband and brother came along to spend a week fishing."

"I'm so glad you decided to make us a part of your week," Shelley exclaimed.

"How do you know Johnny? Sandspit isn't all that close to here," Randy asked.

"My parents moved here a couple of years ago, and I came to visit them one Thanksgiving. Then a few months later, there was an incident they felt I could help with, so I was invited back. Both times I flew from Vancouver to Sandspit, and of course Johnny flew me here. While I was here, I met Gaspar and got to know the rest of the townspeople quite well."

"Johnny sure seems to be a good pilot," Randy said with admiration. "Small planes usually make me nervous, but I didn't feel that way at all on the trip here."

"What's that I'm smelling?" David broke in.

"Could be any number of things." Shelley laughed. "We have tents set up with Russian food, and flowers set in beds all over. Our Business Manager, Mary Ellen, specially ordered in chamomile plants, which is the Russian national flower, for today. Bert, our head gardener, and his assistant have been scrambling since Monday to get them all planted. See, these beds here? The flowers are white with a yellow centre, but their smell is very pleasant, like apples." She looked over her shoulder. "Alice, you were saying you're a professional photographer. I'm wondering if I should introduce you to Mary Ellen. Would you be interested in taking pictures of this event?"

"I certainly wouldn't mind speaking with her."

"Here we are," Shelley said. "You can purchase your tickets and get a map. There is a printout with information regarding the museum, plus the entire day's activities. I need to hurry and get dressed in the authentic clothes I wear, but it has been lovely meeting you all. This is one of the best parts of living here. We're just ten minutes from home. So, bye for now. Oh, I see Mary Ellen now—this is perfect, I can introduce you right away."

Shelley left them talking to Mary Ellen, who was delighted with the opportunity to have a professional photographer record the day, in exchange for covering their costs.

"Greetings everyone, and welcome to New Petrograd," Mary Ellen shouted to locals and guests alike who were gathered in the green space in front of the first-aid facility.

"We are thrilled to have you here for—I'm not sure if it is our sixty-sixth or our first—Russia Day. Why do I say that? Because shortly after our forefathers arrived here, they started a celebration they called Russia Day. We have continued it annually since then, and this year marks the sixty-sixth year. We are extremely proud that *Dedushka* Yusporov has attended every one of those celebrations." The crowd broke into applause. "But this is the first time we have invited others to enjoy this special day with us and consequently we have made some changes. Changes which I am trusting are going to make your time most enjoyable. Incidentally, in another few weeks, on Canada Day, we plan to have another celebration. I can assure you it will also be exciting, and you are all invited back for it. Now I am going to hand the microphone to Martin Shatrov, who will be your emcee for today, or as we say in Russian, the *tamada*. Without further ado, let Russia Day officially begin!"

"See," Marianne whispered to Kevin. "I told you she'd come up with something to make a speech about."

"Yes," Kevin agreed, smiling at her. "She's very good. Very poised, wouldn't you say?"

"She is. I could never do that. I must laugh, because when we left to go to university, I was going for business and Mary Ellen was going to be a teacher. I don't know whatever happened on the trip down in the barge, but before we started our studies, we had switched. She went for an MBA and I for a teacher. *Papa* never could get it straight until now that we didn't carry through with our original plans."

"That is funny. It's a good thing you did, because from what I've seen, you are both well suited for your careers." Giving her shoulder a squeeze, he remarked, "I think Martin will be calling on Don and me soon."

"Have fun," Marianne replied. "I will catch up with you later, since what Mary Ellen has asked me to do isn't until the end of the parade." She craned her neck to see past the crowd. "Say, Kevin, isn't that Charles sitting over there with a lady and a teenage girl? It must be his wife and daughter. I think I should make my way over there to say hi."

When Martin accepted the microphone from Mary Ellen, he applauded, saying, "Let's give Mary Ellen a big hand. Our first event is going to be a parade. Right now, I will call on Don Rosnokov and Kevin Thompson, who are carrying the Russian flags. The flag bearers will be directly in front of our Grand Marshal, who is none other than our one remaining founding father whom Mary Ellen just spoke about. Walking with him are his son and daughter-in-law. He told us earlier today he feels up to walking the parade route, and then some. Please give him a hearty round of applause as he goes past you.

"Next will come the children with their decorated bikes, which I know they have worked so hard on. Just looking at them as they're getting organized, I'm seeing so many artful entries. But remember, kids, the rules have changed, and this is not a contest, like in previous years. It is a parade, and everyone will receive a prize for participating. Now, I see everyone is just about organized. Thank you, Gaspar, for helping with that.

"That's Shelley Rosso, wearing our 1917 policewomen's uniform. If I'm correct, she will be bringing up the rear.

"Now that we've got the children organized, next will come folks who are wearing authentic Russian clothing. At eleven this morning, we have planned a fashion show and you can learn about these garments you are seeing now.

"After them, will come the boys from our tug-of-war teams who are also letting you know of our competitive games event at two-thirty. We invite you, our guests, to participate alongside our residents. Let's begin!"

The parade began its slow rotation. A quarter of the way around the grassy area, a wheel fell off a bike, and much to the disappointment of the boy, the bike had to be removed. A bit further along, another mishap occurred when it seemed a little girl's bike hit a hole and she toppled off, and amidst her loud sobs, she had to be taken away. Fortunately, the parade continued with no further mishaps. There were many appreciative comments from the audience when the folks in their authentic dress passed by. Finally, the teenage boys took great pleasure flexing their muscles and grunting like they were pulling on an imaginary rope. As each child came in, Marianne gave them their prizes—a plastic crown and a coupon for an ice cream at John's kiosk. Of course, she also offered prizes to the two children who hadn't been able to finish.

At the conclusion of the parade and as the clapping was fading, Martin said, "Thank you for your applause. I know everyone appreciated it very much. I would like to mention that throughout the museum we have set out various booths with homemade Russian foods. So certainly, enjoy a taste of Russia. Other than that, wander at will. All our buildings are opening soon. Don't forget that eleven this morning, right here, there will be a fashion show."

At eleven, Martin took up his microphone once more. "Our first model is Olga Petrova who is wearing a typical peasant dress from the south of Russia. We know this because of the plant-like geometric designs embroidered on her clothing, which are very different from what you would see in the north.

"Although women's dresses were very loose-fitting and concealed much of the woman's figure, they drew all eyes to her face. This was accomplished by a wreath, or *vres*, which is sometimes called a crown. The *vres* covered her hair and had a lot of decoration, such as ribbons and flowers.

"Notice the natural colour of the material – white, with touches of red. In earlier generations, red was used to indicate beauty, which meant the women believed that when they added red to their garment, it became attractive.

"Next I will draw your attention to the belt, or *lakomki,* that Mrs. Petrova is wearing. It is a mandatory piece of traditional Russian clothing for women and as you will see later, also for men. They were considered to have protective powers, giving a sense of security. Women tied them under the chest or the belly. It was very useful for keeping money or other small items safely stowed.

"With Mrs. Petrova is her granddaughter, Madeline, who is dressed in a circular *sarafan* dress. This dress is like a pinafore and we will learn more about them a little later. Madeline has a very attractive scarf on her head."

Olga and Madeline twirled and bowed, then parted as Bob and Matthew crossed the grass hand in hand.

"Olga's husband, Bob Petrov, is likewise wearing typical clothing for the male peasant. Grown men, even those with money, dressed humbly. Of course, he is wearing *ports* or pants, but the shirt has a very distinguishing feature, with an oblique collar. Everything was held up with a belt, which could be either homespun or made of leather. The men carried smoking accessories on their belts. On his head is a felted hat made of wool. These came in an endless variety of shapes.

"And with Mr. Petrov is his grandson, Matthew, who is dressed in similar but brighter garments. Also, you will notice his hat is shaped differently."

The Petrov family walked in a circle so that the audience could see them clearly, then moved aside for the next model.

"Alexander Bolitchyn is sporting a Russian shirt known as a *rubakha,* which is a large or oversized shirt. Traditionally, they could be sewn from cheaper fabrics like cotton and linen or more expensive, such as silk. It can also be worn by both men and women.

"Mr. and Mrs. Rosso are going to give us a display of the outerwear for different seasons. Perhaps the most surprising thing is that, again, outerwear is much the same for both sexes.

"Mrs. Rosso is wearing a *kaftan* or a homespun coat, which would be worn in the spring and autumn.

"Mr. Rosso has on a *shuba* or winter sheepskin coat. Note that they were only half-length fur coats with all the fur on the inside. The outside could then be decorated with bright, colourful textiles. They could also be sewn from hare skin.

"Especially notice the *ushanka* on his head. These fur-lined caps with their trademark earflaps protected them from extremely cold weather. Inside, they are lined with a heavily padded leather crown. This not only provided vital warmth to the head, but was also protection from trauma, such as falling on the ice. It may interest you to know that both the coat and hat are still worn today, a safeguard against the often brutal Russian climate."

The Rossos followed the Petrov family's example, walking in a circle and then falling back to welcome the next model.

"My wife, Gayle Shatrov, is wearing another garment that was also popular in the southern regions, a *kosovorotka*. It is a long-sleeved linen shirt that often falls below the waist. The sleeves served two purposes—first, for protection from the weather, and second for beauty, as they were often pleasingly embroidered. Overtop is a skirt known as a *poneva*. The skirt is held in place with a wool string, called a *gashnik*. An apron goes on top of all of that.

"Alexandria Bolitchyn is modelling another dress which is common in the northern Russian regions. Again, over a long shirt they put on a sundress known as a *sarafan*. This garment is known as a *deaf sarafan* as it doesn't have a seam in front. It is sewn from a single piece of cloth. On top of it is a sleeveless vest called a *dushegreya*. *Sarafans* were usually accompanied by a *kokoshnik*, which is the headdress that you will notice is patterned to match Alexandria's dress. *Kokoshniks* can come in a variety of shapes and sizes, but are most recognized as halo-shaped, spanning from ear to ear over the top of the head.

"As a final note on the everyday clothing we have just seen, it was simple, and there were fewer pieces to be worn, no more than seven."

Gayle and Alexandria bowed and twirled, and Gayle stole a kiss from the emcee before she gave way to Marg.

"Marg Filipova is wearing a special-occasion dress. Although its style is similar to everyday clothing, what makes the difference is there could be twenty or more layers. Also, more expensive fabric was used, such as wool, brocade, and velvet. These outfits were only brought out for special celebrations and festivals. Often peasant ladies would keep their wedding dress to be buried in.

"Women of all ages loved decorations. Consequently, Russian clothing was covered in beads or embroidery and worn with elaborate jewelry. The unmarried girls wore bright ribbons, headbands, wraps, and intricately tied scarves. Of note is that all these items have been sewn right here by local women." Martin drew a deep breath. "This concludes our fashion show. Please give a hearty round of applause to our participants."

After a hearty round of applause, he continued, "I would like to mention that in our gift shop, we have specially brought in some ladies' scarves and men's felt hats for this weekend. I believe they have a few other special items, such as Russian flags and chamomile seeds. Chamomile is Russia's national flower and has been planted in flowerbeds throughout the grounds.

"Remember to return at two-thirty to compete alongside our residents in some challenging activities. And our final reminder is ... Don't forget to partake in enjoying a taste of Russia!"

As Alice and Randy made their way to a booth which gave views of the harbour, Randy counted five groups of tables and chairs. Alice was still gushing about how gorgeous the fashion show was. She felt confident she had managed to take several good pictures and could hardly wait until she could get them on to her computer.

After they arrived, they focused on the posted menu.

Main Course

Borscht soup with a slice of rye bread

Olivier Salad
Draniki

Desserts
Sharlotka Cake
Kissel

The staff were so helpful at providing information about the dishes and, to the delight of many, were also passing out printed copies of the recipes.

The staff came around to the patio tables where guests were seated, pouring drinks of lingonberry juice, a variety of sodas, tea, and coffee. But because everyone was conscious that they only had two and a half hours before the competitions would begin, many of the guests hastily ate and were off to take in the exhibits. Of course, there were others who had gone immediately to some of the exhibits and raced to grab something before the afternoon events started.

Many of the folks who had appeared in the fashion show were clustered on the grass adjacent to the founding fathers' plaque so guests could have the pleasure of posing as Nick took their pictures. Then, half an hour before the competitions would begin, they raced home to change into more appropriate attire.

"To start our afternoon's entertainment, we will have an egg and spoon race," Martin said to the eager crowd in front of him. "We are planning to do it a little differently than we have at other Russia Day celebrations. This year, it will be a relay race. The first player will get a spoon with a hard-boiled egg in it. They will run across the field to their waiting teammate, who will return it to the starting line, down the line of four participants. If any of the participants drops the egg, they must retrieve it and begin again. By the way, you can't use your hands. Traditionally, this has been just for our teenage girls because afterward came an event for our teenage boys. Another change today is that we are opening all activities to everyone."

Then with a grin, he began the countdown, which was quickly picked up by the crowd. "Three, two, one!" The first contestant was off to a good start, but everyone could quickly see this didn't last long as chaos soon erupted on the field. It became apparent there was no division between the people who lived in the village and their guests as they called out names, advice, and laughed together all in good fun until the last participant completed the race. The laughter lingered awhile longer.

Over the course of an hour, eggshells could be seen left in the grass, which were removed as Martin was announcing the tug-of-war to all ages. Again, the teams were made up from a combination of locals and visitors.

Before the countdown, Martin reminded them that the winner would be the team who won the best of three. "Looking at how many are lined up, we may need to do a second competition. Unfortunately, this might mean that there is not enough time to do our customary three-legged race."

Amidst much booing, Martin had to agree that they would make time to do one three-legged race afterward.

As earlier in the day, there was no separation between the people who lived in the village and their guests as they called out names and advice, or the bass sounds of *heave-ho* as the participants grunted and groaned until one side let go.

"You know," Martin began, "when the three-legged race was announced and with the large number of adults gathering —" But the flow of people lining up did not stop. "This is going to mean that your supper will be very late."

But for once, it appeared no one was listening.

Bob Petrov and his son, John, were attempting to tie their legs together, but perhaps their efforts were adding to the general mayhem as people were falling down all over. Eventually, everyone was on their feet at the starting line so Martin could begin the countdown for the race. It did not take long until several bodies were sprawled on the ground, laughing uncontrollably. Their laughter though was nothing compared to the shrieks coming from the children watching their parents. Eventually two couples made it across to the other side, but even Martin couldn't tell who had won.

Wiping tears of merriment from his eyes, Nikolai took the microphone, declaring to all that he was very happy that no mishaps or injuries had taken anyone to the first-aid booth. In fact, until now, the only casualty has been someone scalding their mouth on hot *Borscht*. "Let's do our best to keep it that way," he said. "This concludes our programs for today. Whether you are planning to stay overnight or not, we encourage you to stay for supper. Afterward, our day has always concluded with an impromptu dance in the evening and I'm sure this year will be no exception. Everyone is welcome to stay as long as they like.

"Most of the buildings will close at five and reopen tomorrow at nine, other than the gift shop and general store. I understand some of the souvenirs have been moved to the general store because the gift shop was unable to handle the throngs of people.

"At our founding fathers' plaque, Anna Yusporova will give

one more talk on the history of New Petrograd. Other than that, please give your emcee, Martin, and the organizer of today's events, Mary Ellen, a huge round of applause."

As everyone began to disperse, David came up to Alice. "This is great. After the dance, I'm going to the wharf for stargazing. Best fireworks I can think of."

"Yes, I agree, after the dance," Alice replied. "Randy and I may join you. Right now, I think I will take in the talk of New Petrograd's history and then head to the Borscht Kettle for dinner."

CHAPTER SIXTEEN

Good-bye, Russia Day

When he saw them at eight o'clock on Sunday morning, David said to Alice and Randy, "I spoke with Johnny Eagle Feather last night and he wants to leave around three-thirty this afternoon. That gives us a good amount of time to see everything else on this map. The way I see it, we can have a half-hour for breakfast, a half-hour for lunch, and time to see all the attractions with fifteen minutes to spare."

"Well, it's a good thing you're not arranging everything," Alice replied. "First of all, Mary Ellen has asked me to take random pictures that she thought might appeal to my artistic eye. My dear husband can choose whether he wants to accompany me, follow your strict schedule, or do what he wants. Just remember where you are supposed to be at three-thirty for our return flight."

"Randy, what do you want to do?" David asked.

"I think I'll stay with my wife for a while, and then maybe wander off by myself. There always seems to be something I can do to assist her, even if it's only holding her lens cap.

There are a few things I would definitely like to do, but one of them I know Alice did yesterday."

"I think we're all ready, so let's all go to the teahouse for breakfast together, and then we can split up," Alice said, looking pleased at his choice.

"This place is lovely," Pearl, the bus driver's wife, remarked to one of her co-workers on Sunday morning. "I'm sure glad my husband told me we can make our own breakfast in this centre area. I almost have our breakfast together, and I'll leave all the fixings out so everybody else can make theirs when they're ready. I don't imagine we will see many of the young people very early—they got in late last night. But we have until eleven o'clock before Housekeeping comes."

"It sure was nice of your husband to give everyone a Russian flag yesterday."

"Buddy is not good with sitting around doing nothing, so I can easily understand his offering to help when he went for a walk and saw them moving boxes from the gift shop to the general store. He became very attached to this place and the people the first time he had a trip here." As Pearl sat down to enjoy her breakfast, she added, "We were really enjoying ourselves last evening, but decided to retire when everyone else went to see the fireworks."

"Well, you didn't miss anything," her co-worker told her. "There were no fireworks. That David guy got everyone all excited, and then when we got to the wharf, he laughed and said he was referring to the stars in the night sky. He seemed to think he was hilariously funny. To think we'd been dancing under them for some hours by then. We left when some of the students threatened to throw him in the water. By the way, Pearl, what time does your husband want to leave today?"

"He said if we get away around three-thirty, it should be fine, which probably means getting organized about three. It does mean we will get home very late, but I told him I felt everyone would be okay with that. I think that should give us plenty of time to do everything we want."

"I think you should suggest that the students find something other than singing to amuse themselves on our way home. Something quieter, like *I Spy.*"

"You might be right. It was quite noticeable on the way here that poor Buddy's nerves were getting frayed."

"Shelley, I don't want a repeat of the misunderstanding from a couple of days ago, but I've spoken to both Frank and Alex and I'm sure I am correct this time. We took twenty dolls to the general store. Alex's records show fifteen sold, but there are only two left on the shelf. Where are the other three?"

"Mrs. Yusporova, I don't want to sound like I don't care, but with all the tourists that were here this weekend, that doesn't really surprise me. Did you notice some items missing from the gift store as well? I will make a note of your loss in my records, and do not hesitate to tell me if you notice anything else missing."

Betty came back an hour later. "You're right, some of the scarves and men's felt hats are also gone. Mary Ellen special ordered them for this weekend, and as we were boxing them up just now to put into storage, everything didn't add up right."

"Thank you, Mrs. Yusporova, I will include that in my

report as well. Unfortunately, not having seen the person, there is not much I can do at this point about these thefts. I will, however, put some thought into heightening security, even installing cameras. Especially when we have an event that brings in large crowds."

After five on Sunday night, quietness settled on the village even though there was a lot of commotion. Work began, putting tables, chairs and many other special items used during the event back in storage. It had been an exhausting two days, and yet no one seemed overly tired.

As Mary Ellen and Bert were strolling among the flowerbeds, deep in discussion, Bert looked over to where the others were and remarked, "Mother always says, 'Eager beavers, always in a hurry'."

"I like that saying," she replied. "All I could think that was possibly motivating them was an adrenaline rush."

CHAPTER SEVENTEEN

A Busy Week

The next day, Shelley said to her husband, "Gaspar, I was talking to Mom earlier and she invited us for supper tonight. I told her if it was okay with you, we'd accept."

"Absolutely. I'm not going to turn that down," Gaspar said, as he leaned over to kiss her.

"I'll let her know that it is a definite yes." She paused. "Yesterday, when I was talking with Mrs. Yusporova, I suggested we consider ways to heighten security. Especially on the very busy days like we had this last weekend. We have two choices —have someone keep a discreet eye on the shoppers while they are in the store, or install security cameras. For now, I am going to approach Alexander, because I've discovered that he can look intimidating if he has to. I sure hope he agrees to do it. It's the least intrusive option. In fact, I think this evening after dinner I should go and speak to him. Both he and his sister are turning out to be invaluable. I've witnessed them helping in so many different ways."

"That's a good idea to recommend Alexander, my love. Remember when Mary Ellen mentioned at the debriefing that she would look for ways to bulk up his and his sister's education funds?"

"Good point. In fact, I think I'll go right now, and talk to him even before I go and see Mom. Oh, and I almost forgot to tell you, Mom said she got a letter from Lyle. He and Gordy are coming on Thursday on Joe's barge before the Canada Day long weekend."

"That is fabulous! How long are they staying? I want to see if Don has any available times to take them fishing."

Shelley stopped in the doorway and laughed. "I don't know the answer to that. I was just excited when she told me, knowing my brothers would be bringing the rest of my belongings with them! I will ask her when I'm talking to her this afternoon. See you later, sweetie."

At supper that night, she told everyone that when she met with Alexander in the afternoon, he was quite eager to act as security guard, especially when she told him she would let Mary Ellen know he had accepted.

"That's great," he had said with a chuckle. "One more thing to add to my growing resume."

On Tuesday around five, Buddy pulled up with a partially full bus.

"You must feel quite at home here now," Martin said. "You've heard my spiel so many times, you could probably give it on the bus before you arrive."

"You know, I like that idea," Buddy said. "I'll be back on Friday night, and maybe I'll give your suggestion a try. I've travelled the road enough so it is quite familiar to me. It can be very routine sitting behind this steering wheel. This would give me something more to do. My boss has standardized the schedule now, so I'll always be coming on Tuesday night, and leaving on Thursday around noon. Then I return on Friday night and leave Sunday around noon. That gives the passengers a generous amount of time here with two nights and one whole day to see everything." He seemed to hesitate. "I'm glad we're here now, because I've had to keep reminding myself all the time I was driving."

"What's that?" Martin asked him quizzically.

"You remember my wife, Pearl ... well, she saw an article Monday in the classified section of the *Prince Rupert Gazette*. The fellow who wrote it sounded quite pumped about your celebration on the weekend. I know my wife and her co-workers had favourable comments, too."

Early Wednesday afternoon, when Buddy was at the teahouse, he was surprised to see one of the students he'd brought last weekend talking to Mary Ellen.

What's she doing here? he wondered. But as he listened in on their conversation, he realized it sounded like she was being interviewed for a job. His curiosity was piqued, yet at the same time he didn't want to be seen eavesdropping on them.

He had just made it back to the corner when he noticed another person walking purposefully towards the Kettle. He was dressed quite nicely and Buddy realized he had also come on Saturday. Was he being interviewed, too?

This time he wasn't quite so adept at hiding, because the young man called out, "Afternoon, Mr. Rasmussen."

"Afternoon. You here to see Mary Ellen as well?"

"Yes, my girlfriend and I were both very taken with this place on Saturday. At the dance we asked Alexandria who we should talk to about summer work. Right away, she found Mary Ellen and introduced us to her. My girlfriend, Beth, is talking to her now, and I'm next. I guess Mary Ellen has one position available in Housekeeping, but she told us she'd give it some thought and see if she could hire us both. I'm keeping my fingers crossed." He pulled a hand out of his pocket and showed him. "So, what are you doing this afternoon, sir?"

"I'm just kind of moseying around. I'm just like you folks. I quite enjoy it here. Beautiful place, but it's the people who make it for me. So down to earth and friendly. I better not delay you and make you late. Good luck to you both."

"Mary Ellen," Gaspar called, when he saw her walking towards her office. "I've been trying to catch you and tell you about an idea. I mentioned it to Don, but I haven't said anything to Kevin yet."

"So, what is it?" she invited him.

"It's actually an idea I had when I was helping Don on Sunday afternoon, labelling and packaging the salmon. It seems every house is full with summer employees. So, I was thinking, why not build housing for the staff? Did he mention this to you?"

"No, he didn't, but Gaspar, that's a good idea. Although I can't imagine what Kevin might say. He already has several projects lined up. He's just completed another building at the lighthouse station. I'm making plans for building yet another one because *Papa* informed me that they were full this weekend. They were even having to turn people away. Then there is your house and Nikolai and Margarita Petrov's that still need to be built. I have to listen to my sister complaining she never gets to spend time with him as it is. Let me think about it and I'll maybe bring this idea up to Kevin some night."

"And you know," Gaspar added, "when you think about it, at the end of the season when the museum closes, Shelley and I could move into the staff housing until our house is built. But that's another thing when you talk about the lighthouse being full. I heard some people talking Saturday night that they were going across the road to pitch a tent. They were laughing because they would have to rough it, seeing as there are no washroom facilities. Got me thinking maybe we should set up a campground. I could certainly build a structure and schedule a plumber to get amenities installed."

"I don't think it will be necessary for you and Shelley to move," Mary Ellen responded coyly. "I've heard Don say he is enjoying your being there. At least, he's appreciating Shelley's cooking."

"That may be true," Gaspar answered. "But my suspicion is that he may have another cook soon and will be quite happy if we've moved out."

"Now you're talking in riddles and have quite lost me. You have given me two good suggestions to consider. Incidentally, I hired two more people today, so there is more housing I have to find."

"Talking in riddles, am I?" Gaspar laughed. "I'll try to make myself perfectly clear. Before next summer, my prediction is that you will become Mary Ellen Rosnokova."

Leaving a speechless Mary Ellen standing in the pathway, he whistled a jaunty tune as he walked around her.

On Thursday night, Don and Mary Ellen were at the Borscht Kettle having dinner, where Uri overheard Mary Ellen telling him about the people camping out over the Russia Day weekend.

"Have you ever done that, Don? I have absolutely no experience in this area."

"Of course, I've camped out lots of times. What are you really asking me?"

"I mean laying out a whole campground," she replied, looking a little sheepish.

"I haven't any experience planning one either," he admitted, smiling at her. "I do have a suggestion, though. For your next big event, bring in some portable washroom facilities. It will at least create a temporary solution. Also give you a better idea of what you do require when Kevin or Gaspar construct something more permanent."

It was then that Uri stepped in and offered his fishing boat to haul the portables to New Petrograd. "You could carry three or four on it."

"Good idea, Uri. I'll check my bookings tonight and the next time I see an opening in my schedule, I'll go rent them."

"Give me time to phone ahead and make a booking with the rental agency before you go," Mary Ellen interjected. "I also want to have our printers make a sticker for our existing brochures announcing we now offer this amenity."

"Our next big event is Canada Day on July first, so we don't have long to prepare."

"Do you think I can go with you?"

"Good idea," Don agreed, winking at her. "After all, I don't know much about the administrative side of things."

"Anytime you're ready, come by for the keys to my boat," Uri offered, as he started to clear another table, muttering under his breath, "Administrative, my foot."

On Friday, Buddy brought another busload, almost giddy because he knew someone from the cruise line going to Alaska was on his bus. He felt almost certain that they were interested in assessing the living history museum for a possible excursion.

When he pulled off the road, he could see Mary Ellen standing by the entrance, a brilliant smile lighting up her face at the sight of the bus. She stepped forward as soon as the passengers began disembarking, immediately approaching a gentleman with his suit jacket carried over his arm.

"Are you Mr. Shaw?" she inquired.

"I am, but please call me Nathan," he replied with a pleasant smile as he extended his hand.

"And you can call me Mary Ellen." She accepted his hand in greeting. Then she said, "I appreciate the call from your office informing me you were arriving on the bus tonight. I understand your mandate is to determine the feasibility of our museum being added to your roster of excursions for your cruise guests while your ship is docked at Prince Rupert."

"You are correct," he answered. "Our manager read an article in the *Gazette* a few days ago, and presto, I've been instructed to come check things out. The reason I came by bus is so I can assess the entire trip we would be recommending to our patrons—assessing the bus company and the travel time. I must say it was a most pleasant trip."

When Buddy pulled his suitcase out of the luggage compartment, Nathan reached to claim it, and turned towards the entrance.

"If you're ready," Mary Ellen said, "let's get started. After we clear the gate, we'll take your suitcase into the office building. A porter will deliver it to the lighthouse station where you will be staying. This is a service we provide for all our guests."

"I must say, that is quite an idea, to turn a lighthouse into lodging."

"When we were initially planning, someone suggested it," Mary Ellen commented. "The rest of the buildings are just closing for the day, but as we go to the lighthouse station, I can point out some interesting things to you. Right now, we are going past one of our founding fathers' homes. Then we come to an open area where we host special events."

"Like Russia Day," he confirmed. "In the future, it would be great if we could receive information before the events. If not for business, then certainly for me ... and my wife."

"I can do that. In fact, I can tell you right now," Mary Ellen said, "the next special event will be in a week, on Canada Day. Then we will do something for the August long weekend and of course Labour Day. If you leave me your business card before you go, I can certainly send reminders to your office." She led the way down the path. "You can see some buildings in the distance, like the first-aid facility, but for now, we will just continue down here to the crossroads. Tonight, the only other building you need to know about is this restaurant on the corner called the Borscht Kettle. I hope it will be possible for you to join me for dinner at six-thirty this evening."

"I would be thrilled," he replied. "I already have several questions."

"I'm sure I will be able to get all your questions answered tonight," Mary Ellen said, as she pointed out the lighthouse. "Your luggage will be inside your room by the time you check in, and I'll see you at six-thirty." Then she turned to head home so she could freshen up.

It was quite late when they left the restaurant after dinner and walked onto the wharf.

"As you can see, many other folks from the bus have gathered out here to take in the evening—its sounds, as the water gently laps against the pilings, but most of all, to see the stars. The proprietors of the lighthouse station provide a snack and drink to anyone who is interested. Tomorrow night, you may want to consider going to the gallery deck in the lighthouse tower. We have telescopes in both places for our guests' convenience." Mary Ellen added, "Unless you have any further questions, I'll leave you now."

"No," he said. "So far, your help is making my trip most successful."

"Have a good night, and we will see you tomorrow. Just have someone direct you to my office at nine."

"Sounds good to me," he replied. "See you then."

Mary Ellen's plan was to show him everything until closing time Saturday, then allow him to explore on his own for the rest of the evening and until noon the next day, when the bus was scheduled to leave.

By the time Buddy pulled his bus out of the parking lot on Sunday afternoon, Mary Ellen heaved a nervous sigh of relief. She knew Nathan had seen and done everything there was to see and do at New Petrograd. Now to wait for the letter from the cruise line informing her of their decision.

On Sunday morning just after church, Mr. Yusporov sought out Shelley to report that they had noticed items missing from their shop again this week. Because they had not had anything unusual happening all week, this news left Shelley feeling very troubled. Clearly, the thought she had expressed to Mary Ellen after the fishing trip—if the thefts became a common occurrence—was beginning to play a little louder in her head.

When Gayle also approached her Sunday after the teahouse closed informing her that things were missing, she knew she really needed to meet with Mary Ellen.

Just as soon as she could.

CHAPTER EIGHTEEN

Visitors from Vancouver

"I am so thrilled you boys are finally here!" June gushed as she embraced them after they disembarked from the barge. Then she turned to welcome Lyle's girlfriend, Mandy. "Goodness, to think you had only been going out a few months when we moved from Vancouver. I'm thrilled you could join my sons on this trip."

"Your sister has been quite excited about getting the rest of her things," Marvin said. "I sure don't know why, because they'll still need to be stored at our place and at her in-laws'. Her father-in-law, Tony, should be here shortly with his truck." Marvin gave his sons a hardy pat on the back. Then he started looking towards the village.

"Yes, here he comes now, and it looks like he has picked up Shelley from work."

"Lyle, Mandy, Gordy!" she shrieked, as she slid out of Tony's truck. "Oh, it is so good to see everyone!"

"Shel, *what* are you wearing?" Gordy loudly guffawed.

"Hush, Gordy. I'll tell you later," Shelley said, casting him an annoyed look. "Mom and Dad have lunch plans at the house. Then I can take you on a tour this afternoon, I mean, to meet all my new friends. The first person you must meet is my father-in-law, Mr. Rosso," she finished breathlessly.

"Hang on, Shel. Seriously, take a breath," Lyle said, as he reached out to shake Tony's hand.

"Just call me *Papa* like your sister does—after all, we're all family," Tony offered, smiling, as he in turn extended his hand in greeting to each of the other visitors.

"It sure is great to meet the rest of the Palmer family."

"I agree, Lyle," Gordy said as he shrugged off his sister's hug. "Where's that husband of yours? He sent word about us going deep sea fishing with your roommate. I say, let's get this stuff of yours moved, then we can eat. I'm starving. Afterward, we can go find Gaspar."

"Gaspar is working, but Mom did convince him to come for lunch. Consider yourself lucky—it isn't often that he takes a long lunch break."

"In the meantime, Mandy, these guys are going to be busy, so how about coming with Mom and me to finish preparing lunch?" Shelley offered, linking arms with her.

"I most certainly will," Mandy said with a laugh. She gave Lyle a kiss good-bye, and turned to leave with them.

"I was thrilled I could get this week off work to come," Mandy said. "After all the letters I've read describing this place, and you and Gaspar's talk, it is so delightful to finally witness everything firsthand." As they stepped up on the boardwalk, she read out loud the names of the businesses. "Borscht Kettle, New Petrograd General Store, Paul's Barber Shop, Christella's Beauty Salon." When she finished, she looked around. "Seriously, Shel, that's all you have in your business district?"

"We do have one more shop, John's Kiosk, which is where

the Canada Post office is, and I should add, these are the original buildings." Shelley told her, giving the siding an affectionate pat. "Now, along with the living history museum, we have three more businesses—the lighthouse station, the teahouse, and a souvenir shop. Watch your step off this boardwalk, Mandy. The first time I came it was at night and my parents were quite amused to see me stagger off."

"Shelley, that's not really true," June admonished her.

"I guess you're right, Mom, but my story sounds better. In my memory, Dad was sure slow getting the flashlight out." Shelley grinned at her mom. "But this may also surprise you, Mandy—my folks live half a block from this main commercial area. Can you imagine that happening in Vancouver?"

"I can't, not unless you are very wealthy. Even people in the West End aren't that close to downtown." As June opened the gate a minute later, Mandy exclaimed, "Oh, Mrs. Palmer, your garden is lovely. It's just how I always imagined it would look." She paused, taking it all in.

"Shelley is right, Mandy," June began. "My garden at home is nothing compared to past years. This year, because I've been so busy at the teahouse, I haven't had as much time to work on my gardens, so what is visible are my annual plants. The two girls who board with us, Mary Ellen and Marianne, have helped me immensely."

As soon as the men arrived with Shelley's possessions, Gordy said, "I've been waiting long enough. Now can you tell me about this outfit you are wearing? You look so... different."

"Thanks a lot, Gordy, I think you're pretty different, too," Shelley remarked. "I wear it to be part of what we're doing here, and—"

"—because she looks amazing in it," Gaspar added as he came through the door and gave his wife a hug.

"Thanks, sweetie," Shelley said. "In the museum, there are several people dressed in authentic Russian attire, and I am wearing a 1917 policewoman's uniform."

"Now it makes sense," Gordy agreed, as he turned to Gaspar to ask him about the promised fishing trip.

"Don has offered to take us on Monday, as the museum will be closed. At the same time, he wants to do it before the Canada Day festivities begin."

"Well, now that you've got that question answered," June said, playfully, "perhaps now we can have lunch." She handed the plates to Tony and salad forks and serviettes to Daria. Then June brought out some glasses and juice. Shelley and Mandy followed her carrying shrimp salads for everyone.

A lively conversation soon started, or several conversations, until Gaspar finally said, "I should be getting back to work. Why don't you two guys come with me and I'll introduce you to some of my work pals and show you some of the projects we're working on. Mandy, would you like to accompany us or would you rather hang out with Shelley?"

"Thanks, but my idea of fun isn't looking at a construction site," Mandy replied. "I'll go with your wife. I'm sure what she'll be doing is much more to my liking. She has already offered to show me some of the flowerbeds her mom has planned."

The five of them left together, but separated when they got to the corner by the Borscht Kettle.

Shelley pointed out the beds of flowers, and introduced Mandy to Bert. During the afternoon, Shelley was able to introduce her to many others. Just before three-thirty, she took her to Anna and left her there to listen to the presentation on the village's history. Later, as Shelley was making her way back to claim Mandy, she was very pleased to see Olga had joined them. Finally, she left her at the souvenir shop, where she stayed until closing. Shortly after five, as they were walking home, Shelley quizzed her on whether her brothers had any plans other than fishing for the week.

"Not really," Mandy admitted. "All I've heard is Gaspar and fishing. Which leads me to believe I'm free to make my own plans."

"Exactly what I suspected and wanted to hear." Shelley snickered. "I think you'll have a much better visit."

"I agree," Mandy replied. "So, tell me, Shel, what is married life like in New Petrograd? It sure is obvious everyone here loves you."

"I know, I feel so at home and my sweetie is wonderful. My parents have also been warmly embraced into this community."

"Mom," Gordy announced when they returned that evening, "we had such a great time this afternoon. By the way, I've also invited Gaspar's friend Kevin for supper."

"What's different about that?" June replied. "I often have Kevin and Don for supper."

"You do?" Shelley queried her mother. "I didn't know that."

Gaspar looked on and smiled knowingly.

"You know, Mrs. Palmer," Mary Ellen said, shortly after she and Don arrived home, "I really don't think this is fair. We shouldn't all be intruding on your first night together. I think it makes much more sense if we go to the Borscht Kettle or the garden at *Papa's* and leave your family alone."

"Heavens, no, it's no bother," June responded, smiling at everyone. "This is just the way I have always liked it—my children and their friends at home in my kitchen. There will be time enough for us to be together later. After supper, Dad will help you boys organize your camping gear in the yard. For now, I suggest going outside and helping him set up another table. And while you're there, you may as well set it," she said, as she handed Gordy a stack of dishes. "Mandy dear, the twins have kindly offered to share a room, so you won't have to sleep on the couch. While the boys are getting their camping gear out, we'll get you settled into one of the rooms upstairs."

"Mine," Marianne immediately spoke up. "I just have a few more things I want to take out and then it is all yours."

After all the accommodations were sorted, Marvin shooed everyone out, stating, "I'll help Mom with the dishes while you kids all go and meet some of Shelley and Gaspar's friends."

Friday night everyone convened early in the evening for fish and chips night at the Borscht Kettle and of course, it was a huge hit. Afterward many of the young adults gathered together for the remainder of the evening. Which started a trend, the visitors getting together most evenings with Shelley and Gasper's many friends.

Over the next few days, the variety of activities the visitors enjoyed included a pleasant hike along the trailhead that started at the lighthouse garden, taking in some of the various village attractions, casually throwing a few horseshoes in June's and Marvin's backyard, or just doing nothing, or reading a book for an hour or two. The days seemed to fly by as everyone enjoyed doing what interested them most. Sometimes together, sometimes apart.

On Saturday morning, Marvin loaded up Gaspar's truck and took the boys fishing in one of the lakes towards Hartley Bay.

Mandy, not wanting to join them and satisfied she had

done everything else that interested her, chose to settle down on a park bench beside the wharf to read a book. Noticing a plant in the middle of a planter beside her that she didn't recognize, she called to Bert.

He stopped his work and came over. "Yes, miss, is there something I can help you with?"

"I was just wondering about this lovely flower bordered by these red and white carnations. What is it?"

"This is a chamomile plant. It is Russia's national flower that we planted for Russia Day a few weeks ago. After the celebration, Mary Ellen instructed me and my co-worker to pull them out and then plant these carnations for Canada Day. Mrs. Palmer helped me to design these beds combining the two. When Mary Ellen saw what we had envisioned, she was thrilled because the plants in the gardens represented both countries."

He picked up his trowel again to go back to work. "Only two more days to get the job done." As he was leaving, and as Mandy opened her book, she heard him mutter, "Mother always says, 'Love is a flower you have got to let grow'."

June spotted Mandy as she was walking home from her day's work at the teahouse and called over to ask her if she was ready to come home.

"I am, but Mrs. Palmer, before we go, I am curious how it came about—your designing these planters with Bert. They are beautiful."

June started to laugh as they headed home. "The day after Russia Day, I saw Bert pulling these plants out of the planters, but oh my, he had such a long face. When I asked him why, he told me he was so upset because Mary Ellen had instructed him to pull out the chamomile plants. I could easily understand why he was grieved at pulling out perfectly healthy plants, so we put our heads together and designed this. When I left, he was already starting to replant the ones he had pulled out, except for the one I had taken for my own garden."

On Sunday afternoon, Gordy and Lyle were lazily throwing horseshoes with Marvin, when Mandy put down her book and asked Lyle if he would accompany her on a tour of the lighthouse.

Finally, it was Monday and time for the boys' much anticipated deep-sea fishing trip. Only a faint glimmer of pink sky was showing in the east when, starting with Lyle and Gordy, ten people clambered up the gangplank of the *Neptune of the Sea*, Uri's old fishing boat.

"What is this, a fishing trip or a leisure tour?" Don, the proud new owner of Uri's boat, chuckled good-humoredly.

"It's about half and half," Mary Ellen said as she gave him a cheeky smile. "Fishing for you guys, and sun for the rest of us. We promise to just sit quietly, but after all, this is just too good an opportunity to pass up."

"Suntanning on the high seas," Shelley sighed dreamily.

At the end of the day, as everyone slowly meandered off the boat, they offered their thanks to Don. Many of them were a little burnt from sitting under the beating sun. All were anticipating a fish fry that evening—some a little more than others, as they had caught the fish.

CHAPTER NINETEEN

Canada Day

"Welcome to New Petrograd, everyone," Mary Ellen greeted those gathered on July 1 for Canada Day. "It certainly gives me much pleasure to see so many folks here. I have observed family cars, vans, campers, and a bus pulling into our parking lot this morning. I understand our accommodations are full tonight. I am pleased to tell you that we have also cleared some space at the south end of our parking lot for a new camping area. There are four portable washroom facilities set up there for everyone's convenience.

"As a special event, Johnny Eagle Feather, a frequent visitor here, has arranged for some of Canada's Indigenous people to perform for us. Shortly, I will introduce you to Gerald Gladstone, who will explain the cultural dances they will be performing. Later, we invite you to visit the wharf, where there will be two Tsimshian canoes on display. There are also booths set up where our people will be giving carving demonstrations and displaying their finished work.

"And for a grand finale, there will be a potlatch this evening. For those who don't know what that is, Gerald will explain—and I am certain he will do a much better job than I!

"I can well remember when I was growing up my *babushka* speaking about the freedom her generation had appreciated finding in this new land. So, to officially begin our celebration today, let us start by singing *O Canada*."

The crowd jubilantly sang as they waved the small flags that had been handed to them as they entered the gate that morning, while the larger Canadian flags were hoisted by Marvin and Bob. As the last words of the anthem died away, the drums began to beat as Tsimshian dancers began chanting. Gerald took the microphone from Mary Ellen and the dancers moved into the foreground to begin their performance.

"Thank you, Mary Ellen, for a very warm welcome. Our first dance is a song called, 'Paddle to Metlakatla,' which describes an instance during the canoe trip of 1887 when some of our ancestors were going from Metlakatla in B.C. to establish a new village, 'New' Metlakatla, in Alaska. Many in the group were complaining about leaving their homes, when one woman stood up in her canoe and rather forcibly told everyone, *'Wha! T'iina tleexgn!'* which means 'stop crying!'

"Please note their clothing. All the dancers are wearing basket hats made from cedar bark. The designs of these hats often showed a person's position and family ranking. Over their shorts, our men are dressed in breech clouts and long cloaks. Some of these are very nicely decorated with bead work. The women may be clad in knee-length bark skirts over which they have on poncho-like capes, the backs of which are woven with the person's tribal designs. These capes or robes can be worn by either men or women. All our clothing was traditionally woven out of fiber made from cedar bark, or else made from deerskin and otter fur. Our women wear their hair long and loose or braided, but men's hair is often in a topknot."

As the drummer began to beat faster, and the chanting got louder, the dynamic of the dance changed.

"Our dancers are going to paddle even harder, as the fear of starting over slowly begins to leave them. One of the dancers has on the spectacular Chilkat blanket, which was woven from cedar bark and mountain goat hair. Traditionally, they would have been worn only by the very prominent, for example a shaman or chief. Our dancer's grandfather owned one, so he was very fortunate to have inherited it."

"This is pretty neat stuff," Gordy whispered to Shelley, sitting beside him. "I've never seen anything like this anywhere else. In fact, I have to admit I'm more impressed with everything than I thought I would be."

"And just where else have you been, my worldly wise little brother?" Shelley gave him a push on the shoulder—only realizing a little too late that she had pushed him right into Alexandria.

"Sorry," they both said to her, looking at her startled face. Gaspar began to laugh uncontrollably and June frowned at her daughter.

"Hush," Alexander said, annoyed.

Which only caused Gaspar's laughter to turn into hoots.

Gerald raised his voice a little. "Often our dance is secondary to the words we are singing, which unfortunately are not translatable. Watch and see if you can notice the dancers doing this very prominent position of a slightly tilted, forward stance. Then they will raise the knee, and stamp with a flat foot. Another step is a toe-heel action, and muscular easing and control in gesture. This basic style varies from dance to dance and even from the different dancers.

"See if you can pick out the movements for the Raven dance, next, which is from the Haida. This dance has two parts to it. The first half starts with the women paddling a canoe. It stops and then begins again when someone comes out wearing a raven mask and performs the dance of the Raven. Haida people have two clan names. The eagle, who is most majestic, and the raven, who is considered highly intelligent. Ravens do remember people and faces, which you will witness during this dance. I might mention, while you are watching, see if you can spot Johnny Eagle Feather."

This time the dancers seemed to be circling around each other, their beautiful robes shimmering with their movements, especially those with the long fringes on them.

When the dance concluded, Gerald explained, "Before our dancers leave to prepare for the next dance, I would like to draw your attention to some of our warriors, who have painted their faces. They have used different colours and designs, which are tribal tattoos or stylized animals.

"We also like to decorate our drums. Some of the more popular items painted on them are feathers, the moon or sun, and animal footprints. As I mentioned before, our voices create music. The dancers also shake rattles in time with the drumbeat. Sometimes they will carry different objects in their hands. Today I have seen paddles, and it looked like some warriors also brought clubs. I don't know why, because today we have come in peace," Gerald smiled.

When the drummers from this dance finished, Gerald announced, "We have one more dance to perform. One thing I have not mentioned is footwear. In nice weather, the Haida choose to go barefoot. Of course, when it gets cold and rainy, we put on moccasins.

"Mary Ellen was mentioning earlier about a potlatch. To

the Haida band, this is our biggest celebration and means *to give*. The host would give his guests gifts. Of course, the richer the family, the better the gifts would be. This ceremony was for any major event in a person's life, even death. Much like today, it included food, drinks, singing and dancing. A big difference, though, was that traditionally it could be held for as long as three weeks! One interesting fact you may find humorous is the Dignity Potlatch. If a chief or shaman had fallen off a canoe and lost their dignity, they would throw a Dignity Potlatch to regain their importance in the tribe." Then he added, "This is our gift to you today for including us in your celebration. We are preparing a meal consisting of barbecued salmon which has been cooked on an open fire over alder branches, along with baked potato and two vegetables. The meal will be finished with a mixture of different berries for dessert.

"Appropriately, our last number this morning is called the Salmon Dance. It looks like all the dancers are ready. Again, I draw your attention to their footwork. This is a very special dance to our people because we, of the Pacific Northwest coast, rely upon the Salmon People for food. Each year, when the salmon return, we hold a First Salmon Ceremony to recognize the spirit of the salmon. Also, it was very important to show our thanks for their reappearance. We are about to perform for you a song which shows our reaction when we see the fish jump out of the water, and our gratitude when they yield their lives to us. This dance recognizes the significance of wild salmon in our culture, and to man's survival in the world."

The drums and chanting began again...

At the conclusion of the dance, Gerald handed the microphone to Martin, who asked, "Can we please have the dancers back to give them one last show of appreciation? Truly you have enlightened everyone so much with your performances."

The clapping was as thunderous as the drums had been a few minutes before.

"Next we invite Anna Yusporova, who will speak about what life was like when our forefathers first arrived in this land as new immigrants."

"Morning, all," Anna said in greeting. "The details I would like to share with you come from my husband's *dedushka's* memory of when they first arrived after their long journey. It was a June afternoon, and they were hungry and tired as they concluded their travels. They planned to anchor at sea and take rowboats to shore. But as they got closer, they could see pilings protruding from the water. He said at first that they couldn't believe their eyes. They used the pilings to tie and anchor their boats. Then they rowed to shore with their moods bolstered.

"The men needed to start work immediately setting up shelters by creating tentlike structures stretched between two trees. Again, they marveled at finding cleared space to be able to do this. While this was being done, the women were gathering huge rocks for the men to arrange into fire pits. Once this was accomplished, the women began to prepare a meal with food they had brought with them." Anna stopped and said, "They couldn't even have a cup of coffee until this was done!" This brought laughter from her listeners, as some murmured that they would have died waiting all that time.

Anna smiled at their comments, and continued, "You can only imagine what their conversations might have been during their first meal. The following morning, when some of the men returned to the shore to go back to their boats to fish, they found a boat's anchor had not held. They could barely make out their boat as it drifted away on the horizon before it vanished from their view. This was a huge blow to them.

"They soon recognized other signs of earlier habitation. In the brambles, there were a few tumbledown buildings. Each time the tide went out, they saw more items on the beach that had been left in the sand. Other than perhaps an old bowl which could have some use, they left these objects for the tide to wash out to sea again.

"But that the area had been lived in became especially apparent later, when they found fruit trees and berry patches. Certainly, a much welcome addition to their diets. Soon the women were planting vegetable gardens, eager for fresh vegetables to add to their meager cooked meals to feed the hungry men. A few women had had the foresight to purchase sewing machines in Vancouver. These were put to good use now mending everyone's worn clothing.

"Meanwhile, *Dedushka* spoke about how he and some of the other men were felling the cedar trees and dragging them across the land. Within a few weeks, he recalled that they had enough logs to begin building the nine homes they needed. Unfortunately, they had only managed to build eight before winter's storms set in. They could endure the rain, but not the snow. This meant Pyotr and Elena had to share a home with his parents, Vasily and Tatyana Filipov, until spring.

"Slowly, life in New Petrograd was beginning to take shape. With winter's storms, everyone's tasks soon turned to ones that could be done indoors. I do not know what the men did to fill their days—perhaps sleeping on the couch," Anna said, with a twinkle in her eye. "We know that the women were still able to prepare hearty meals and clean their homes."

As the laughter died down, she continued, "I'm joking, because *Dedushka* said they took to trapping small animals and shooting large game. We also know the tireless job of chopping and stocking wood for the fires would have been done by the men.

"In the spring, when outdoor work began again, some folk witnessed a devastating accident just off the craggy point, when they were coming home from a day's fishing. It soon became apparent there was an urgent need for them to erect a lighthouse. This further delayed the construction of Pyotr and Elena Filipov's house, but it was finished before their second winter. They also managed to construct a church and rectory that summer. The remains of this original church is where the founding fathers' plaque stands today.

"*Dedushka* mentioned they could hear the patter of little feet as some of their offspring were beginning to walk. In his household, he was referring to my husband's *papa,* and later their home was blessed with his three siblings.

"The following year, they built the New Petrograd General Store. The current store is very reminiscent of the original one, which incidentally was built almost at the same location. The Borscht Kettle came a few years later. The barber and beauty shop were added a whole generation afterward, as originally the wives cut their husbands' and sons' hair at home. The women never even thought of going to a beauty parlour in those days, but let their hair grow long, often putting it in a bun at the nape of their neck. *Dedushka* often speaks lovingly about how his beloved wife would have laughed at the very thought of visiting a beauty parlour. But he quickly adds, she had no need of being beautified, because even her hands, with all their cracks and broken nails, were perfect to him. What was important was that her hands were so loving and gentle, and a song always adorned her lips.

"Two of those original homes you are still able to see inside today, and there are a few more still standing, although in disrepair. Of course, a few years later those pattering little feet *Dedushka* mentioned, grew up and married, creating a need for new homes and a schoolhouse. With each generation, there has been a need to continue building. The greatest construction has come recently as we prepared our village to host this living history museum. As you will see, it is still going on as more needs are identified. The difference is that today, as we clear land for building, the government is taxing us.

"I encourage you to take the lighthouse tour to learn more about its early days. In another half-hour, I will be resuming my regular talks on the first part of our forefathers' journey, by the plaque. These will begin at one-thirty and then again at three-thirty."

"Thank you so much, Anna," Martin said, as the clapping slowed to just a few people. "The entertainment this morning has been outstanding. All exhibits will be open in a half-hour. Also, don't forget to take in the canoes and the Tsimshian artisans' carving demonstration.

"I heard the Borscht Kettle has two items on the menu today, Beef Stroganoff and Chicken Kiev because, although Russian, they have become familiar meals on Canadian tables. The teahouse has likewise prepared a similar but lighter meal. I understand they will also offer some child-friendly food. Plus, don't forget the Potlatch this evening, which sounds wonderful. I know that is what I am looking forward to.

"This concludes our program until this evening, when we gather here again to enjoy the dance."

"That was amazing, all of it," Mandy exclaimed enthusiastically, as soon as everyone clustered together to discuss their next move. "I suppose you have to go to work now, Shelley?"

"I do, although I can take time to grab a quick lunch with

everyone. One nice thing about my position—anytime I am dressed this way, essentially I am working. I suggest we go to the teahouse. You do have the pleasure of Gaspar's company for this afternoon. What about you, Dad?"

"I really haven't decided on my plans," Marvin said. "I don't think they will need my services at the gas pumps until later in the day, when people might be leaving. I'll have lunch with everyone, but I'll leave you young people to entertain yourselves. I may wander around by myself for a while and then sit under a shady tree until Mom gets off work. If I change my mind, I'm sure I can find you."

They started off when Lyle stopped, looked around, and asked, "Where's Gordy? Did we lose him? He's usually leading the pack when it comes to food."

"You did," Gaspar guffawed, "To Alexandria, whom my wife so nicely managed to push him into earlier. It seems they started chatting after that, and..."

"Are you serious, Gaspar?" June asked. "I wonder if she remembers she is supposed to be working at the teahouse right after this?"

When they went into the teahouse, they learned that indeed, Gordy had been ahead of the pack, way ahead. He was standing off to the side while Alexandria loaded a tray for him.

"Goodness," June exclaimed, as she headed off to begin work.

Gordy did come over then to inform them he wanted to be included in their plans for the afternoon, as Alexandria would be working. Then he left, presumably to eat on the deck.

CHAPTER TWENTY

Canada Day Exhibits

Much to the surprise of everyone, when they gathered around the carver who introduced himself as Cooper, it was not wood he was carving, but argillite, a type of black slate. As he worked, he explained that the stone had become very popular in the late 1960s. On his table were carved otters, whales, birds, totem poles, and canoes. What he was presently working on looked quite intricate—a family crest he had been commissioned to do.

A few feet away, another carver was working on a cedar mask, which Mandy thought resembled something mythical. While they watched him, he chipped off pieces that reminded her of rings. For all the conversation going around him, the carver never broke his concentration.

Still another carver was working on what he explained were bentwood boxes. These were gorgeous wooden boxes which, when finished, would be inlaid with abalone shell.

Near the the circle of carvers, was a collection of items for sale. Gaspar and Shelley's family made a few purchases and then made their way to the wharf.

A striking young woman who introduced herself as Emily kept them entertained while they waited in line. She shared some information about the longhouses where originally her people lived. Food was readily available to them, so they did not need to move in search of it. This made a permanent home feasible. Their houses were assembled from one-hundred-foot-long cedar trees. A bark roof was then put on top to complete it. The roof was low, so it easily kept the room warm in the wintertime. Indoors, there were fire pits that provided light and heat to cook with. The downside to this design was it soon became smoky inside. Besides the door, the only other opening was in the roof, which allowed the smoke to escape.

"Do you live today in what we'd call an ordinary house?" Gordy asked.

His question brought a brilliant smile to her serene face, even as Emily continued, "They slept in bunkbeds. The family kept open shelves above the beds. It was cool below them, so that's where they dug a hole to store their food. The longhouse lodged several families from the same clan. There were often as many as fifty people in one house. When it became full, another house was built alongside it, and this created a village. In the front of the house was a totem pole with the family's crest."

Emily waved at Lawrence, who approached to take them to see the canoes. "Haida have often been likened to Vikings, but we say Vikings are like Haida."

Lawrence quietly waited until she finished before introducing himself. He then began to explain that there were five different types of canoes—freshwater, ocean-going, head canoe, river, and northern. As they walked along the wharf, he said, "Canoes are usually made by a specialist carver with one or more assistants. Traditionally, this master canoe maker also required a spiritual helper. This was true of anyone involved in its construction. These men were subject to several constraints, such as not combing their hair during construction."

At Lyle's confused look, Lawrence added, "This was thought to avoid splitting the ends of the canoe. Perhaps a more difficult constraint was that ideally, the carver needed to abstain from sexual relations so the timber would not rot. In total, it often would take three men about two months to complete a twenty-five-foot canoe. As you can tell," Lawrence said with a twinkle in his dark eyes, "this would not be very agreeable to many of our men."

When the laughter died down, he continued.

"A tree is chosen not only for size, but also for its straight and even length. Finally, for its proximity to water. Canoes are made from a single hand-picked log. Cedar was certainly preferred, but other woods, like cottonwood, could be used. It was cut in the fall, and then over the winter months it would be burned and shaped into the basic canoe form. In the springtime, the incomplete canoe would be turned over and then the carvers would begin hollowing it out." He concluded by stating, "We have brought two types with us today. Let's move along to the first one."

When Gaspar and the visitors were standing beside it, he told them, "This is a river canoe." Lawrence explained that it was made from the softer, deciduous wood of cottonwood, as it was a simple dugout. Not much thought was given to the quality of workmanship or decoration as it was always used close to home. As often as it was paddled, it was poled and even towed by ropes from the riverbank.

The other canoe they had brought was called a Northern

canoe. Lawrence proudly explained, "Although other tribes made it, it was often called a Haida canoe. This was because they had the best red cedar logs to construct it from. This allowed their carvers to make the most sophisticated and speedy boats possible. It was meant for long trips on open stretches of ocean."

Other features, Lawrence told them, were its size and its high prow and upright cutwater designed to throw off the waves. Lastly, he said, "These long lengths are like a painter's canvas as they often had elaborate paintings. For this, they used red, black, or ochre."

Gaspar could not help but admire its beauty as they were moving to the next exhibits, but not before giving Lawrence and Emily a hearty thank you, which was echoed by the others.

The next person they met was Robert, who enlightened them on the care and maintenance of canoes. He emphasized this was extremely important, as not only the lives of the crew depended on it, but also their family and household. Steady maintenance involved polishing the hull to maintain speed. Also, whenever it was beached, the canoe was turned over and old matting, boards, or branches were thrown over it to prevent its cracking from the sun.

What was most interesting, and perhaps unexpected, was when he explained the various types of paddles. "There are seven different types—the Haida, two different types of Coast Salish, the Kwakiutl, our neighbours the Tlingit, and lastly the steering paddle." Robert spoke of how the whaler's paddle tapered to a fine point so they could enter the water more stealthily. Still on his display stand, he pointed out a steering paddle, used in the stern. It was more stout and broader than the others. He also told them about the poles that could be used in propelling and steering freshwater canoes.

"Like the river canoe," Lyle interjected.

Robert paused to give him a thumbs-up, before saying, "Lastly, as a final touch, master canoe carvers and the men working with them would elaborately paint a set of paddles for each vessel. Of course, they used the same colours as the canoe."

The next item they were shown were canoe bailers.

Robert carefully explained, "These were a protection from the heavy pounding the canoe would receive in open water. Without them, there was a fear the canoe's hull would crack or even split in half."

"What are those?" Gordy asked, pointing to some rocks.

Robert answered, "These stones could be used as an anchor. Alternatively, they could be used as ballast when freight canoes were travelling empty. Another use for them was as weapons. There were many battles on these coasts, amongst ourselves and with other bands. Our people also kept large stone rings. These were tied with a lengthy cedar bark rope and fastened to every war canoe. They could be up to two feet in diameter and weigh up to fifty pounds. Our warriors were able to throw them at attacking canoes and split them, while still retrieving their weapons. These stones were called canoe breakers."

"I can't thank you enough for all you have shared with us," Gaspar said. "All of you. I've enjoyed myself immensely this afternoon. I sure hope you'll be able to join us again next year."

"This has been so informative," Gordy agreed. "Last thing I expected coming to a Russian-Canadian village. Thank you."

"Yes, I agree," Lyle stated.

Mandy looked on and nodded before saying, "I feel I need to digest all that I have learned today. This day has been so amazing."

"I agree, Mandy, I feel like I've been transported out of New Petrograd," Gaspar acknowledged. "Maybe if we go for a cold Russian drink, it will remind me that I'm still here."

As they were leaving, Robert called after them, "I hope to see you at the Potlatch this evening. I can smell the aroma of the salmon from here."

"Let's go to the Borscht Kettle for drinks before we meet up with the others for dinner," Gaspar suggested. "If we're lucky and we see Shel, we can invite her to join us."

"She is right over there," Mandy pointed. "She is talking to your friend Anna's husband on the boardwalk outside the general store. You should be able to get her attention."

"You're right, I could get her attention but I'm not going to. Look at her stance and at Alex's face. I think something has happened."

"I think you're right," Lyle agreed. "Gordy and I've been on the wrong end of that stance many times."

"I think we'll just go without my wife," Gaspar finally concluded.

As they began walking towards the Kettle, Gaspar listed the drinks he thought they could order. "We could get a *kvas,* which is a fermented non-alcoholic beverage, or a *medovukha,* which is a honey-based drink and, I might add, very refreshing."

"It seems to me we've tried some of these drinks already since we've been here," Mandy answered. "So, I'm going to order the honey-based one."

"Speak for yourself," Lyle laughed. "I don't think it's too early to have a *tarasun*. Mandy, please order one for me. I have a quick errand to run. I'm sure by the time the drinks have arrived, I'll be back," he finished, already heading off in another direction.

When they were seated at the table, enjoying their dinners, June looked around at everyone, feeling so happy her whole family was together. Then she exclaimed, "Where are Lyle and Mandy? I didn't see them leave. Really, earlier today, it was Gordy who went missing. Now, he and Alexandria are here, and his brother and girlfriend aren't."

"I wouldn't worry about them," Marvin replied, grinning at her. "I saw them slip away as soon as they finished their meals. I didn't think anything of it. After all, since they've been here, they really haven't had much time alone. I'm sure they'll show up later." Then Marvin continued, "This is the most delicious salmon I've ever tasted."

"It is," Gaspar answered. "But no better than the fish you prepared last evening."

His father-in-law smiled at the compliment. "Thank you, Gaspar. As soon as you're finished with your meal, June honey, shall we move to the dance?"

Looking up, Gaspar said, "Oh, there's Robert with Emily, who were at the canoe display. I would call them over now, but before I do, Shel, I wanted to ask you about the conversation we saw you having with Alex around three-thirty."

Shelley sighed, before looking around to make sure they couldn't be overheard.

"Alex was telling me he hadn't noticed any souvenirs missing, but other confectionaries were. He only noticed because a customer asked for some potato chips. When he went over to show him where they should be, they were all gone. He knew for a fact he hadn't sold them all, because he knew the number of bags he had procured for today. Don had suggested last week that he carry them in his store. Alex is going to suggest to Mary Ellen that she speak to John about the kiosk staying open later to serve the guests who want some late-night munchies."

"What is going on?" Gaspar wanted to know.

"All these incidents happen without anyone catching them," Shelley replied. "My guess, of course, is children. So, other than adding the incident to my notes, there's really nothing more I can do."

Gaspar took her hand in his. "I have to say, I don't like what's going on, but I guess it's like you said earlier. When you're bringing in tourists, it's to be somewhat expected."

While they were at the dance, Alex approached Shelley and told her nothing had gone missing from the souvenir shop. His *mama* felt it was due to Alexander being there, therefore, the only incident he was aware of that day had been the one at the general store.

CHAPTER TWENTY-ONE

Port Essington

The day after Canada Day, Shelley came bounding into her parents' home. She excitedly explained their plan to spend the day at Port Essington, but paused as her mom began to speak.

"Lyle has something to tell you about why he and Mandy disappeared last night."

"Oh," Shelley exclaimed, "I hope one of you wasn't ill."

"Not at all," Mandy declared brightly. "Your brother proposed to me."

"What? Oh Mandy, this is the best news ever! Congratulations!" Shelley enveloped them both in a hug. "This is so exciting! I am thrilled for you. Both of you. Now you really are going to be my sister. I couldn't imagine what was holding my brother back from asking you."

"No, me either," June said. "It is so lovely and I'm so pleased he did it while they were visiting us. Mandy is going to phone her parents today to share their good news with them."

"Shelley, it was so romantic," Mandy said. "Earlier, he had arranged with Mr. Filipov that we would have permission to go up to the gallery deck at the lighthouse. Lyle figured—and rightly so—that everyone else would be at the dance so we would have the whole gallery to ourselves. Only us and the stars. Oh, and the stars were so magnificent," she recollected breathlessly, before she continued. "They were all spread out like tiny diamonds in the sky, and then we saw larger ones, but neither of us knew what they were called. Then the sky got all dark, kind of a navy-blue colour, and this tableau of shimmering vibrant green raced across the sky. Then he got down on one knee and asked me. It was so sweet. He said, 'I was—'"

"Mandy, darling," Lyle broke in, "you don't have to tell my sister and mother *everything*."

"Oh, okay," Mandy said in a soft voice, as she turned to face him adoringly. Then turning back to face her audience, she continued, "Of course, I know he didn't plan to do it before we left home, because all he had was this wooden ring. But that's okay, I just love it."

"Where did you get it?" Shelley asked, looking at her brother, puzzled. "It's actually quite attractive." She took Mandy's ring finger in her hand to have a closer look.

"From the Indigenous carvers," Mandy explained, going into peals of laughter.

"I had to pay dearly for it," Lyle said indignantly. "It took me a long time to describe what I wanted, and then of course to get the right size."

"I see," Shelley said, nodding seriously, before looking at Mandy with a smile.

"Well, that should save Lyle a bundle," Gordy said slyly, as he came into the kitchen. "If you're happy with it, I suspect you won't get a diamond until your tenth anniversary."

"And what about you, may I ask?" Shelley said, turning her attention to her younger brother. "What about your Rosie? It seems you've forgotten all about her since you met Alexandria."

Lyle guffawed. "Rosie, she's long gone. I think he's had two girlfriends since she was 'the one,' if you know what I mean."

"That's enough," June broke in. "If we're not going to talk any more about the engagement... Shelley, what were you saying when you came in?"

"Oh, that Gaspar is getting his truck filled with gas. For your last full day, we thought it would be nice to go for a drive. I imagine he will be here soon."

Shelley had no sooner finished speaking when Gaspar came through the door, which of course meant the news had to be shared all over again.

"I suspected something like this was up, because your *papa* hinted about a wedding when he was filling my tank. And well, I didn't think Gordy had moved that fast with Alexandria," Gaspar finished, slapping Gordy playfully on the back. "Congratulations to both of you. It is a real delight to think you'll soon officially be a part of this family, Mandy. I can tell you from my own personal experience, you couldn't wish for better in-laws."

"Why, thank you, Gaspar. That is really sweet of you," June said.

"Shel, did you manage to tell them the plan for today?"

"Barely, sweetie. In fact, I just finished as you came in."

"So, what does everyone say? Does that sound like a good idea?"

"It sounds fantastic as long as we get back here by the time Alexandria gets off work," Gordy said.

"I don't think we want to promise anything like that," Shelley responded. "They have a fabulous Japanese-Canadian restaurant in Port Essington. I would like to leave our day open to having supper there if we choose. When we were there before, Gaspar told me the canneries and original area are a ghost town. He mentioned then that it might make a pleasant afternoon to walk around. I think, Gordy, you are going to have to choose between your family and your latest flame."

"Now, not so fast, Shelley," June interrupted. "First, Mandy needs to phone her parents, so you can't leave right away. I need to get to work, and you and Gaspar need to think of another way this might work. Since you need a second vehicle if Alexandria goes too, what about asking Don for his truck, Gaspar? If he would agree to that, I'll talk to Gayle about letting Alexandria have the day off work to go with you all."

"Oh Mom, would you?" Gordy exclaimed. "That would be the best."

"Don left early this morning with a fishing group. In fact, two boats full, because Kevin and Marianne went with him. I told him I had plans for the day, but I could ask to borrow my *papa's* truck."

Mandy and Lyle went off to the lighthouse station to use the phone. Gaspar and June went across the street to talk with Tony. Upon receiving an affirmative from him, June went to work to see what she could arrange with Gayle. It was about eleven before all these details were straightened out, and a very excited Alexandria showed up on the Palmer porch. With everything finally arranged, the vehicles departed.

Of course, it was necessary to drive across the bush road so they could take the visitors to see Rushing Falls. The spray of the water was so appealing as it misted them.

As always, the squirrels came out to scold, and the birds harmonized with the falls. As they were standing there watching, they heard a rustling behind them. Expecting to see a squirrel, they looked straight into the startled face of a deer. It paused for a moment, before it turned and bounded away. Everyone stood quietly taking in this very beautiful gift from nature. Then they decided to return to their vehicles, conscious of the fact that they got away much later than they had anticipated.

Back at the main road, Shelley said, "Sometime I would like to go the other direction. Our biggest problem is that Gaspar is used to taking the weekend off, and I get Monday and Tuesday off. He likes to take his regular days off and help Don with his customers. It means Don can book more than one boat that way. Sometimes Kevin goes too."

"Besides," Gaspar finished for her, "I like you spending your days off cooking and baking." Then turning to the others, he added, "My *mama* likes to spend time with Shelley teaching her Russian dishes, which they both enjoy."

"Instead of going to a restaurant tonight," Lyle declared, "you should have been slaving in the kitchen for your favourite brother."

"On your next trip, dearie," Shel answered him, laughing. "By the way, you never did say—have you two set a wedding date?"

"Not yet," Mandy answered her. "We know we have to do it before next May, when the museum opens again, and you and Lyle's folks start work. I kind of like the idea of doing it this winter, but I don't know if we can arrange things that quickly. When we talked to my mom this morning, she was so excited, and is already starting to plan. She was going to call Regency Caterers tomorrow and start getting ideas about menus. I had to tell her, slow down, wait until I get home at least!" She laughed.

"Gaspar," Lyle asked, pulling everyone back to the

present. "Is there anywhere along the road you can stop so I can take pictures of the river? By the way, which river is this?"

"It's the Ecstall River, which is the same river that runs alongside Port Essington. I can stop anywhere you like and as often as you want, Lyle." He pulled off the road and onto the shoulder.

As Lyle was getting out of Gaspar's vehicle, Gordy honked his horn as they waved and passed by in theirs.

Watching the Bronco pass, Gaspar said, "I hope he knows where he is going."

"Don't worry about him, sweetie," Shelley said with a grin. "Lyle and I always say our little brother constantly lands on his feet."

The photo session over, they continued on their way. For the afternoon they strolled through the remains of eighty years of dreams. They noticed a large sign that informed them that a fire had destroyed the town fifteen years earlier, so there wasn't much left to see.

"This place is more of a ghost town than I realized," Gaspar apologized. "I suppose those few houses that we drove past when we first came in are the homes built since the fire. This makes New Petrograd look like a metropolis. I do know the gas station primarily serviced the water traffic in the past. I imagine with the new road coming through now, business has picked up."

There were a few feet of boardwalk that was in such disrepair that even Gordy had difficulty walking along it. After making several attempts and almost falling, he had to admit defeat and jumped off, laughing.

Shelley and Mandy were both interested in wandering through the very overgrown cemetery. Mandy was glad that

Gaspar and Lyle indicated they would rather wander over to the pilings, the remainder of one of the canneries.

Once they were out of earshot, Mandy said, "Lyle told me last night he'd been thinking of proposing for a long time. The reason he hadn't was he was waiting for a perfect idea or place to do it and nothing ever seemed right. But when we did the lighthouse tour last Sunday, he knew he'd found his answer. Isn't that funny? If he hadn't found the perfect place, maybe he never would have asked me... Oh look, here is one for a reverend and his wife. He was only in his early forties when he died."

When Shelley turned her head, she realized Lyle and Gaspar were approaching and now understood Mandy's quick change of topic. Still she knelt and bent her head, brushing the moss away so she could read the tombstone Mandy was pointing to.

"Reverend Nakamura," she read out loud and then the birth and death dates. The next line read *Mary Nakamura* and her dates.

"That's interesting," Mandy commented. "Over there, we saw grave markers with Japanese characters. The reverend seems to have a Japanese last name, but Mary is English. Maybe that is why it is written out in English."

"Or because he was a reverend and everyone knew him. I guess we'll never know," Shelley replied, as she stood, dusting off her hands.

"So how did it go looking at the pilings?" Shelley asked. "See anything interesting?"

"The most exciting thing we found down there was a rusty old muffin tin," Gaspar said cheerily, reaching for Shelley's hand.

Quickly drawing her hand back, she exclaimed, "I hope you didn't touch it."

"Not a chance, *moi medvezhono*," Gaspar said with a laugh. "Only because I'm not interested in getting tetanus or the shot. It is about six, so my suggestion is we go for supper," he added. "Do you know where Gordy and Alexandria are? I haven't seen them since the big goof was trying to walk on the boardwalk."

"Not since then," Shelley answered. "But I did give him directions to the restaurant, so they could take off. This way he doesn't have to worry about us and more importantly, we don't have to worry about them."

"Good job," Gaspar smiled at his wife. "I don't think he is very interested in tagging along with us."

"Never was," Lyle agreed. "Although admittedly, he is three years younger than Shelley, so to a kid, seemed way younger," he finished, reaching to hug Mandy.

"I'm going to repeat what Shelley said earlier," Mandy said. "Did you touch anything?"

"Not on your life. But I disagree with Gaspar, because we saw an old fishing boat lying on its side in the reeds. Would you like to see it?"

After a few minutes of discussion, they all finally agreed to walk over to it. But when they looked at it, Mandy noted with some disappointment that the name had worn off.

"I agree with you, Mandy," Shelley said. "Seeing its name would give it some personality rather than just an old hull."

"It doesn't look too bad. Maybe it belonged to a resident when they had the big fire," Gaspar finally offered as they turned to go back to the truck.

"This place has so many mysteries and unanswered questions," Mandy said, wistfully. "I wish there was a book so we get answers."

As they pulled into the parking lot at the restaurant, Shelley exclaimed, "Look Gaspar, there's your dad's Bronco," at which they both broke out laughing.

As they made their way to the entrance, they had to explain what was so funny. The last time they were there, they had spotted his *papa*'s Bronco in the same parking lot.

"This time, Gaspar," Shelley said emphatically, "leave them alone."

When they opened the door, Gordy and Alexandria were just in front of them, standing there holding hands. Gordy was asking the hostess for a table "somewhere secluded."

Shelley quietly closed the door and said to the others, "We'll just wait here a minute and give them a head start."

She flicked a bug off Gaspar's shirt, then smiling, said, "Good," and casually entered the restaurant.

When the hostess approached them and asked, "A table for how many?" Shelley quickly responded by asking for a table for four, "somewhere over there," pointing in the opposite direction from where she saw her brother sitting.

The food was just as good as the last time. And they were all preoccupied with their meal and conversation when Gordy and Alexandria quietly slipped out.

As they finished their meal, Gaspar said, "With these long summer days, it's hard to imagine it's so late. I suppose we should head home. Both Shel and I have to work tomorrow. It sure has been fun spending the day together."

"I just had an idea," Shelley interjected. "Before you go tomorrow, I want to show you where Gaspar and I plan to build our house."

"Sure," Lyle said. "It won't take me long to pack and take the tent down. What about you, Mandy?"

"Easily," she replied. "That will be the topper to this jam-packed week. I think Joe mentioned we don't need to be on the wharf until noon."

"You could probably even be later than that," Gaspar replied. "In my observation, Joe usually has a meal before starting the trip back."

"I'm not sure you need to take the tent down. Just yesterday, Don told me they're expecting his brother and family for two weeks at the end of July. I imagine Shelley and I will camp with your *roditeli* while they are here."

"They are?" Shelley asked, startled. "I know my parents won't mind us staying there, but Lyle, can you check if they are okay if we leave the tent up that long?"

When they arrived back at New Petrograd, Mandy said, "I've been thinking, Shel, ever since we left the graveyard. If you ever learn more about those people, write me."

"That reminds me," Gaspar said. "As I was paying for our meals, I read an article at the cashier's desk about the boat we saw in the reeds. It was a crab boat, but I didn't have time to read the whole article before the waitress came to take my payment. I wouldn't mind learning more about it, next time we are up that way."

As they were driving back to Don's, Shelley commented, "Brad's your best buddy, isn't he?"

"He was when we were growing up. But you know, it seems I've become closer to Don. When Brad was home eighteen months ago, we found we really didn't have as much in common. I guess there is a big difference between someone who majored in construction and someone who majored in accounting."

"I didn't know you could major in construction."

"That's it—you can't, my love. I'm just an ordinary guy."

"But you are exceptional at being an ordinary guy, sweetie," she teased.

"I'm glad you think so," he said, flashing her a brilliant smile. He lightly kissed her nose, before opening the door and ushering her inside.

As soon as she heard the door open, Mary Ellen hurried from the living room. "Shelley, earlier today my *papa* was looking for you."

"Oh, okay. I'll stop by their place tomorrow. It is always a pleasure to visit with both of them."

"I can tell you now that it won't be so this time," Mary Ellen warned. "He was saying that they've been thinking for some time now that some books are missing. *Mama*-Marg categorized all the books in the lobby and when she found she couldn't locate some, they knew there was a problem."

"I think we also need to talk, Mary Ellen," Shelley replied. "I'm thinking I need to start interviewing all of the employees, because others have approached me with similar concerns."

"Anytime you want," Mary Ellen agreed. "It does sound like a discussion we need to have."

CHAPTER TWENTY-TWO

Security Check

The next morning Shelley was still very upset, but she kept the promise she had made to her siblings the night before. She was a little surprised that Gordy decided to come along. And even more surprised when, later in the day, Alexandria was not there to see him off. Lyle's raised eyebrows in her direction were the only indication that he was questioning Alexandria's absence, too. Shelley hoped nothing was wrong other than that she had to work, because she knew that they were in for a miserable trip if Gordy was out of sorts.

at the last minute, Gaspar came driving down the wharf to see everyone off. Amidst all the activity of everyone saying good-bye, Joe sounded the horn, which alerted the travelers to get on board the barge because it was ready to leave. As they were waving good-bye, Shelley moved closer to her mother, hugging her tightly. Despite her putting on a brave face, she was finding it tough to see her sons leave.

"Don't worry, Mom. It won't be long before we get a date for Lyle and Mandy's wedding and we'll all be planning a trip to Vancouver."

"You're right, honey. Besides, I am so glad I still have you."

Of course, everyone waved until the barge rounded the craggy point and then Gaspar drove Shelley back for her meeting with Phil and Marg Filipov.

"I really hate to see you so agitated, *moi medvezhono*," Gaspar commented, as he leaned over to kiss her before she got out of the truck. "Even last night, I knew how upset you were. You tossed and turned most of the night."

It was quite late in the afternoon when Shelley came home and saw Gaspar was already there. Immediately, he could tell she was in an even worse state.

"I'm just going to have to take more decisive action," she moaned, wringing her hands. "I just can't delay any longer. Mr. and Mrs. Filipov talked about the books that went missing but in addition, they told me they think money is gone. They were rather hesitant to say anything because they don't know for certain. I think I should go right now to meet with Mary Ellen to make some recommendations and discuss our options. I never used to get so upset when I worked in Vancouver, but somehow it just seems different here. It's more personal."

"I'm going to take you to the Borscht Kettle for supper when you come home," Gaspar remarked. "Other than fish and chips night, we haven't been for ages."

Despite how frustrated she felt, Shelley had to smile when she saw Peter Molodtsov talking to Bert while he worked. Peter was very expressive, his arms flailing around, and she wondered what story Bert was listening to. As she drew closer, she heard Bert say, as he sat back on his haunches, "Well son, my mother always says, 'History will be kind to me, for I intend to write it.' Actually, it really was a man named Winston Churchill who first said it. Do you know who he was?"

Intrigued now, Shelley stopped walking to listen for Peter's answer.

"Yes, he was the British Prime Minister during World War Two," Peter replied. "Do you know what my teacher told us? She said that he proposed to and was rejected by three women before he married his wife."

The last word coming out a little muffled, as by that time Peter was doing a cartwheel.

"You don't say. Well, I reckon that's an important fact for any young man to know."

"Mr. Bert, do you need me to bring anything else, or can I go play?"

"I think we've finished for today, Peter. I can sure use your help tomorrow though."

"All right," Peter said, as he happily ran away.

Noticing her, Bert stood up and said, "Evening, Mrs. Rosso. Peter and I are just finishing up another beautiful summer day's work."

"Good evening, Bert. I just overheard your conversation with Peter, and I just had to hear what Marianne had told him. What a little charmer he is. He's obviously enjoying working with you."

"Ah, he's great company for Miles and me. Never a dull moment with him around. Good night."

"I'm sure there isn't. Night, Bert." Her mood had turned a little lighter than it had been.

"Hi Shelley, I expected you a little earlier," Mary Ellen greeted her. "Not to worry, this is actually good timing because I've finished everything I set out to accomplish today. So, now my mind is clear to concentrate on our conversation. I'll just say good night to Nick and then we can be on our own."

Shelley could hear Mary Ellen exchanging a few words with him. A minute later, she came back in carrying two large glasses of water, one of which she offered to Shelley.

"There, now we are alone. How did your meeting go with my *roditeli*?"

"Worse than I anticipated. Only because Mrs. Filipova told me she thinks some money has also gone missing."

"Well, I can at least put your mind at ease about that. My *papa* raced over here to let me know they had made an accounting error. He was huffing, he was so out of breath. In fact, I made him wait until his heartbeat slowed down before letting him leave. I'm surprised you didn't pass him on your way here."

"Well, I am certainly pleased to hear that good news!" Shelley interjected with a sigh of relief.

Mary Ellen continued, "You certainly have a whole lot more experience than I do in investigating this kind of thing. What do you suggest we do?"

"I'm going to suggest a couple of things. I would like your approval to begin interviewing the staff—the new hires and Kevin's crew. On the way over here, I came across Bert and Peter working and having a delightful interaction, which I just had to stop and listen to. Since Bert is the one I least suspect, I am planning to interview him first."

"Isn't it the one you least suspect that turns out in the end to be the guilty person?" Mary Ellen commented. "At least, that is the way it always is in the movies."

"Well no, I just think he would be the easiest. When I think about it, the proper way would be to talk to them alphabetically. Can you get me a list of all their names? And do you know the names of the men on Kevin's crew?"

"I can print off the names of my employees for you in a minute. I'll talk to Kevin about his list tomorrow. Now, you said a couple of things. What is the other one? Or was it the two lists?"

"No," Shelley said, "the other thing is that there are three security cameras that I think you should consider. Even if we installed just one in the souvenir shop, it may deter anyone from trying to steal from other places. Especially once we have put up signage informing customers we have installed one."

"That is a great idea, Shelley. It is worth looking into," Mary Ellen responded. "I think you've made two brilliant suggestions."

"So now that you have agreed to it, Mary Ellen, I am going to contact a reputable security company in Vancouver. I am sure there are some in Prince Rupert, but I am more familiar with the businesses in Vancouver. To purchase several cameras would be extremely expensive, so I'm recommending that you review a few in different price ranges. I'll write to ask for some brochures."

"Once you get me all the details, it will become my top priority," Mary Ellen said, smiling.

"Okay, I will start looking into that in the morning."

"Appreciate you taking care of this," Mary Ellen said, as she was getting up from her chair. "Let me get the list of my employees' names for you. Don has suggested we go to the Borscht Kettle tonight for dinner, so I may as well walk you home."

"Gaspar said the same thing to me," Shelley said, as she accepted the list from Mary Ellen.

As Shelley stepped outside, Mary Ellen turned the lights out. "Did your siblings get away on time?" she asked congenially. "I'm sure they would have, because Joe's barge has run like clockwork for as long as I can remember."

"They did, but I guess that is why I'm so late. I had a busy morning and afternoon before I came to meet with you."

"I've had a busy day too," Mary Ellen answered. "Mandy sure is a joy, isn't she?"

"She is. I've waited forever for Lyle to propose. Who would have thought I would be married before he even got engaged?"

"By the way," Mary Ellen said, "I stopped at the teahouse at noon today and Alexandria appeared to be floating on cloud nine. She was talking about your brother to anyone who would listen. Buddy appeared to be a contented, captive audience, just eating his meal and taking it all in."

"He would," Shelley said with a laugh. "I'm glad to hear that. I was a little concerned when she wasn't on the wharf to see him off. Gordy is a little charmer. His problem is that he can't seem to commit to any one person for any length of time. But who knows, I heard her say she wants to move to Vancouver in the fall for school."

"I think in her mind, she has the most important thing organized—a boyfriend." Mary Ellen giggled and Shelley joined in.

"It will be interesting to hear what Mandy tells us Gordy's side of the story is," Shelley remarked, as they arrived at Don's house.

The next day Shelley started her workday as usual, but by noon she took a break, pulling out the sheet of paper Mary Ellen had given her. Then taking out her notebook with the various incidents listed, she began to write out questions. She paused often in her writing, putting some thought into them. *Where were you when?* She realized that didn't work because clearly, they would know they were being interrogated.

"I've left it too late," she thought, "but how could I have asked them any earlier?"

She started to work on another idea that seemed more friendly and casual.

"Hi, so what do you enjoy doing in your free time? Have you made any friends with other employees or village residents since you came?" Yes, that was better. The main point was to get them talking so that she could observe their reactions, their hesitations, or any signs of sweating or nervousness. She was so absorbed in what she was doing that when someone came up and spoke to her, she jumped and dropped her pen.

"Whoa, are you ever skittish today," Kevin said, laughing. "Jumpy like a bunny rabbit. Mary Ellen mentioned you wanted the names of my crew, but I won't disturb you."

"Thank you, Kevin. Don't worry, you're not disturbing me. I was just absorbed in what I was doing. How many men do you have working for you?"

"Actually, as I explained to Mary Ellen, it isn't quite as simple as you might think. I have about six guys now that stay here. But then, depending on what we are doing, I may have electricians, plumbers, even cabinet makers here for a few days, even a week. When they finish a job, they leave. Everyone comes from Prince Rupert, but some weeks, it is almost like a ferry run going back and forth. You see, rather than driving, which takes a lot of time, they just hop on a boat and come across."

"That's interesting," Shelley remarked, looking impressed. "Have you mentioned the boat to Mary Ellen? I mean, not related to your men working, but otherwise? It seems to me that would be a great way to have additional tourists come to the museum. Of course, it would mean we need another building on the wharf for an entrance booth, but that would be easy. In fact, the more I think about it, the more I like the idea. Even when Johnny Eagle Feather flies in, no one would have to meet the seaplane and take the guests to the front to purchase their tickets."

"No, I haven't mentioned it to her," Kevin replied tentatively. "Marianne and I have talked about it, I guess, because that's how we often sneak away. To do what you're suggesting, I would have to build the booth, but my workload right now is jam-packed, so unless that good man of yours is going to take on this project, it isn't going to get done for awhile."

"I see your point," Shelley said. "Okay, back to your men. I need only the names of the staff who are living here. I don't think I need the names of the men who are temporary, at least not yet. Does that make it easier?"

"Sure does. I have that list right here," he replied, handing her a rather smudged sheet of paper. As he took note of Shelley's expression, he excused himself by saying, "Apologies, Shel, that was all I could find to write their names on after Mary Ellen came to talk to me this morning. I might add that they're all great guys and I am sure you don't have to worry a thing about them. I work them hard enough during the day that they go home for supper exhausted, and I suspect they stay that way until the next morning."

"Thank you, Kevin. I really do appreciate your bringing this to me. I will start with the other list Mary Ellen gave me and then if I still haven't figured this out, I'll call your men in for questioning. You have given me some good tips, though. I imagine I will have to go to their homes in the evening. I really don't relish being around a worksite."

"You got that right," Kevin agreed, as he prepared to leave. "Time is short enough these days. Anyway, I'd best get back to work. See you around."

"Thank you again, Kevin. I'll talk to a Gaspar about building a booth on the wharf."

Later, while Gaspar and Shelley were enjoying a quiet evening at home with Don and Mary Ellen, Shelley casually commented, "You know, this afternoon when I was talking to Kevin, he told me something quite interesting. He mentioned his casual labour just take a boat between here and Prince Rupert. He even said that he and Marianne quite frequently do that themselves."

"Yes," Mary Ellen replied brightly, giving Don a shy look. "We do that too."

"You do? Here I was going to suggest something, but that's okay, I guess maybe it doesn't matter."

"I'm always up for suggestions," Mary Ellen said, as she perked up. "Please tell me."

"Well, after the man from the cruise company was here, didn't you tell me he was very impressed by everything he saw? But the company had concerns about the distance coming by road. They felt it would take too much time. The excursions are only a day."

"Yes, that is correct."

Then as the realization dawned, she gushed, "Shelley, you are brilliant! People could come via boat. Kevin could build a welcoming booth on the wharf... I am sure I still have Mr. Shaw's business card."

"Actually, the reason Kevin hasn't mentioned the idea before is because he doesn't have time to take on any extra projects right now," Shelley said. "He doesn't need to worry, though, because I volunteered Gaspar."

"What?" Gaspar asked. "Why did I know that was coming?"

Shelley began questioning the employees the following Monday. She had spoken to three of them so far without noticing anything suspicious in their demeanor that would cause alarm. On Saturday, when Bert's name came up on her list, and she almost had a jaunty step when she approached him.

"Good morning, Bert. Isn't this a lovely day?"

"Good morning, Mrs. Rosso. It sure is, a grand day. What's on your mind?"

"Well, I was just wondering if you could take a break so we can have a little chat."

"What for?" Bert spoke abruptly. "It doesn't matter what for because, no, I don't have time for a break. I have too much work to do."

"Then tell me when you might be in the vicinity of the teahouse and when it would be more convenient to take a break."

"I don't work with the flowers or do yard work at the teahouse. Miles does. Besides, here comes Peter with the tool I asked him to bring me. Sorry, but I must get back to work. Mother always says, 'Idle hands are the devil's playground.'"

"But—" Shelley began.

"People who just stroll around all day talking to other people have too much idle time on their hands. Thank you, Peter, that's just the one I needed. See, we can work around here without disturbing anything."

And Shelley knew her plans to talk to Bert had been defeated, at least for now. Dejectedly, she walked away.

That evening, when she was preparing supper, she relayed the conversation to Gaspar. He suggested that maybe next Friday they could invite Bert to join them for supper.

"Good idea, sweetheart," Shelley agreed. "If during the week I haven't already found the culprit, I'll invite him. Or better yet, maybe you should ask him. After all, everyone goes for fish and chips night. He is a funny little man, always with words of wisdom from his mother, but such a dear. I obviously caught him at a bad time today because he was so busy. Still, I must admit that although he was abrupt as usual, something about his attitude did trouble me."

Shelley did manage to interview Patricia Reynolds, whose name was next on the list. During their discussion, she was surprised to learn that she was seeing a Craig Southerland, who was working on Kevin's construction crew.

"So much for your friend's idea that he works his men so hard they go home too tired to do anything after their supper," Shelley exclaimed to Gaspar. "Apparently, they met at the wharf one night while stargazing. She also indicated that there are quite a few other friendships blossoming around our little village."

For much of the week, Shelley kept interacting with the guests. She really enjoyed seeing the tourists, their happy expressions a very good indication that they were all having a good time. It amused her to see the adorable twins accompanying their grandparents on their daily mingling with visitors. Olga and Madeline wore their *sarafan* dresses, with their bright aprons, while Bob and Matthew looked very dashing in their shirts with oblique collars and black *ports* which they had worn for the fashion show on Russia Day. Often, she stopped to watch them as they posed with the guests for pictures—when she herself wasn't being asked to pose.

The only downside to her week was when Gayle approached her on Wednesday to report some items missing from the teahouse.

On Thursday night, Gaspar let her know that Bert had happily accepted and would meet them at the Kettle.

"Thank you for arranging the appointment for me," Shelley sighed with relief. "I'm not quite sure I know how to handle this situation, but am trusting my experience will keep me in good standing with everyone."

"I'm sure you'll do fine," Gaspar said, kissing her. "I even spoke to Uri and asked him to reserve a table in a somewhat secluded spot."

"Anna and Uri don't take reservations, and I'm sure on such a busy night, they won't even consider it."

"That depends, my love, on whether you have a drippy tap that needs to be taken care of."

"You're sneaky," she commented, with a twinkle in her eye.

"Bert, glad you could join us," Shelley said, as Anna led them to their table.

"Well, only an old fool would turn down an offer for a free meal. And Bert Montgomery ain't a fool."

"Not advice from your mother, Bert?" Gaspar grinned.

"Nope, like I say, 'an old fool'."

"You're not old, Bert," Shelley assured him, as she sat down in the chair Gaspar had pulled out for her.

Their conversation during dinner was pleasant and light as they all shared stories from their varied pasts. When Shelley started casually asking Bert if he had made friends with anyone at New Petrograd, Bert responded, muttering something about Peter. Then when she asked him what kind of activities he did in his free time, he seemed to get defensive. And his spine seemed to become rigid.

Completely caught off guard by his reaction, Shelley was not sure how to proceed. "I understand that you enjoy working with Peter, but isn't there anyone you enjoy spending time with in your after hours, like Miles? What do you do in your off time?"

Then Bert set his knife and fork down. He looked across the table at her. "Do I need a lawyer for these questions, missy?"

Knowing not to pursue this topic any further for now, she quickly backed off. But it seemed the remainder of the meal had lost its light mood.

After their dinner with Bert, she had another meeting with Mary Ellen, when they decided to advise all the shopkeepers to keep an eye on Bert when he was in their stores.

The same evening, Mrs. Yusporova reported to Shelley that items were missing from the souvenir shop again. Then *Dedushka* Yusporov also reported some of the small wooden toys Martin had made were gone. It almost seemed like the thief was getting more brazen. This was troubling, because despite all her questioning, she was no closer to resolving this situation. Worse, she had no doubt there would be gossip amongst the staff.

Despite this unpleasant turn of events, as Shelley continued to speak with the casual labour, she was surprised how much she enjoyed feeling like a real police officer again. She was also enjoying learning much about their social life and appreciating the many good friendships that were forming.

On the Friday of the third week of July, she found herself once again in Mary Ellen's office dropping off the brochures on the security systems she had recommended. She took a few minutes to explain that one was stationary, the second one had a wider range, and the most expensive one rotated, covering every angle of a room.

In addition, she mentioned that although she didn't understand why Bert had gotten so upset, she felt certain he was not behind the thefts. Because after almost a week, all anyone reported to her was that Bert had bought toothpaste and a bar of soap at the general store. Then he left. He had not even visited any other stores. In fact, it seemed Bert went to work in the gardens, home for his supper, and to his room to read for the night.

"I feel in such a quandary because I just have Ned Turner and his girlfriend Beth Walker left to speak to. I really don't want it to be either one of them, because on several occasions Gaspar and I have gotten together with them socially," Shelley admitted to Mary Ellen. "But then again, I'm also reluctant to interview anyone from Kevin's crew and am hoping if I need to speak to any of them, Gaspar will accompany me. I guess this is one of the downsides of living amongst your suspects. I am still hoping it might be someone from outside."

After talking with Mary Ellen's remaining employees, she also felt quite certain that none of them was the culprit. She had to face the fact that the end of July was just a few days away and she hadn't reached her goal. Yet this thievery seemed to be going on right under their noses.

Slowly, she pulled out the sheet of paper with the names of Kevin's crew written on it.

CHAPTER TWENTY-THREE

Visitors from Ontario

"I can't believe it is almost August already," Shelley exclaimed one morning. "We'd better get ourselves organized to go camping at my mom and dad's. It's going to be fun, almost like a holiday!"

"You're right. Don still doesn't think it's necessary, but I'm not sure where he thinks he's going to put everybody. Besides, I think he'll have a much better visit with Brad and Cheryl without us being there. I did agree with him that we don't need to pack for a whole two weeks. Seeing as I usually go through a pair of overalls a day, it seems to be reasonable to stop at his house occasionally to get a clean set of clothing. What is Kevin doing? Staying at Don's?"

"No, he muttered something about my *papa* suggesting he could camp in their yard. Kevin seemed quite happy with that idea. I think he feels like he's going home, too."

"More like, happy he is in the same vicinity as Marianne," Shelley replied with a knowing smile.

"You could be right, my love," Gaspar agreed, giving her a kiss.

On Thursday, July 31, Brad, Cheryl, and their son, Eric, flew to Prince Rupert, and Don and Mary Ellen picked them up.

Although Mary Ellen hadn't really planned a big celebration for British Columbia Day, the living history museum was open on the Monday. The only special events were carnival activities for the children.

Beth, one of the summer students, had offered to paint their faces. Everyone was getting so much pleasure out of seeing the children's transformations into cats, zebras or butterflies, and even very beautiful and artistic abstract designs were emerging on their faces. Shelley had heard more than one adult wistfully sigh and wish they could get theirs done, too.

Beth's boyfriend, Ned, also had a huge audience of delighted, squealing children surrounding him as he artfully twisted balloons into dogs, cats, and even monkeys in a rainbow of colours. These were fun and amusing carnival crazes which even the local children were having a great time enjoying.

Shelley had earlier seen Matthew and Madeline in the line of children. She knew that if Madeline saw her, she would come running because she had lost all shyness towards her in the months since her arrival. She had to smile when she spotted Eric holding onto Cheryl's hand a few children down the line.

Alexander had to be talked into getting dressed up as Raggedy Andy to accompany his sister in her Raggedy Ann costume. But once outside, when he saw all the children's excitement as they clambered all over him, his demeanor changed and he embraced the experience.

As noon approached, the aroma of wieners roasting was heavy in the air. Soon the children began to walk around nibbling on their hot dogs, dripping with mustard and ketchup, much to the chagrin of many parents. The rest of the meal consisted of potato chips, pop, and popcorn. As Mary Ellen observed the children's happy faces, she realized the carnival day she had planned was turning out to be a big success.

As Shelley was observing all the activities going on around her, she stopped to admire the bright red faces of the poppies. These had replaced the chamomile and carnations, the featured flowers from last month. Earlier, Bert and Miles had planted gladiolas and poppies and they were now beginning to bloom. Mary Ellen had explained that she had chosen these flowers to feature in August as they were the month's birthday flowers. For contrast, Bert had added in daisies with the poppies. Shelley knew mums and asters were growing in her mom's greenhouse to be planted next. Bert had also recommended purple fountain grass for the fall. Although the museum would be closed after Labour Day, the grounds would continue to look lovely with all the flowers alongside the remaining wildflowers in the meadow.

Shelley was thankful that a friendly relationship had resumed between her and Bert after their disastrous meal at the Borscht Kettle.

Shelley had begun to interview the men from Kevin's construction crew. She had a limited amount of time to gain access to them because as the days were getting shorter, they were working longer hours. As well, she wanted Gaspar to accompany her. One of the names on the list Kevin had given her was Alexander Bolitchyn, but she really wasn't planning on talking to him as he was a local. She had no intention of questioning any of the people who lived there full time.

Besides, both Alexander and his sister had proved multiple times to be great assets to their community.

Alexandria was proving to be a great help at the teahouse. It was obvious she had a great rapport with all the guests. She also often entertained children of all ages on her own time. Alexandria was getting very excited about leaving for Vancouver in the fall to work on her travel and tourism diploma. Shelley had to wonder how much this excitement had to do with getting her education and how much was because Gordy would be there. She did know her brother was still interested in her, because Mandy had written several times saying Gordy often brought up Alexandria's name in conversations with her and Lyle.

Alexander was planning to go to Prince Rupert to further his education in one of the trades. This way he would be close enough to continue working for Kevin on weekends.

Rumour around the village was that they had both assured Mary Ellen they would be home in the summer for work. No one in the village doubted that Mary Ellen would be thrilled to hire them for the upcoming season.

Shelley often saw Cheryl out visiting exhibits, although she figured it was mostly to give little Eric a chance to expend some energy and enjoy his freedom. This gave Shelley a great opportunity to stop and chat with her and get to know her better. After a few mornings of observing her, she had a funny feeling Cheryl might be pregnant again.

Surprisingly, Brad often joined Don's fishing trips with his clients or sometimes even went fishing on his own. Gaspar and he were having a great week catching up, and she was happy for her husband. Gaspar told Shelley how happy Brad was being home, unwinding, and getting back to his family's roots. He was pleased Cheryl was enjoying time alone, entertaining herself, and certainly appreciated Shelley's growing friendship with her.

For the first week, Brad and Cheryl had stayed at Don's house, but they surprised everyone by announcing that for their second and final week they were moving over to the lighthouse station. And not in one of the buildings that comprised the guest accommodation, but in with Phil and Marg. His *mama* insisted and she was not going to have it any other way.

Shelley and Gaspar had decided to continue camping just in case things got too crowded at the lighthouse. Besides, they were enjoying this little reprieve from normal life.

Mary Ellen had organized a class reunion on the Monday afternoon of their second week. They had planned to hold it in the lighthouse garden. Bob and Olga had offered to prepare a meal at the Borscht Kettle, allowing Uri and Anna the time off to join their friends. Everyone was rather surprised how many of the old gang were still around. Much laughter was involved recalling their childhood antics. It was certainly a high-spirited event, especially as the partners entered into the experiences and general merriment.

At five o'clock, when the party was scheduled to move to the Kettle, Sandy stood with the rest, then gasped, grabbing for John's hand. She then cradled her stomach and moaned and it was obvious to the mothers in the group what was happening. Sandy's time had arrived.

"Don't let her fall," Cheryl cried, immediately springing into action. "I'm a maternity nurse. Brad, you need to get your mom to open one of the rooms at the station and go stay with our son."

"I'll go, and you stay, Brad," Don said, looking a little pale. "I will be quite happy to keep my nephew entertained."

Shelley stepped forward. "Just let me know how I can help, Cheryl. I used to work for the Vancouver Police and periodically, we would get a call when a woman had gone into labour."

"Thank you, "Cheryl said, in acknowledgement. "First we need to get my patient inside and lying down."

Everyone began coming in from the garden area, where Marg and Phil met them.

As she was unlocking the door to the large room, Marg said, "Thankfully, it is Monday and the museum is closed. It seems we are fully booked on the days we're open. This room will work best, not only because it is roomier than the others, but it has a complete kitchen too."

John and Nick half carried Sandy into the room and then John helped his wife onto the bed. Marg raced to the laundry room to get clean linens.

Meanwhile Martin had leapt into action, and said, "I'm going for Mr. Petrov, I mean Nikolai Petrov. He may even want you to move her to his first-aid room."

"I'll let Bob and Olga know what is happening," Phil calmly stated. "At least they'll understand why no one is coming to dinner."

"While you're at it, dear," Marg said briskly, "go and let Sandy's *roditeli* know, too."

"Right," Phil said. "I'll go as quickly as I can."

Anna spoke up then and said, "Don't worry, Mr. Filipov. Uri and I were just getting ready to leave to take over the restaurant for my *roditeli*."

"*Papa*," Marianne offered, "and I'll go let Sandy's *roditeli* know."

"Good thinking, sis," Mary Ellen nodded, for once seeming not to know what to do.

Gayle stated, "The rest of us should just leave. That means all of us—Kevin and Gaspar. Brad, you should come with us, too. You're just in the way here. Now that the emergency is over, what is most needed is privacy."

It was obvious Gaspar and Kevin were only too eager to go as they had been standing by the wall, clearly not knowing what to do.

"Honey, are you sure you'll be okay if I leave?" Brad inquired. "Are you sure you're okay?"

"Honest, I'm totally fine," Cheryl assured him. "This is what I do, honey. Just go with Gayle. As soon as this little bundle has arrived, I'll come and get you."

After the first shock was over, John dared to say, "Sandy always said she wanted me in the delivery room. I just didn't know how important it was to her until now."

Which made everyone smile, even Sandy, until she let out another gasp as yet another contraction occurred. Again, she reached for John's hand, holding on even tighter.

Bob and Olga arrived shortly before Nikolai did. Olga hugged her son and told him, "Darling, this is not the way we anticipated things would happen, but that doesn't matter. Our only concern now is how our dear Sandy is doing. We'll just wait on the couch, near but out of the way."

As Nikolai entered, he said, "What's this I hear about delivering a baby? All I can say is, I'm sure glad there's a qualified nurse available. I admit my services have only been needed a couple of times before when some of the ladies at work found themselves in a similar predicament. Before I came, I grabbed the supplies from the first-aid trailer I used last time I helped deliver a baby. I brought along the autoclave to sterilize the scissors and a clamp. You do have a kettle in here, don't you, Marg?"

"I do," Marg told him, as she bent down to remove it from the cupboard. "In fact, I should probably prepare a cup of tea. Because as we know, sometimes little ones arrive quickly and other times not. I remember my boys. Brad took his time—twelve hours, if my memory doesn't fail me. Whereas his brother arrived before I knew it." As she spoke, Marg was busy bustling around putting the kettle on. "Phil, I found some teabags here, but can you please go back to our place and get some milk and sugar? Then dear, I think we'd best go home and wait for word of the new arrival. We've done our part and they sure don't need an audience here. Be sure to call us if we can help with anything else, though."

They opened the door to leave, and could hear a long scream, which got louder the closer it got to them.

"Sandy-y-y, Sandy-y-y..." Sandy's *roditelimo* came into view, looking quite shocked.

Even though the Molodtsovs were rather reserved, Marg couldn't resist giving her a hug before moving away from the door.

Katerina was still calling, "Sandy-y-y-y," as she came into the room, her husband Roman right behind her.

Olga patted the spot beside her as she too stood to give her a hug. Then she exclaimed, "Marg just put the kettle on. Let me make a nice hot cup of tea for everyone. I'm sure that will help settle you."

"Oh, thank you. John dear, how is my girl?"

"I've never seen her better," he said with a reassuring grin. "She may not agree, though."

"*Mama*, I'm just fine," Sandy said, as she attempted to smile.

It was another six hours before a beaming John stood just outside the Borscht Kettle and announced he was the proud father of a baby boy, John Robert Petrov, Jr. Not that anyone was around at this late hour—eleven o'clock at night. So, it wasn't until the next morning that the residents of New Petrograd became aware of the new arrival.

In everyone's eyes, Cheryl had become a hero by helping with the birth. But she just brushed it off. "It was nothing. Something I do every day. Sandy did all the work."

Shelley had one last person to interview. She already felt instinctively that Craig Southerland, Patricia's boyfriend, was not the culprit. After her little chat with Patricia, she had often seen them about the village and just knew the tall, lanky man who often stopped to do a kindness for someone was not guilty of a misdeed.

Still, one day in the second week of August, she managed to speak to him. This wrapped up her investigation, and she had to admit she had drawn a blank.

Later, she was making her way to Mary Ellen's office when she heard a commotion. Turning, she saw Nikolai Petrov and a few of their guests hovering around a small boy who was crying. She walked over and suddenly seeing Cheryl, realized the child was Eric.

"I think he's managed to break his ankle," she heard Mr. Petrov say. "Most likely, the way this little man landed on it. Of course, I can't be sure without an X-ray. For that, you'll have to take him to Prince Rupert."

Shelley could hear Eric crying, "Don't like it here. Bad place."

"Hush, baby," Cheryl crooned. "We need to go with Great Uncle Nikolai to that building over there. He is going to tape up your ankle and give you something so you won't feel your 'owie'. While Great Uncle carries you over, we'll talk about all the fun we've had the last two weeks. Hasn't it been so much fun running around and not needing to be careful of cars? And wasn't it fun getting your face painted, and when *Dedushka* took you up the big tower? Do you remember what he called it?"

"Big house," Eric answered excitedly.

"What an awesome mom," Shelley thought, as she accompanied them to the first-aid facility. "I hope I can be just like her." She smiled at the secret that she hadn't even told her parents yet. Only she and Gaspar knew.

"What happened to Eric?" she asked.

"Oh, he was racing after some flying bug and tripped. Thank goodness we were going to Prince Rupert tonight anyway, as tomorrow we fly home."

"I am so sorry this happened, Cheryl, right at the end of your trip. It seems to me you have had a most enjoyable two weeks."

"We have," Cheryl replied. "I am so thankful my husband has had time to unwind with his family and friends. Plus, a little adventure thrown in with Sandy delivering John Junior. Brad and I have gone to visit them a couple of times since."

"First major injury I've dealt with all summer. Here I thought I was going to get away lightly," Nikolai said, looking up from taping Eric's ankle. "We can hope that it's only a sprain and this young man will be on his feet again real soon. There you go, sonny. I've taped it up, and I think your *mama* will just have to carry you."

Turning to Cheryl, he added, "I know you know more than

I about nursing, but I suggest he not put any weight on that foot until after it's been X-rayed. Would you like me to carry him over to my sister's for you, or call Phil?"

"I'll be fine. I'm sure when I get home, your sister will pamper him to bits."

As she brushed Eric's blond locks out of his eyes, she soothingly said, "How about we go to *Babushka*? I'm sure she'll find a book to read to you while Mommy finishes packing."

As Cheryl lifted and settled him in her arms, Nikolai took out a soft chocolate chip cookie and after asking Cheryl if Eric could have it and receiving an affirmative, offered it to him.

Cheryl intercepted it and said, "For this cookie, mister, I think you'll just have to wait a minute. Mommy doesn't want you to get cookie crumbs in her hair," which started the wailing again, worse than when Shelley had first seen him lying on the grass.

She once again had to admire Cheryl as she held firm to her words, carrying him but stopping occasionally to let him have a bite. Someone must have let Brad's parents know though because Phil was hurrying towards them. Shelley smiled at the scene they made as she turned to continue on her way to the office.

When Shelley walked into Mary Ellen's office, she explained, "I've interviewed everybody on the lists that you and Kevin gave me and feel confident our thief is not any of them. I feel at my wit's end, so my job will be to keep vigilant and on the lookout for suspicious behaviour that until now I've obviously overlooked."

At the conclusion of her meeting, Mary Ellen commented, "I've read all the brochures for security camera systems, and contacted the companies to get answers to the few questions I had. And I have decided on this one." She pointed to one particular brochure.

"This one is in the mid-price range. I've found you usually don't want to go too cheap, but then again, the most expensive design I often find to be overkill. I am disappointed, however, as it will be another few weeks before the order arrives and then we'll need an electrician to install it. In the meantime, I can at least have the printers make signs telling customers a security camera is onsite."

"Sounds good, Mary Ellen," Shelley said. "By the way, little Eric has fallen. Mr. Petrov thinks he may have landed in such a way that he broke his ankle. Right after our meeting, I'll drop by and see how he is doing."

"Oh, dear, I am sorry to hear that," Mary Ellen responded. "Don's brother's family have so enjoyed their visit. Eric is so adorable. He has been reveling in his *Babushka's* attention, and I often heard him calling my *Papa Dedushka,* which sure made *Papa* beam."

"Mr. Petrov said that's the first serious injury this season," Shelley said. "It would have been so nice to have escaped the season with—"

"—nothing a Band-Aid strip couldn't fix," Mary Ellen finished. "I'd go with you, but I want to order this equipment first. Now that a decision has been made, I don't want to wait another minute before acting on it. Let Cheryl know I'll come see her and Eric as soon as I'm able."

Later that evening, a small cluster of folks gathered around one of Don's boats as his whole family and Mary Ellen boarded it to go to Prince Rupert. Brad was holding his son tightly, a worried frown on his usually cheery face. They were planning on going straight to the hospital, and then spending the night in a hotel before going to the airport the following day.

Marianne would take care of the lighthouse accommodations so her *roditeli* could get away. As for Mary Ellen's job, well, as she had told Nick, "I can't imagine there being any emergencies that my right-hand man can't handle."

"There won't be," Nick assured her. "Nothing that I can't take care of on my own."

John and Sandy were there, proudly showing off their sleeping baby boy.

"So, sweetheart," Shelley said, "what do you say? Are we going to move home tonight or have one more night to camp out?"

"I must admit, my love," Gaspar responded, smiling at her, "I am quite enjoying camping. We do have a deadline, though, because I got a letter this morning from Greg. He and Barbara are planning to visit at the end of the month and into early September. I was going to recommend they become the next occupants."

"My parents will be thrilled to have them. But I have to ask—are you sure, because I'm not so certain Barbara would enjoying camping."

"You might be right, but she probably doesn't have a choice. Greg might be spoiling her, but I doubt if he is willing to go back and forth from Prince Rupert every day, and I'm quite sure all the rooms at the lighthouse station are already booked."

CHAPTER TWENTY-FOUR

Mystery Solved

Following her last meeting with Mary Ellen, Shelley resumed her normal duties. Admittedly, she was paying closer attention to all the businesses in the village.

A few days after Brad and Cheryl left, Bert approached Shelley. "Mrs. Rosso, I just want to apologize for my behaviour the night you took me to dinner."

"Oh, think nothing of it." Shelley laughed it off.

"No, I need to apologize. Mother always says, 'Honesty is the best policy.' Well, you see, I read a lot of cop and robber stories. When the police question the suspects, they always ask for a lawyer. I guess I just overreacted. But Mrs. Rosso, I would never think of doing anything wrong."

As he finished speaking, Shelley forced herself to choke down her laughter, so she would not hurt his feelings. Until his next words sobered her completely.

"Me and that doctor guy, we think the person you really should be questioning is that bus driver."

After a stunned silence, Shelley managed, "Who do you mean? Buddy Rasmussen?"

But Bert had just taken hold of his wheelbarrow and trundled away.

"Bert," she called, after his retreating back. Then shaking her head, she realized that for him, this conversation was finished. She walked over to the first-aid facility.

When she went in, Nikolai greeted her. "Well, Shelley, this is a pleasant surprise. What can I do for you? A Band-Aid strip or something more serious?"

"Something much more serious," she replied.

"Oh," he said, taken aback. "Do you have serious morning sickness?"

Her mouth fell open. "You know?"

"I wasn't certain until now, my dear. But I must admit I've been observing you and I've certainly had my suspicions. This will be our little secret—well, along with Gaspar and your *roditeli*."

"You are the first to know, other than Gaspar, that is. We haven't even told our parents yet. We plan to tell them this evening before we go back to Don's. So until the village gossips start spreading the word, please keep our secret to yourself."

"Trust me, I suspect your *mamas* already have an idea," Nikolai said, chuckling.

"I suppose so," Shelley responded with a smile. "Anyways, the real reason I came is, I was just talking to Bert. He mentioned something very strange and then typically for Bert, just walked away. I understand you both suspect that Buddy Rasmussen, the bus driver, might be behind the thefts."

"That's right," Nikolai said. "I was going to come talk to you myself this afternoon. I heard you've been questioning staff, and when I was leaving the other night, Bert and I got talking. Both of us have noticed some strange behaviour from the driver, and at other times I've seen his pants pockets bulging with weird shapes. When I think back, I've been noticing it for a long time. In fact, I'd say most of the summer. It wasn't until I heard about you doing some asking around that I started putting two and two together." He paused to let his information sink in. "Now, about that morning sickness... just keep a couple of crackers by your bedside to nibble on before you get up and that should settle your stomach."

"This news about Buddy comes as such a shock," Shelley finally got out. "But thank you so much for all the information. I certainly will pay close attention... to both."

As she left, she saw Bert watering the garden. He looked over and when he saw her, nodded. She returned the nod as she went past him.

Over the next week, when she saw the bus in the parking lot, she did try to observe Buddy. One afternoon when she saw him leaving the teahouse, she approached him to just start an idle conversation about the weather, and summer almost being over and after that, his plans. Anything she could think of to keep him talking.

She could see him getting fidgety, his body weight shifting from one leg to the other. Beads of perspiration formed on his forehead, even though it wasn't that hot outside, only around seventy-two degrees. And it was true, as he was shifting, she could see something bulky in his pocket. When she stopped him again a few days later and received much the same reaction, she decided it was time to act.

"I think our mystery is solved," Shelley announced to Gaspar at dinner that evening.

"What mystery?" he asked. "If you mean the thefts, I'm not sure I would label it that way."

"That's the one I'm talking about," she replied. "However, I'm not at liberty to discuss the case any further. I will talk to Mary Ellen tomorrow about what I've learned. Can you pass the salad, sweetheart?"

"Is that all you're going to say?" Gaspar said, a hint of exasperation in his tone. "Make a statement like that and then go on with conversation as if we were talking about how beautiful the day was? Which, I might add, it was, although you can feel the change as fall is drawing nigh."

"It is. I have worked far too hard on this case to have rumours floating around this village and have my suspect get away," Shelley responded seriously.

"Suspect, you say. You're not even going to tell me whether it's a man or a woman?"

"You're right, I'm not," Shelley agreed, smiling at Gaspar. "Tomorrow will be time enough for that when I meet with Mary Ellen. And before you get your hopes up, I won't be able to tell you anything until this is all resolved."

"I understand. I'll just have to be patient," he replied, still looking a bit dejected. "But now that you don't have to spend every spare minute interviewing people, especially during the evening, I have a secret of my own. But I'm going to share mine," Gaspar teased. "I think we should go for a walk. How about tonight?"

"Oh, that would be delightful, Gaspar. Have you and your dad been making the baby's crib?" Shelley asked eagerly.

"Honestly, Shel, after all this do you really think I'm going to give you a hint?"

"Please?" she pleaded.

"Not on your life. How about I serve us some dessert?" he

finished with a grin, as he got up, planting a quick kiss on her cheek.

"Okay, I get it. What you're really saying is, 'Two can play at this game'."

"That's right," he replied smugly. "In fact, if I were Bert, I'd be saying '*Mother* always says' so."

The air was lovely as they walked past the many sunflowers growing beside the buildings in the business section. Shelley couldn't help but think they were showing signs of getting ready for the harvest, another indication that autumn was fast approaching. She felt somewhat surprised that Gaspar was going in this direction. Usually when they went for a walk, he would lead her to the trailhead near the gardens at the lighthouse station.

When Gaspar led her past all the shops and continued towards his parents' place, she knew. "I was right. You *are* working on the baby's crib." She quickened her step.

"You think so, do you?" Gaspar laughed. "Okay, go ahead. Go to my *roditeli* and see."

When she arrived, she barely knocked on the door before entering, then said to Tony, who was coming to the door, "Gaspar said he finished the crib."

"He did?" Tony replied questioningly, looking at his son, who was now standing in the doorway smiling.

"Please excuse my out-of-control wife, *Papa*. I told her I have a surprise and she has got it into her head it's about the crib."

With amused looks, they both watched as Shelley walked briskly in the direction of Tony's workshop. Daria came out of the kitchen, curious to see what the commotion was about. After a few minutes, they heard a loud grunt coming from the direction of Tony's workshop.

Turning to his *mama*, Gaspar jokingly asked, "*Mama*, do you have a scarf that I can blindfold my wife with? We only told you about the baby the other night. How could we have the crib made already?"

"Pregnancy brain," Daria said with a knowing nod, ignoring her husband and son's puzzled looks. "Now that you are here, though, why not stay and have a cold drink with us?"

"Pregnancy brain, huh?" Gaspar repeated. "I'd better warn Don that my wife is going to act weird on occasion."

"You have the right idea, son. She is liable to become teary-eyed or start crying at the slightest provocation," Daria said, giving him a hug. As she handed him a scarf, she said, "Just be kind and patient with her. I am sure going to tell June about this little episode, though," Daria admitted. "She will get such a kick out of it."

"Maybe we'll come back," Gaspar said, as amidst much sputtering from Shelley, he blindfolded her and led her back outside.

Once they arrived at their land, he took the blindfold off, enjoying her shocked look as she gaped at the foundation and lumber piled beside it.

"Oh," she said, her eyes brimming with tears. "Oh, Gaspar! You and Kevin are starting to build our home."

"Actually, Kevin is still pretty busy, but he did find time the other day to get his crew to dig the trenches, make the forms, and ask his cement driver to pour the foundation," Gaspar answered, pleased. "The lumber, well, I decided I couldn't wait any longer. I can't have my son living in a tent, or moving into Don's, now, can I?" he asked her in a very serious tone.

"Your son, my dear, won't be coming for another few years," she replied, just as seriously. "My daughter, however, will be arriving in a little under six months."

Laughing together, they joined hands and walked back to Tony and Daria's for the promised cold drinks.

CHAPTER TWENTY-FIVE

Labour Day Weekend

When Mary Ellen and Shelley got together, Mary Ellen asked, "What do you think we should do now? I'm right about one thing—he is probably the last person I would have suspected. Anyway, what do you suggest now?"

"If I may, I am going to use your phone to call Corporal Freedmont of the Prince Rupert RCMP detachment. I sure hope he is still stationed there," Shelley answered. "I plan to invite him to visit on Wednesday. It may take a few days of observation because, as both of us are aware, although the thefts occur most days, they certainly don't happen every day. Plus, they are not always in one place so he and I will have to cover the entire grounds. I will also discuss with him the need to be in plain clothes. I'm sure he will already assume that, but I want to make certain. Of course, he will need to stay over, but I certainly hope everything can be wrapped up by the end of the Labour Day weekend. It is really our last chance to catch our thief. My concern is that the lighthouse station might already be booked up for the entire weekend." Shelley gazed at her. "Your task is to put some thought into how you want to handle it now that we know who the culprit is."

"I sure hope you're going to help me with that, because I have no idea what to suggest," Mary Ellen replied. "What about his wife if he goes to jail? She was so nice."

"I can ask Corporal Freedmont to bring information on what sentences were given to other people who committed similar crimes," Shelley advised. "I'm sure you will find this information most helpful. We have to file a complaint. We can't just do nothing. What if he's stealing from shops all along his bus route?"

"You're right," Mary Ellen said unhappily. "But Shelley, I do have to end our meeting, as I need to get back to making the final arrangements for the Labour Day events. I still have a lot of work to finalize the details and I am running out of time."

"Absolutely," Shelley agreed. "I've said all I need to anyway. I'll be out of your hair as soon as I make my call to Corporal Freedmont."

"I will take you to another room to give you more privacy."

As they emerged from Mary Ellen's office, Nick turned in his chair and remarked, "So, Shelley, you got your man. I knew you would."

"Nick, please, please keep this to yourself," Mary Ellen pleaded. "You are certainly right, I had faith in her as well, but all Shelley's work could be for nothing if anything gets out."

"Mary Ellen is right, Nick. Gaspar tried to worm it out of me last night at supper and I wouldn't even give him a hint," Shelley said, smiling. "We should have known not to talk here. The walls have ears."

Shelley did put through her call. Corporal Freedmont was very surprised but pleased to hear from her. But he did have disappointing news as he mentioned that they were close to wrapping up a case they had been working on for months. Therefore, they could not spare anyone until the end of the week. He also mentioned he was aware New Petrograd had become a living history museum. But with all the extra work required to 'get their man', he had not been able to get away all summer.

Shelley, of course, let him know she understood. Secretly, she was very disappointed because it meant he would be here during the long weekend, and she would have preferred him coming at a less busy time. He informed her he would be coming and another of his colleagues would accompany him, a Constable Denis. The conversation ended with him saying he would certainly have someone look up information on similar cases and bring that with him.

Greg and Barbara flew into Prince Rupert on the last Friday in August. Don loaned Gaspar one of his boats to pick them up. Seeing as it was Friday, their visit began with fish and chips night. Sitting at the table along with Gaspar and Shelley were Kevin and Marianne, plus both the Palmer and Rossi couples. Throughout the meal, Greg was received with welcoming hugs as not only Gaspar's friends greeted him but many of the other village folk. Later in the evening, Greg's closest friends retired to their latest haunt, the lighthouse gardens.

As they were leaving the Borscht Kettle, Shelley smiled at Gaspar. "Sweetie, I know I'm fading fast, and I have some pretty busy days of work ahead of me. I think I will just go home now, but that doesn't mean you shouldn't enjoy your company."

'I'll just see you get home safe, *moi medvezhono*," Gaspar

said, as he wrapped her in his arms. "Then I will rejoin everyone."

"Promise?" she said, smiling up at him.

"Promise."

Despite all the Labour Day celebrations going on around her, Shelley's only thought on Saturday morning was to meet Corporal Freedmont and Constable James Denis when they arrived on the RCMP boat around nine-forty-five. They had settled on that time knowing Mary Ellen would have all the other visitors preoccupied with her opening address.

"Good morning, Corporal. Welcome back," Shelley greeted him when they disembarked and tied up. "I hope the case you were working on was completed to your satisfaction. I can't thank you enough for coming. I know your time will now be busy with all the follow-up paperwork."

"That is true, but I admit that your case seems like, well, almost a reprieve from the one we just finished up," Corporal Freedmont responded, smiling at Shelley. "I brought the paper along so a little later today you can look at the write-up. As well, I certainly appreciate what you were saying the other day that these are the last few days before your museum closes for the season. I just hope we can be as successful for you as we were on our other case."

"Before too much time passes, allow me to introduce to you Constable Peter Unger."

Shelley started to speak, but Corporal Freedmont cut her off.

"I know I told you Constable Denis was coming, but, we ran into a little problem. I contacted the proprietors of the lighthouse station like you suggested, and like you also suspected, they were all booked up. Constable Unger and his family were already coming here this weekend to meet some friends and had booked a large room. It seemed to be the only way we could arrange everything."

As Shelley shook hands with Constable Unger, she said, "You were here before with another couple. I remember because my husband and I were having supper at the Borscht Kettle that night and I mentioned to him that you looked like a cop. Welcome. Who would have ever thought you would be here now on official duty?"

"You're right, Miss Palmer," Constable Unger said. "I was having dinner with another couple, but that is only because we left our children with Alexandria in the lighthouse garden. Last time, we were just here at the same time as the other family, but this weekend, we had arranged to meet them again. That is why Corporal Freedmont suggested I come instead of Constable Denis."

Shelly was still smiling at the words Miss Palmer. "Oh my, I suppose Corporal Freedmont told you they asked me to come back and investigate this situation, like the last time. The truth is, I live here now. I married Gaspar Rosso a few months ago. You will remember him, Corporal Freedmont, from the skeleton case. Come to think of it, Kevin Thompson also lives here now, and Greg Ramsey and his wife Barbara just arrived yesterday for a visit."

"Yes, Shelley, I remember them well. It will be good to see them again," he responded.

"I imagine by now that Mary Ellen has finished her welcoming address," Shelley continued. "So, we should take your luggage and leave it at the lighthouse station like any other guest, and then go to the office to meet with her."

They strolled down the wharf and the butterflies that had been floating in Shelley's stomach all decided to take a nap. They completed their first task with Phil, who promised to put their luggage in the room Peter's family had reserved, and then they went to meet Mary Ellen.

"Nice to meet you, Mary Ellen," Corporal Freedmont greeted her. "Allow me to introduce Constable Peter Unger. As promised, I have brought along some files of other sentencings for similar crimes. Basically, you will see that the offender is usually charged a fine, to a maximum of a thousand dollars, and ordered to do community service."

"I like that sentence already, except a thousand dollars seems a little steep," Mary Ellen responded. "I don't think the things he stole would add up to that."

"I would advise that amount because it suits this situation," Constable Freedmont answered her. "It could have meant the future of the museum. Those details can all be worked out to the satisfaction of all parties, though. For right now, the biggest question is, how do you want us to handle things? When we arrest him, do you want us to use handcuffs, or..."

"Oh, no," Mary Ellen gasped. "I will say only if it becomes absolutely necessary, like if he is resisting you. Wouldn't you agree, Shelley?"

"I do. Also, Mary Ellen and I discussed earlier that instead of arresting him, you take him to the first-aid facility. That way, anyone seeing the incident would just assume he's been injured. Then Mr. Petrov can get Mary Ellen and me to come."

"Mr. Petrov," Corporal Freedmont frowned. "Isn't he the acting sheriff?"

Shelley started to giggle before saying, "Not that Mr. Petrov. His brother Nikolai moved back from Trail and is now handling our first-aid requirements."

"The Bob Petrov you met a couple of years ago is now wandering around with his wife and grandchildren wearing authentic Russian clothing. I am sure you will see them as you begin your surveillance around the village."

Constable Unger, who had been sitting quietly through the discussion, now broke into a brilliant smile, "I remember them. Bob and Olga were very helpful to us on our first visit."

"Now that this is settled," Corporal Freedmont said, "I think we should get outside and begin our surveillance."

"I know you are here on RCMP business," Mary Ellen said as she was rising from her desk, "but before you leave, I would just like to inform you of the special activities that we have for the Labour Day weekend. Throughout the summer we had some special events. In recognition of Russia Day, I decided to bring back the assortment of Russian dishes which you will find at six locations throughout the museum. In recognition of Canada Day, we had Johnny Eagle Feather bring back some Indigenous carvers, who are set up with their displays down at the wharf. For the August long weekend, we had children's face painting and balloon animals. These were a big hit amongst the young people and so we were happy to bring both of these back. At two of our events, we had a dance on the evening of the opening day, but for this weekend we have planned a dance for every evening. We have invited musicians from Prince Rupert to provide live music. It seems our plans are quite simple for a grand finale, but I am trusting everyone will enjoy themselves with everything we have planned."

"I can tell you right now that my son will be all over this," Peter said with a laugh. "It won't surprise me if he already has something painted on his face. I don't doubt that everyone will have a good time. I sure know we did at your opening weekend. We met another family here and our children have stayed in contact with them all summer. The other couple are also here this weekend."

"I appreciate your giving us this information, Mary Ellen," Constable Freedmont said with a smile. "Peter, it is time you and I got to work."

By five o'clock Saturday, Shelley hadn't heard anything from the RCMP officers, but saw Corporal Freedmont walking to dinner with Constable Unger and his family. She recognized another family walking with them. Corporal Freedmont joined Mary Ellen and her sister, plus Don's household, including Kevin. Barbara and Greg arrived partway through the meal, and were invited to join them.

On Sunday by midafternoon, Shelley was enjoying a casual conversation with Marianne at the day-care in the schoolyard. Two more days until another school year would begin. She looked up to see Nikolai striding purposefully across the lawn, heading towards her, and somehow instinctively knew that he was looking for her. Out of the corner of her eye she also saw her husband and Barbara walking towards her.

"Please, not now," she thought, as she hurriedly finished her conversation with Marianne, and began walking in Nikolai's direction.

"There you are, Shelley," Gaspar called. "We were looking for you."

It sounded like an echo as Nikolai called almost the same words, except he added four little words at the end that made all the difference. "There's been an incident."

She gave a little wave of apology to Gaspar and Barbara as she said, "I'm sorry, it seems like I'm needed elsewhere. I will catch up with you later." She only hoped she sounded sincere as she joined Nikolai.

As they walked away, Nikolai said, "Constable Unger just came into the first-aid facility with someone a few minutes ago. I'm going to see if I can find Mary Ellen. We'll meet you there as soon as possible."

"Thank you for coming to find me," Shelley said. "I don't relish the next few minutes, but neither was I enjoying the situation being unresolved."

"Well, I understand Constable Unger caught him red-handed in the souvenir shop," Nikolai said. "I've left them both in my facility, but could you look for the Corporal? Do you have any idea where Mary Ellen is?"

"I'm sorry, I don't, but my suggestion is to try her office first. If she isn't there, Nick will know where she can be found."

"Sounds like a reasonable idea," he agreed. "I'll catch you later."

"Okay," Shelley agreed, "but about the Corporal..."

"Good luck, my dear." Nikolai laughed, as he turned and walked away.

Shelley stood a few minutes realizing she had no idea where to begin looking for Corporal Freedmont, and wishing she had a radio, or a walkie-talkie, or a pager, anything. She had walked towards the crossroads when her eyes caught sight of a man striding purposefully across the grounds heading towards the first-aid facility. That's Corporal Freedmont, she thought and quickened her step, catching up to him a few feet from the first-aid facility.

Corporal Freedmont's face had already taken on a stern look. "Constable Unger just paged me."

"Here I was wishing I had a pager. I should have realized you and Constable Unger would."

As she finished speaking, Shelley and Corporal Freedmont entered the first-aid facility, but even before she opened the door, she could hear Buddy expressing his remorse. As soon as he turned and saw her coming in, his face fell and he broke down.

"Oh, Buddy," she cried. "Why?"

"Shelley, I am so mortified. I don't know what came over me this summer. It all started when I helped move the items from the souvenir shop to the general store on Russia Day. I would come with my busload twice a week and wander around. I guess after a while, I found it got to be routine and monotonous. My mind went back to moving the items on Russia Day and I don't know why, but the solution to my boredom seemed to be that I got a bad case of sticky fingers. It started off as a challenge and then it got out of control. Then I just couldn't stop myself. I would leave and drive home and tell myself, never again, and the next time I came, it would happen all over again. I am almost glad I got caught by Constable Unger today."

He had stolen from them out of boredom? Somehow that seemed worse than if he had needed the money from selling the pieces himself.

"Well, Buddy," Shelley finally said, "I don't think you should say more until Mary Ellen gets here. We don't want you to have to repeat everything."

"What is Pearl going to do to me? What is my boss, Jack, going to say?"

"It's a little late to be asking those questions now, don't you think?" Corporal Freedmont said. "Maybe if you had asked them sooner, you might have stopped what you've been doing."

A few minutes later, Mary Ellen came in. Buddy turned to her and said, "I am so ashamed of myself. I am guilty of stealing multiple times. I took things every time I came, so I've lost track of exactly where and what I stole, but I know they were from the souvenir shop and the tea house."

Corporal Freedmont spoke again. "Mary Ellen, Buddy has already explained to us what happened and why he did this. When he gets to your office, Constable Unger and I will have him write an official statement."

Then, sheepishly, looking down at his feet, Buddy added, "Oh yeah, and I took chips and chocolate bars from the general store but I ate those on the way home. I do have all the other items piled up in my garage. I can return them, if that will make a difference."

"Restitution will help your case," Corporal Freedmont said. "The magistrate might have a slightly better opinion when it comes to sentencing. But don't count on that. But before that, I need to discuss with Mary Ellen what her decision will be. Shelley, would you like to come with us and leave Constable Unger here to watch Mr. Rasmussen? Is that okay with you, Nikolai?"

"Absolutely," Nikolai, replied. "I suggest we move him into the back room, so if something comes up, I will still be able to attend to my duties."

"Certainly, I would like to come," Shelley said, as she opened the door for them all to leave.

When they returned to her office, Mary Ellen closed the door behind them and said, "Since this is not a public investigation, do you think it would be possible for the village to come up with an appropriate punishment?"

Corporal Freedmont sighed and said, "I suppose that might work, but since it's been going on all summer, I'd like to see you file a complaint. Let me think about it for a few minutes. Shelley, what are your thoughts?"

"I still agree with what we all discussed when you first arrived," Shelley stated. "I also like the comment Mary Ellen just made and am going to suggest that he make a formal apology to the entire community."

"Yes," Mary Ellen said, nodding. "I feel comfortable with that."

"All right, if that's your decision," Corporal Freedmont said. "Mary Ellen, I would like to use your phone to call Constable Unger and ask him to bring Mr. Rasmussen over here."

Mary Ellen nodded in assent as she dialed the number and handed the receiver to him.

"Nikolai, can you please ask Constable Unger to bring Mr. Rassmussen to the reception area where Mary Ellen's office is?"

As they entered the office, Nick said in shock, "Buddy, you are so pale and your hands are shaking. Are you all right?"

"I'm guilty of all of it. I am so sorry!" Buddy blurted out, as tears welled up in his eyes again.

"What do you mean?" Nick asked. "I don't understand." Corporal Freedmont stepped out of Mary Ellen's office, and beckoned to Constable Unger, ushering them in, and leaving behind a puzzled Nick as the door closed.

Constable Unger motioned for Buddy to sit down. As Buddy started to do that, he looked around at all the stern faces, noticing only Mary Ellen had a kind expression.

Corporate Freedmont said, "Before I begin, Mr. Rasmussen, would you please look at me and not that spot of spilled coffee on the floor? I must say, you are one fortunate man. Mary Ellen has chosen not to press charges and send you through the court system."

Buddy lifted his eyes, for the first time with a look of relief on his ashen face.

The Corporal then continued, "Do you truly understand that you have deeply wounded and betrayed the residents of New Petrograd? From what I understand, they took you in and have treated you with utmost kindness. Are you ashamed of how you have behaved?"

"Sir, you cannot imagine the shame I feel right now," Buddy replied brokenly.

"Before we continue, Mr. Rasmussen," Corporal Freedmont said as he handed him a pen and a writing pad, "please write out a confession statement and tell us everything, to the best of your recollection, about what happened after Russia Day."

It took a good twenty minutes. After Buddy completed it with his signature, Corporal Freedmont went on, "Mary Ellen has decided that you will pay a one thousand dollar fine, you will serve five hundred hours of community service, and give a formal apology to the entire community."

"Five hundred hours!" Buddy gasped.

"Mary Ellen has calculated it at twelve hours a week for nine months—from now until May, when their living history museum reopens."

Buddy stammered, "I appreciate that. I—I should easily be able to do it on my days off. Thank you, Mary Ellen and Shelley, for pardoning a man like me."

"Mr. Rasmussen, that is assuming you still have a job with the bus line," Constable Unger said, sternly. "You may be looking at some months of unemployment. Who is going to hire you after all this comes to light?"

Buddy turned white again. “If I lose my job, there goes the new living room furniture Pearl wants to buy. She is going to be really mad at me.”

“I can send a letter to your boss explaining our position in this matter, Buddy, if you think that would help,” Mary Ellen suggested.

“I would not suggest you do that, Mary Ellen,” Constable Unger said. “Mr. Rasmussen must truly realize that he has done wrong. If I had anything to do with his sentencing, in addition to a formal community apology, plus the restitution of the stolen goods, I would take him around to each individual he stole from and have him apologize to them directly.”

Corporal Freedmont said, “Shelley, Mary Ellen, if you don't have anything more to say, I will have him give me all his contact information and then he is free to go.”

Buddy slunk outside into the late afternoon just as he saw Nick lock the entrance.

After they left, Constable Unger heaved a sigh of relief. “Well, I guess for the rest of the weekend and the drive home, I am once more just Peter. Feels good. Corporal Freedmont, ladies, if you don't require my services, I think my next task is to find out where my wife and children have gotten to.”

“Thank you so much, gentlemen, for all your assistance.” Mary Ellen sighed with relief. “Although I am not looking forward to the next step, I am glad to have this behind us, especially before we close our doors for the season.”

“And I become unemployed,” Shelley agreed, as the men left.

“Pardon?” Mary Ellen exclaimed, looking at Shelley. “It would seem to me our little meetings aren’t quite finished yet. Could you perhaps come to my office tomorrow? There is something else we need to discuss.”

"Sure, but I just assumed tomorrow when the gates close that my job would be finished until next season," Shelley answered, mystified.

"We need to talk about when we're going to put those security measures in place to ensure this doesn't happen again next year. Cameras, a security guard... we can't count on Bert's powers of observation all the time, that's for sure."

"I agree," Shelley said, nodding. "As part of Buddy's community hours, you may want to include him in these discussions. After all, he learned where our weak points are this summer."

On Sunday evening, the casual labourers slowly drifted away from the dance early to attend a farewell party given in their honour at the teahouse. As they were heading home afterward, Shelley drew Gaspar's attention to two figures walking hand in hand down to the wharf and mouthed the words, "Patricia and Craig."

Many of the summer students had indicated to Mary Ellen that they would be pleased to return the following season. "If this new boat idea being talked about materializes, I am quite sure you can come and visit everyone before then," Mary Ellen had said in invitation.

Shock reverberated through the village for a week after the identity of the thief was revealed. Many people flooded Mary Ellen's office relaying stories about all the good deeds Buddy had done. At times, Mary Ellen felt her head was spinning as she listened to their comments, and had to remind herself of all that had taken place, and all the worry he had put them through, starting with the first conversation she'd had with Shelley months ago.

One person from the seasonal staff who had agreed to stay for now was Bert, because there was still lots of work to do to prepare the gardens for winter. Mary Ellen had also assured him that she was certain she could find other things to keep him busy around the village until spring.

But as he told Shelley, "I'm not the least bit concerned, because I can certainly entertain myself reading the fifteen Tony Hillerman mysteries that Mary Ellen presented me with, in recognition of the little bit of help I gave you in solving the crime. As Mother always says, 'All's well that ends well.'"

EPILOGUE

After Labour Day and the school year began, life in New Petrograd reverted to a semblance of normalcy. Well, as much as that word fit into anyone's life anymore. It may have in the past, but clearly it no longer did.

The closest thing to routine that the villagers of New Petrograd knew was when Joe's barge arrived weekly at almost the exact same time. In fact, many of the old-timers bragged they could set their clocks by its arrival. Recently even Joe had shaken the village by announcing he would be retiring at the end of the current month. None of his crew wished to take over the route, choosing instead to take on new jobs. This meant that from now on, his customers would have to come up with alternative arrangements for their shipping requirements.

Joe had kindly inquired into their options regarding the mail. He had learned there was only one possibility and that was to have it delivered to Prince Rupert, and picked up from there. This was certainly a feasible arrangement for New

Petrograd, however, for places like Hartley Bay and farther south, it was going to cause a lot of hardship.

The day after Joe dropped his bombshell, during fish and chips night everyone was voicing their apprehensions and concerns over what would happen to them now.

As Kevin listened, an idea began to form in the back of his mind. It began as a passing idea, but as the evening wore on, he visualized everything more clearly. Could he finance a boat that could be operated between Prince Rupert and New Petrograd? And maybe even go as far south as to include Hartley Bay? He wouldn't plan on going farther, but who knew what the future might bring? Of course, he'd have to hire someone to operate it for now, because he had so many jobs to finish—a list as long as Santa's.

He knew, of course, that he would have to do some research into costs and such. This did not trouble him because really, he would be using the same basic principles as costing any other job. He wouldn't mention it to anyone except perhaps Mary Ellen—she might be able to help him put a concrete plan together. He certainly wasn't going to say anything to Marianne until he finalized his decision. He needed to keep his nose to the grindstone, working on the construction of the casual staff residence.

He was just starting to think about his current workload and what he had to do the next day when Marianne startled him out of his reverie by snuggling up to him. "Are you feeling okay?" When he looked around, he saw several concerned gazes.

"Sorry," he said apologetically. "Long day, I guess."

"Long day in the rain," Gaspar concurred. "The overcast skies alone are enough to get a man down. It sure isn't like the dry cold you're used to, Kevin." Even as he spoke, he thought,

Don't kid me, my friend. You have something else on your mind. Aloud, Gaspar said, "I sure am glad my *papa* and I have done so much work on our house. We have a good start on the framing. By the time it starts to snow, I intend to have it dried in so we can work on finishing the interior without the elements being a factor. It sure doesn't hurt that Alexander comes home most weekends and is giving us a hand."

Gaspar wrapped his arms around Shelley. "My love goes to my mother's kitchen almost every day to learn some new Russian dish. Sometimes her *mama* goes also. It always sounds to *Papa* and me like quite the hen party. But I'm not complaining, because we benefit from their hard work when Shelley brings her latest creation for our afternoon coffee break. As much as I regret saying this, I may have to suggest she stop, because it's getting mighty slippery around our worksite. We sure can't afford her doing any acrobatics." He looked up at Don. "So, Don, I've talked a bit about what's happening in my world. What's happening with you these days?"

"I guess my main focus now is hunting," Don admitted. "Also, when the fishing season ended with the chum run, Uri helped me take his old fishing boat, *Neptune of the Seas*, out of the water and put it into dry dock. Uri is going to help me do a minor overhaul and give it a fresh coat of paint over the winter. Mary Ellen and I were talking the other night and we both feel quite satisfied that this first season went so well, with really not many hiccups."

"Don, seriously—not many hiccups?" Shelley and Mary Ellen cried in unison.

"That's not what I said at all, Don," Mary Ellen added. "What would you call all the stealing that went on this summer? I do have to admit I am pleased because Buddy has taken full responsibility for his crimes. He paid his fine on time, and is doing well accomplishing the tasks I've assigned to him and in a timely manner. And most important, he has still kept up his usual cheerful demeanour!"

"Sorry, sorry," Don said, holding up his hands in mock surrender, turning to Mary Ellen to plant a light kiss on her nose. "Yes, I know the thefts plagued you all summer. All of us were pleased to have these issues resolved before the season ended. So, Gaspar, now I've resolved that issue with your wife and my girlfriend, back to what I'm doing now. As soon as I took my boats out of the water, I needed to get my hunting gear out, as I already had bookings coming in. It has been nice getting outdoors in these cooling temperatures and watching the Canada Geese flying overhead, honking their good-byes as they head to warmer climates. The bookings started with black-tailed deer, but these last few days, I've also had a few clients interested in moose hunting. I'm thinking of taking a drive this Saturday to do some scouting. If you and Kevin are interested in coming with me, just let me know by Friday."

"Um, Don," Anna said, as she cleared the table of the last few dishes. "This is Friday night. In fact, it's ten minutes before closing time."

"Thanks, Anna," Don said, sheepishly. "Okay guys, I guess you need to tell me now."

Everyone sitting at the table got up then and started trickling out into the darkening night.

"I'll let you know in the morning, Don," Gaspar said as he and Shelley were leaving. "It sounds interesting, but the truth is, I'm not sure if I can take the time off. I might manage it for a few hours, but certainly not a whole day."

"I have to agree, Don," Kevin said. "If you don't mind, I'll also let you know in the morning." He smiled at Marianne and reached for her hand.

As Don and Mary Ellen left, he thought, It's fine going scouting on foot, but I need to get my stock back. And a dog. New Petrograd in all these years has never had a dog. Just one more thing they need to learn about.

"Now you're the quiet one," Mary Ellen teased, as he walked her home. "Penny for your thoughts, love?"

"I have to ask you a serious question, Mary Ellen."

"Yes?" She turned to look at him, with a catch in her breath. "Now? Right here?"

"No, not now, but I need to talk to you about land for my animals soon. Questions like, do I need permits to build and/or what all is required? You must have done all these things last year when you were putting together this living history museum. I'll need to know all this information before I can speak to Kevin about constructing a shelter, or preferably a full stable and paddock."

Recovering quickly, Mary Ellen replied, "Just let me know when you are ready. I'm not in my office every day now, but I'm sure you know where to find me." She was suddenly glad it was dark so that Don couldn't see her blush, or the disappointment that had flitted across her face.

Just after Thanksgiving in October, early one morning Frank raced through the rain to Bob and Olga Petrov's house. When they answered the door, in a panicked voice he cried out, "Where's Nikolai? It's *Dedushka*. He's not himself."

As they walked swiftly back to his house, Frank said, "Last night we noticed he was pushing his food around on his plate more than eating it. Then when he excused himself from the table, he went straight to his room. This just wasn't like him.

After discussing it, Betty and I felt that really, we all have those kinds of nights, so nothing alarmed us. I went in to see him before I retired and he seemed to be sleeping soundly. This morning, he didn't come for breakfast at his usual time, so Betty went into his room. She called to me in a frightened state and told me his breathing seemed laboured. I did not waste any time in coming to get you."

"We may need to get him to the hospital in Prince Rupert," Nikolai said.

"The fastest way to get *Dedushka* there would be if Marg's son, Don, is around and he could take us in his boat," Bob agreed. "I sure hope he is in the village and not off somewhere hunting."

But when they got back to the house, they found Betty weeping into a tissue. They had not come quickly enough and when they entered his bedroom, they heard him sigh. Frank raced to his *papa*'s side, as *Dedushka* took two more short breaths.

His body went still.

As Frank began to cry, he haltingly said to everyone in the room, "There really wasn't much warning, and not much more that anyone could have done. Really, it has been a very peaceful death, as peaceful as we always wanted for him."

Frank had not had time to call any of his siblings, so not even Alex and Anna knew until after he was gone.

To honour *Dedushka*'s wishes, the family carried out the Russian traditions he had requested. Betty, with Olga's assistance, went about covering every mirror in their home, because she certainly didn't want any more deaths in her personal life.

Frank went from room to room stopping all the clocks to assist his *papa*'s soul to move more quickly into eternity, where there is no time. Bob and Nikolai offered to go tell Alex and Anna what had just happened.

Frank's younger brother, Steven, arrived the next day and helped Frank bathe the frail body and dress him in white. Then Betty assisted Frank's sister Isabel who was lovingly binding her *papa* with a belt, as this would ensure his soul would be bound to his body. Anastasia, Frank's youngest sister, was the last to arrive home and by then, everything was set for them all to sit with the body for the customary twenty-four hours until the funeral. The four siblings and their spouses reminisced over their memories of their *papa*'s long life. Neighbours kindly brought meals for the family so Betty and Anna wouldn't need to prepare food.

At his *keriah*, or wake, the villagers solemnly circled his open casket. Many tears were shed while they kissed his cold cheek. Still others brought bouquets of flowers, having raided Bert's gardens. Finally, his children placed a burial shroud over him.

On the day of the funeral, his four children, along with his ten grandchildren and two great-grandchildren, were all gathered together. There was a cold wind that day and thankfully it didn't rain while the service was held at the church. Immediately afterward, his body was lowered into the ground in the cemetery next to his beloved Anastasia. Grief shrouded the village for weeks as they recalled the dear old man they loved, who had always shown so much spirit.

For the customary forty days afterward, Betty and Frank, along with Alex and Anna, hosted gatherings on the third, ninth, and finally the fortieth day to again help hasten his soul into eternity. The rest of the family had all left shortly after the funeral. However, some of Frank's immediate and extended family were able to make it back for these important dates.

One evening early in November, Kevin invited Marianne for dinner at the Canadian-Japanese restaurant in Port Essington. When they arrived, Don and Mary Ellen were already there, so naturally the four of them decided to enjoy their meal together.

But what happened later no one could have predicted in their wildest dreams. The couples left in their respective vehicles, but did not drive straight home. Each of the men found somewhere under the green and yellow waving Northern Lights to stop and propose. And received an answering yes! It wasn't until later that night, when each of the girls showed the other her engagement ring, that the strange but wonderful coincidence became clear.

Out of respect for *Dedushka*'s death, it did not seem right to announce their engagements until after the forty-day ritual had ended. This meant that they were left to wear their engagement rings only around their bedrooms, or at least within the confines of Marvin and June's home. Naturally, Kevin wouldn't have known about the tradition around respecting the forty-day mourning period after someone's death. But for Don, knowing this tradition, it showed how impatient love could be.

Those first weeks after the engagements were announced, there was much speculation around the village. Would it be a double wedding? Some were convinced it would be. Others were equally adamant that it would be in April, prior to the second summer season beginning.

When news of Kevin and Marianne's engagement began to spread around the village, a common question was whether he would become a permanent resident, or whether Marianne would be moving away again. The answer soon became apparent when the news that he had decided to invest in a boat began to circulate. A boat not only to carry mail and other small items from Prince Rupert to New Petrograd and Hartley Bay, but in the summer months, to bring tourists to the village as well.

During Don's off-season months, Kevin had hired him on, and Mary Ellen was accepting applications for spring on Kevin's behalf.

As Marianne proudly showed off her diamond engagement ring, she was just as eager to tell her captive audience that her fiancé was now considering investing in a delivery truck that could bring larger items to the village.

Despite all of this exciting news, Kevin needed to stay focused on the next project on his to-do list: Nikolai and Margarita's much anticipated home. Then Mary Ellen had asked him to put in more buildings at the lighthouse station.

Somewhere in all of this, he thought in laughing despair, he needed to start working on his own love nest.

Toward the end of December, Alexandria was fairly bursting with excitement. She held onto Gordy's arm when they and Gordy's big brother Lyle and his fiancé Mandy went to the airport to meet his family.

They were all going to celebrate Christmas together at Gordy's Uncle Melvin and Aunt Wendy's place. Then on New Year's Eve, they would gather in St. Matthew's Church in the Renfrew district to celebrate Lyle and Mandy's wedding. Alexandria felt so delighted because Mandy had honoured her with the task of receiving and recording the gifts.

The day after the wedding, Lyle's and Mandy's families waved good-bye to them in the International Terminal of the airport as they were flying to San Francisco for their honeymoon. After saying good-bye to Mandy's family, Gordy, Alexandria, June, Marvin, Shelley, and Gaspar raced to another gate in the International Terminal to see June and Marvin off on a brief holiday to the Caribbean for two weeks, before returning home for the much-anticipated arrival of their first grandchild. After a brief lunch, Gordy, and Alexandria went to the Domestic Terminal to see Shelley and Gaspar off for home.

One evening early in February, as Shelley and Gaspar were talking about how much they were looking forward to moving into their new home, Shelley stopped, and in the same tone said, "Sweetheart, I think it's time we were on our way to the hospital."

Don and Mary Ellen were working at the kitchen table, finalizing their wedding guest list for out-of-town folks, addresses strewn all around.

Panicking, Gaspar raced down the hallway and shouted, "It's time."

Like a well-oiled machine, the plan they had rehearsed went into action. Don fired up his truck and he and Gaspar helped Shelley in. At Kevin's boat, Don started the engine, while Gaspar ensured there were no hazardous obstacles around the area before allowing his wife to exit the truck.

Meanwhile, Mary Ellen raced over to Shelley's parents to inform them, and then returned to the lighthouse station to call the Prince Rupert Regional Hospital to ask them to have an ambulance waiting at the dock.

She arrived breathless at Don's boat, and when Don felt they couldn't wait any longer, they saw the headlights of Tony's truck racing down the wharf. It skidded to a halt on the slick surface, and all four parents jumped out and ran toward the gangplank and the anxious people waiting.

And a gruelling twenty hours later... Shelley delivered a baby girl. She and Gasper named her Ashley June.

At the first sign of the meadows coming alive again with a new carpet of spring flowers, Father Nikolas officiated at the double wedding of Mary Ellen and Don, and Marianne and Kevin. Kevin's family had arrived from Olds a few days before.

The wedding party consisted of Kevin's brother, Kent, as his best man and Marianne's bridesmaid, Anna Yusporova. Don's brother, Brad, who had also arrived a few days earlier, was his best man, and Mary Ellen's bridesmaid was Anna Golobuva. Cheryl was very disappointed she was not coming this time, but had decided not to, as the family had been blessed with another son, Wade, earlier in the year. Her parents had offered to keep Eric, but the whole trip would be too much, especially when during the wedding Brad wouldn't be available to help her. The twins, Madeline and Matthew, were asked by both bridal couples to be their flower girl and ring bearer. Needless to say, all of the residents of New Petrograd were in attendance, including Alexandria, who had returned home to begin working again in the living history museum. Gordy had accompanied her, but his plans after the wedding were still unknown.

Instead of returning to the Borscht Kettle afterward, the reception was held in the meadows, delightfully similar to the Rosso reception the previous year. Gaspar and Shelley were only too happy to relinquish the title of newlyweds.

Immediately afterward, Kevin and Marianne left in his car for a two-week adventure holiday. Kevin kept the destination a secret even from his bride, although the Rocky Mountains were a favoured speculation. All Marianne knew was what she needed to pack in her suitcase. Olga had been only too pleased to come out of retirement for a couple of weeks to be the substitute teacher.

Don and Mary Ellen had chosen to fly to the Maritimes, and flew from Prince Rupert to Toronto on the same flight as Brad, a few days later. Mary Ellen had thought that she could only get away for a week, but Don had convinced her to take more time and leave the responsibilities with her right-hand man. And with the last click of his camera, Nick had mouthed the words, "Don't worry, everything is in good hands."

After the weddings, everyone's fervor was rising, as it wouldn't be long until again they would open their doors to the world. The most surprising day was when Buddy Rasmussen and his wife arrived, being the first to take up residence in the seasonal workers' accommodations. Word went around the village that he would be working with Shelley on security because after all, Ashley June was barely three months old. Pearl had taken a year's leave of absence to accompany her husband.

As the cars arrived with the other seasonal workers, Nick discussed with Pearl the position of attending to the booth on the wharf. Mary Ellen had earlier seen to it that all the tourist bureaus were aware of this new arrangement. Kevin and Gaspar still hadn't got around to building the booth at the "water entrance" to the wharf, as it was now called. They had promised it would be done by opening day.

As Bert was planting flowers in the pots by the wharf, Miles strolled up and greeted his old workmate. "Good to see you. I see you've been busy already, planting geraniums in these containers."

"Good to see you, too," Bert said, looking up. "Peter and I have been working hard preparing the gardens for the new plants ever since the snow melted. I guess I'll have to move out of Paul and Christelle's and into the seasonal workers' accommodations temporarily."

"Temporarily? Can't you live there during the winter months?" Miles asked.

"Well, no," Bert replied. "Seeing as I have been asked to work all year round, Kevin has offered to build me a permanent house. For everyone, a new season is beginning, and as I told Mary Ellen, Mother always says, 'Don't focus on the past but look forward to a bright new future.' That is what we can all do in New Petrograd."

PART TWO

Recipes

GRENKI

"It's so nice to be starting our lessons again," Daria greeted Shelley and June, early one September morning,

"Yes, I agree. It is kind of nice that fall is here, and we have resumed our lessons," June responded.

"Today I am going to teach you one of my son's favourite recipes and all you need to start with is yesterday's baguette and a couple of eggs. It is such a simple meal that even Gaspar started helping me make it when he was quite young. Of course, Tony and I made sure he was safe around the stove before we would let him help us. This recipe is for a breakfast version, and is usually served with a hot drink."

"I remember this," Shelley said. "Gaspar ordered it at the teahouse just after we came home. It reminds me of a very fancy French toast. I'm going to take him some as soon as we're finished."

INGREDIENTS

- One dry baguette
- Two eggs
- One tablespoon of sugar
- Jam to taste

DIRECTIONS

Slice your bread into two equal halves. Add a large spoonful of jam to one half.

"I have found strawberry and plum to be two of the best jams to use," Daria suggested.

Cover with the other half of the bread to make a sandwich. Be sure to press down on all sides of the bread, ensuring that it is sealed tightly so none of the jam oozes out.

Add the eggs and sugar to a bowl and mix thoroughly with a fork.

Dip both sides of the bread in the egg mixture.

Add approximately 2 teaspoons of vegetable oil or butter to a pan. Then turn the heat to medium.

Fry the *grenki* on both sides for 3–4 minutes.

Serve with your choice of syrup.

"Isn't it good?" Daria said as they enjoyed the treat. "Today we made a sweet version of *grenki.* However, depending on the fillings, it can either be a sweet or a savoury dish. Some fillings to use are seasonings, vegetables, fruit, meat, cheese, and other things. As you can tell, the options are endless!"

RUSSIAN BAKED APPLES

"I think, prior to learning how to make Russian Baked Apples, I would like to tell you how important apples are to our table," Daria said as she poured another cup of *sbiten* for Shelley and June. "Apples are commonly found in every household, just like bread or butter. It's so nice to bake apple pies and enjoy a cup of hot tea with apple jam during the winter. It brings everything special to our lives, like warmth and coziness, and binds the whole family at the dining table. Now, if we've finished our hot drink, let's get busy," Daria said. "This is a very simple dish to prepare with a huge variety of options.

"Like the Chak Chak recipe, it can be prepared with children. I assure you Gaspar used to beg me to make this dessert with him. He delighted in filling his apple with all the different goodies. After all," Daria said with a laugh, "I was quite happy to let him play because even if in the end the apple wasn't all that tasty, it wasn't a big expense for him to entertain himself for the afternoon."

"*Mama*, I am beginning to get a sneaky feeling that you are showing me all these child-friendly recipes for a reason," Shelley exclaimed.

"You think so, do you?" Daria smiled as she handed her a bowl. "Really, my dear, the truth is, only because they are still some of your husband's favourites. It is possible to fill the apples with curd, and with a variety of toppings such as chocolate, candied fruits, and/or whipped cream. Or it can be as simple as sprinkling sugar on top. Today, I have planned one that has been Gaspar's favourite since he was a teenager. For myself, what I most enjoy is that it fills the whole house with a very pleasant aroma."

"I think I like it all ready," June exclaimed. "What is in it?"

"The main ingredients are nuts, honey and cinnamon. Besides the apples, of course."

INGREDIENTS

- Apples
- Walnuts
- Prunes
- Honey
- Cinnamon
- Powdered sugar

Note: All quantities are dependent on how many you plan to make. For two apples, we used five walnut halves, two prunes, and two tablespoons of honey.

On the recipe we have listed several ingredients. Don't be afraid to play around with these items and combinations to know the exact amounts to satisfy your individual taste. And consider other ingredients you might like to experiment with.

For future reference: you may find it helpful to note the amounts of your favorite combinations.

DIRECTIONS

Preheat the oven to 350 degrees F.

Remove the middle section of the apple (core).

Put a pan on the stove, but do *not* add any oil. Add walnuts, and toast them. Remove from stove and chop finely.

Cut prunes into bite-sized pieces and mix in a bowl along with nuts and honey.

Fill the apples with this sticky mixture, and sprinkle cinnamon on top.

Place apples on a baking sheet, and wrap each apple in foil for baking.

Bake the apples for 20–30 minutes; when the apples are soft to your touch, they are ready.

When you take them out of the oven, dust them with the powdered sugar.

This would be a great idea for a children's birthday party or get-together.

CHAK CHAK

Fried Honey Cake

"Good morning," Daria greeted Shelley and June as she opened the door to let them in. "Quick, come in out of the rain."

"Yes, good morning, *Mama*," Shelley said, as she gave her a hug. "Your home is so lovely and warm on a chilly day."

"Good morning, Daria," June added. "Warm in more ways than one," as she too hugged her friend.

"Today, I'm planning to teach you how to make Chak Chak which is also known in Russia as a Fried Honey Cake. It is frequently served to guests at weddings or other celebrations."

"That explains why Gayle made it for the grand opening," June said enthusiastically. "That was a day of celebration like no other."

INGREDIENTS

- 3 large eggs
- 1½ tablespoons cognac or vodka
- 2 cups flour

- 3 cups of oil
- 1 cup of honey
- ⅓ cup sugar
- 200 grams toasted slivered almonds (optional)

DIRECTIONS

Beat the eggs together with a whisk or beater.

Add in the cognac or vodka to egg mixture and stir until well blended.

Put the flour into a bowl, and then stir in the egg mixture.

Daria, stopped here to comment, "During this process, if it becomes lumpy, be sure to break the lumps up because you want your dough to be soft."

Next, knead your dough on a floured surface and let sit for 15 minutes before starting step 5.

Roll the dough to about ½ cm or ¼" thick. Then cut into strips, about 1 or 2" wide.

"When we finish this step," Daria advised, "we will have many long strips of dough. A tip is to sprinkle enough flour so they don't stick and then layer them by placing 3 or 4 strips on top of each other."

"Oh," Shelley cried, "this makes cutting much easier. Thank you for suggesting it."

Cut these long strips into pieces about ½ cm or ¼" wide.

"Another suggestion I can make is to give them a good shake to separate them into individual pieces. When we fry them, they will double or triple their size."

Heat the oil on high until hot.

"A way to test if your oil is hot enough is to put one piece of dough into the pot. It should crackle and begin to expand. Then we know we can add more."

Fry the dough portions in small groups in the hot oil until they turn golden yellow. Remove and set aside on a paper towel to drain the oil.

"With this step," Daria said, "I caution you to not overdo them. Be sure to take the pieces out when they are lightly golden."

Put the honey and sugar into a pot and cook on low for about 5 minutes. Make sure all the sugar is dissolved into the honey.

"Could I use a double boiler for this step?" June asked.

"Absolutely," Daria agreed. "That is actually a very good idea."

Use another frying pan to toast the almonds on medium heat until they are toasted to a golden brown.

Prepare the serving plate before putting the fried dough pieces and toasted almonds into a large bowl.

Then pour the hot honey mixture over everything. Mix together using 2 wooden spoons until it's evenly coated.

"With this step," Daria advised, "you must work very fast, before the honey sets."

Now place your finished product on the plate you prepared and using your hands, form a hill or a pyramid.

"We're almost finished," Daria said. "My final tips are, again, work very quickly before it sets. And you may find it is helpful to wet your hands with cold water to help you form the pyramid. It can be refrigerated to cool and set, or served while it is still warm in smaller portions."

RUSSIAN SOURDOUGH BORODINSKY (RYE) BREAD

"I've noticed, Shelley dear, how tired you are by the end of a lesson. Your Mom and I have decided that today will be the last one for a while," Daria said one rainy day in November, as she hurried Shelley and June inside.

As Shelley began to dispute her comment, June quickly intervened. "No arguing, Shelley. As the baby's grandmothers, we insist."

Shortly thereafter, as the three of them were sitting around the table enjoying hot mugs of tea, Daria smiled and said, "Our pleasant mornings of getting together certainly don't need to end, though. Before we begin to bake Gaspar's favourite bread, let me tell you some of its history.

"There is a widespread tale, as lovely as it is tragic. In 1812, Russian General Alexander Tuchkov died at the Battle of Borodino. His heartbroken widow decided to erect a convent at the location where the gory battle took place. Some believe the nuns originally prepared this bread. At first it was called Memorial and later, the name was changed to Battle of Borodino. The bread's deep, dark colour is meant to signify mourning and grief and the coriander seeds represent bullets and grapeshot. Despite this romantic story, another theory is that it was created in Soviet bread-baking factories and the first recipe emerged in the 1930s.

"I have my suspicions," Daria said with a chuckle, "that it was because of this story that Tony and Gaspar decided it was their favourite bread. I asked you to plan on spending your whole day here because the prep time will take us several hours, and even with that, I did the first few steps last night. Then, we need to bake it for another fifty minutes."

"I'm ready," Shelley said, already rolling up her sleeves. "What is the first thing you would like me to help you with?"

INGREDIENTS (PRE-FERMENT OR SOURDOUGH STARTER)

- 5.3 ounces rye starter*
- 9.9 ounces cold water / 1-1/4 cup
- 3.5 ounces rye flour / 1 cup

*A package of rye starter can be purchased at Amazon (please follow the instructions on the package).

The day before you wish to make your bread, mix the sourdough (rye) starter, cold water, and rye flour together. Let it sit for at least 12 hours, or overnight.

"Of course, the first step is what I did last night," Daria said, "because it was just mixing our starter together, in anticipation of the real work today."

INGREDIENTS (BREAD DOUGH)

- 10.6 ounces white bread flour / 2 cups
- 3.5 ounces whole meal flour / 1 cup
- 1.8 ounces rye flour / ½-cup
- 0.4 ounces salt / 2 teaspoons
- • 0.4 ounces caraway seeds / 2 teaspoons
- • 0.5 ounces coriander seeds / 1 tablespoon
- • 2.1 ounces molasses / ¼ cup
- • 1.4 ounces dark cocoa powder / 1/3 cup
- • 10.6 ounces cold water / 1-1/2 cups
- *Smetana* (sour cream)

INSTRUCTIONS

Begin by adding the first nine items listed under Bread Dough to the pre-ferment. Hold back 0.2 ounces of caraway seeds and coriander seeds for later use.

"I know you will be very tempted to add more flour," Daria stated. "Because it will be very wet. It is correct being wet, so do *not* add more."

Work the dough for around 5 minutes using your hands or a wooden spoon. The reason for doing this, is to allow the gluten to form a bit in the dough. Now oil your hands to stretch and fold the dough, then cover it up and set it aside for three hours.

"We can make use of this time by lining two bread tins with parchment paper," Daria said. "I also prepared sandwiches for a bite of lunch." Daria took a plate out of the fridge. "June, can you please put the kettle on and make a fresh pot of tea?"

"Of course," June agreed. "I also brought a green salad for our lunch."

Apply oil to the tins, line them with parchment paper, and then lightly oil again.

Sprinkle the tins with a bit of *smetana* (sour cream), and 0.1 ounce each of coriander seeds and ground caraway seeds.

When your dough has risen, do not knead it, but lightly tap it down to release the air.

With oiled hands, divide it in two.

"We could have prepared one tin to make just one loaf, but my tins are quite small, so that is why I gave you two," Daria admitted.

"I'm in favour of that idea anyway," Shelley agreed. "This is a lot of work for just one loaf. All summer long, Gaspar has been bringing a loaf home from the teahouse on a weekly basis."

Gently even out the top. Then sprinkle with the remaining 0.1 ounce of the coriander and ground caraway seeds.

Next, lightly cover it with an oiled plastic wrap and let the dough rise again.

"I suggested we oil the wrap a bit because we do not want it to stick to the bread. This time, we only need to leave the bread for 90 minutes. Our bread should now double in size."

Turn your oven on to 220C.

"The idea with doing this," Daria advised as she handed Shelley a bowl, "is to create some steam. This is how we get that nice crust on the bread, which makes it so lovely and crisp. The bread will also finish rising in the oven without the crust forming too quickly."

When it is ready to go into the oven, fill a little metal bowl or tray with water and place it in the bottom of the oven.

Bake the Borodinsky rye bread at 220C for 20 minutes. Then turn down the oven to 180C and continue baking for another 10 minutes.

After the ten minutes, carefully remove from the tins and put back in the oven, bottom side up, for another 5 minutes.

Remove and place on cooling racks.

"I know how enticing the smell is, but be strong and resist slicing a piece. It is best to let it cool down first. And just a word of caution, you will have to be strong for both you and my son," Daria grinned, hugging Shelley.

Then she stopped and looked at Shelley before exclaiming, "That was a big job. You look so tired, dear. I know your mother and I made the right decision to put our lessons on hold for a while."

"You're right, it was a big job. Do you mind if I lie down for a bit?" Shelley smiled wanly at her. "I decided this afternoon, I think we will continue to buy our bread until after the baby comes."

"You won't have to buy it, honey," June replied. "Because I will make your bread."

As Daria and June sat down with a glass of *stewler* each, Daria whispered to June, "I know we made the right decision to stop the lessons."

“We did. If Shelley even gets a whiff of your giving me a lesson, she’ll be determined to come, though. I have to say, I am quite proud of the Russian foods I can prepare. I’m getting pretty good at this—or at least Marvin is starting to compliment me.”

RECIPES PUBLISHED PREVIOUSLY

Lighthouse in the Mist:

- Blini
- Olivier Salad
- Kissel
- Sharlotka Cake

Deep in the Mist:

- Sbiten
- Draniki
- Rassolnik Soup
- Russian Honey Cake

GLOSSARY

LANGUAGE

- **Babushka:** grandmother
- **Dedushka:** grandfather
- **Mama:** mother
- **Papa:** father
- **Moi medvezhono**: my teddy-bear
- **Roditeli:** parents

FOOD

Baked Apples (Russian Style): This is an easy dish that even children can enjoy preparing because they will like filling the apples with different goodies. There are a huge variety of filling options. You can fill the apples with curd, and with different toppings such as chocolate or candied fruits, whipped cream, or just sprinkle sugar on top.

Beef Stroganoff: Begin with a nice piece of beef such as steak and cut it into little strips. Mix it in *smetana* (sour cream).

Blini: A Russian pancake sometimes called *blin* or *bliny*. Traditionally it is made from wheat or buckwheat flour. For toppings, it can be served with sour cream, quark, butter, and other garnishes you may have in your fridge. They are also known as blintzes, crepes or *palatschinke*.

Borodinsky bread: Sometimes called borodino bread, it is a dark brown sourdough rye bread. The traditional way of making it is sweetened with molasses and flavoured with both coriander and caraway seeds.

Borscht: A sour cream soup made from beetroots. The main ingredient gives it a distinctive red colour.

Chak Chak: A sticky and sweet dessert that's absolutely delicious. It is actually from the Soviet Union, and not Russia. Another name for it is Fried Honey Cake with Almonds.

Chicken Kiev: A dish made of a chicken fillet pounded and rolled in cold butter, then rolled in a mixture of eggs and bread crumbs, and either fried or baked. It is traditionally served with rice or shoestring potatoes, both of which help to soak up the delicious herb butter filling. The meal is often completed with fresh string beans, peas, and broccoli.

Draniki: A very popular dish; Russian-style potato pancakes. The potatoes can be mashed, fried, baked, boiled, and then served with sour cream or apple sauce. Regardless of how you prepare it, it is very likely to become one of your top comfort foods. *Draniki* is very versatile. Some like it in the morning with eggs; others prefer it with a salad at lunch. It is a wonderful side dish to any entrée.

Grenki: Small slices of stale bread (different kinds of bread can be used) fried in oil or baked in the oven. They can be made sweet or savoury by adding seasonings, vegetables, fruit, meat, cheese, and other things. The choice of options is simply vast!

Kielbasa: A meat sausage that comes from Poland.

Knish: A Jewish snack food. Made with a savory filling covered with dough and then baked, or sometimes deep fried.

Kissel: A fruit dessert of sweetened juice, thickened with arrowroot, cornstarch, or potato starch.

Kvas: A fermented non-alcoholic beverage made from black or regular rye bread or dough.

Lazy Vareniki: A cross between traditional Russian dumplings and a traditional Russian pie. They can be served with your choice of toppings: jam, sour cream, honey, or any other type of sweet sauce. And you can freeze any uncooked leftover *vareniki* for next time.

Medovic Torte: This cake consists of eight paper-thin cake layers with sour cream spread on them, hence the other name it goes by, Sour Cream Cake or Smetana Cake. It tastes like dreamy graham crackers that have been frosted.

Medovukha: A traditional Russian honey-based drink.

Mors: A non-carbonated Russian fruit drink prepared from berries. It can be made from many varieties of berries, but commonly from lingonberry and cranberries. Sometimes blueberries, strawberries, or raspberries are used.

Olivier Salad: A Russian version of potato salad. So of course, we start with diced potatoes, eggs, chicken or bologna, sweet peas and pickles, with a mayonnaise dressing. Other vegetables such as carrots or fresh cucumbers can be added.

Okroshka Soup: A refreshing kefir soup that is thought of as a summer soup because it is served cold. The ingredients are similar to Olivier Salad but the taste is very different.

Pastila: A Russian sweet originating from the 17th century.

It is a cross between candy and meringue cookies—light and airy puffs made from egg whites, sugar, and fruit.

Pirogi: Made of a flaky or puff pastry. They are often used as a dessert. They may be sweet and contain quark or cottage cheese. This base is then filled with fruits such as apples, plums, or berries. Other varieties have honey, nuts, or poppy seeds. A savoury version is filled with meat, fish, mushrooms, cabbage, rice, whole grain buckwheat or potato. These tasty little morsels are often served as an accompaniment to clear borscht, broth, or consommé.

Rassolnik Soup: A classic soup made with barley, beef, potatoes, carrots, and... pickles? You mean cucumbers, right? Nope, pickles.

Sbiten: Since the twelfth century, *sbiten* has been consumed as a traditional wintertime honey-based beverage. The key to excellent *sbiten* is good quality honey and spices.

Sharlotka: There are maybe a few facts we can tell you about Russian Sharlotka. Interestingly, it was actually invented in London in the nineteenth century by French cook Marie Antoine Careme. The Russian part came when it was served to Russian Tsar Alexander I. In the beginning, the name of the dish was Charlotte à la Parisienne (Parisian Sharlotka). Later on, the dessert was renamed Charlotte Russe and became famous all over the world.

Smetana: sour cream.

Stolichniy Rye Bread: One of the most well-liked types of Russian rye bread. It is made from a mixture of rye-peeled flour and wheat flour of the very best grade. This healthy bread has been around since Soviet times and is near to their hearts.

Tarasun: A highly alcoholic colourless liquid prepared by distillation and fermentation of mare's milk. It is described as a form of milk whiskey.

CLOTHING

Dushegreya: A single-breasted sleeveless vest.

Gashnik: A wool string which holds the *poneva* skirt in place.

Kaftan: This coat was originally from the Middle East but it became so important to the Russian wardrobe it soon was thought of as being local.

Kosovorotka: A traditional shirt with a collar that fastens on one side, usually on the left. It can be worn by men or women.

Kokoshnik: A conventional headdress worn by women and girls to go with the *sarafan*.

Lakomki: A beltspocket, a belt which also had a pouch to carry small items in it. It was worn by both men and women.

Poneva: Was considered a complete costume which consisted of a plaid or striped skirt gathered by a string or wrapped around the hips, a long loosely fitting shirt featuring embroidery on the sleeves. The final piece was an apron.

Ports: Men's pants.

Rubakha: A basic piece of any traditional Russian wardrobe, which could be worn by both men and women. They were worn as street clothes among the peasants and as home clothes among the rich. It is now called oversize, as it didn't have any real shape.

Sarafan: A loosely fitting, long jumper-like dress worn over a long linen shirt and belted. A necessary piece of traditional Russian dress was the belt often worn under the garment. They were sewn from homespun linen or inexpensive printed cotton.

Shuba: The Russian word for fur coat, the shuba was an intrinsic part of both male and female wardrobes. Traditionally the fur was left on the inside of the coat, while the outside was decorated with bright, colourful textiles. Although still very popular, they have evolved to match current styles.

Ushanka: A winter fur cap with ear flaps that hang low, covering the ears, jaw, and chin, or which can be tied up to the crown of the cap.

Vres: A wreath that the women wore on their heads, decorated with ribbons and flowers. This was sometimes referred to as, or called, a crown.

WEDDING

Gor'ko: A protest that the wine is bitter, and the guests are wanting the couple to kiss for a long time to take out the bitter taste of the champagne or vodka.

Tamada: Master of Ceremonies

Za-Molodykh: A toast for the newlyweds: "Cheers to the young couple that is presently getting married."

INDIGENOUS

Wha! T'iina tleexgn: Stop crying!

Potlatch: To the Haida tribe, this is a big celebration and means *to give*. However, it was the host who would give gifts to his guests. Of course, the richer the family, the better the gifts would be.

Made in the USA
Monee, IL
27 April 2021

67077024R00180